STRAWLITTER TALES

Volume 1

KOFI

AND
THE CLIMBING BOY

By
Mike Healey

1. Kumasi, West Africa
September, 1762

The Great Shadow moves across the globe with a speed that is breathtaking, plunging whole continents into sudden darkness. Animals fall silent and men, women and children cower in fear.

In Kumasi, on the plains above Africa's equatorial forests and south of the Sahara, the tribal gathering waits. Every villager knows that something extraordinary is about to happen – not least Maloa. She is 'Mother' of the tribe, a frail, crumpled bag of bones. She lies, bent in an arthritic curve, on the cushioned floor of a tiny wooden cart. She is dressed entirely in black, swaddled like a baby. It is said that she is one-hundred-and- three years old.

Nearby, Lumana squats beneath his oracle tree and contemplates his future for he is the tribe's Shaman. Above his head the branches of this ancient jacaranda tree writhe and twist, like the convolutions of the old trickster's drug-induced imagination. It has been decades since this holy tree was covered in blossom but each year it plunges bony fingers deeper into the ground, throttling the earth with its iron grip.

Today it will witness portentous events while the fate of the Shaman himself hangs in the balance - like a clenched spider suspended on a frail thread above a fire.

Kofi sees nothing of this. He is the king's nephew and is only nine years old. Already he is bored and has begun to pick his nose and fidget.

'Kofi, stop that at once! Remember who you are. And for goodness' sake sit still - unless you want another smack!'

Ashtari is a tall, handsome woman in her late twenties. Kofi is her first and only child but now, after several barren years, she is pregnant once more. Her second husband died in battle three weeks ago. She is, therefore, in mourning but the new child, now growing in her belly, gives her fresh hope.

In the outer corral magicians, snake charmers and acrobats ply their trades, trying to distract the crowd. Kofi longs to be amongst them but protocol requires that he sit at the foot of his uncle's golden throne - as befits a royal prince. He yawns and scratches his arse, shifting uncomfortably on his wooden stool

'Kofi! What did I tell you? Sit up and behave yourself. What would your uncle say if he saw you fidgeting like some commoner?'

Maloa is Kofi's great, great grandmother and because of her age gives the tribe a living link with its past. Her weather-beaten skin is a parchment upon which are written the tribe's triumphs and defeats - an intricate map of past years, some fat, some lean. Within in her prodigious memory inside that bony, hairless skull can be found the tribe's collective past, its identity.

Kofi has always been afraid of this old woman yet when he holds her thin, monkey-like fingers she always squeezes his hand affectionately.

The Great Shadow has now plunged the tribal lands into unnatural darkness - at which point Maloa's suddenly trembles. From her thin lips there escapes an involuntary sigh. Only Kofi, being nearest to her, hears this. He grasps the handle of the cart and rocks it gently.

A profound stillness now descends upon the village, spreading from the outer defences of briars and cacti to the inner corral of thatched huts where the throng are gathered. Within moments it reaches the hill on which stands the royal palace and before which sits King Kwasi Obodum - Tribal Lord and Leader of the Ashanti.

All eyes are now turned to the king and the elders of the tribe, sheltering beneath ornamental umbrellas. Even these wise men, dressed in their ceremonial cloaks and beads, shift uneasily on their cushions, troubled by the darkness that has engulfed them. Behind them loom the towers of the king's palace, its whitewashed walls punctuated with short beams - like rows of wooden teeth. Standing two storeys high, these mud-brick buildings with their conical minarets, dominate the hill.

In the fields beyond the outer perimeter, cattle fall silent. In a corab tree five goats, perched precariously on the upper branches, stop eating. Their slit, orange eyes stare at each other in astonishment at this freak of nature.

Kofi too is frightened but as the darkness deepens he feels his mother's grip on his shoulder and is comforted by her strength.

Some, wiser in the ways of nature, see this circle of darkness as a warning. With the right sacrifices and salutations, the tribe's gods will prevail and the light will return. These devout members of the tribe therefore crouch in prayer, their heads bowed beneath the black rim of the sky. Others, tempting fate, stand and wave their spears at the sky while uttering great oaths. For them this is an omen to be shouted down, to be scorned - as they would an inferior enemy.

Meanwhile, Lumana - still crouching beneath his jacaranda tree - is intent upon the salvation of the tribe.

3

'Great gods!' he cries. 'Save us from the Dark Spirit that would devour us!'

Some years before there had been a lunar eclipse. Those that knew of such matters had hidden their animals in their huts, fearful of the moon's baleful light. Others, less wise, had left their animals in the fields, exposed to the shadow that covered the tribal lands for an hour or so. Their goats and pigs, thus exposed, promptly fell ill. The mouths and feet of these unfortunate animals became covered in blisters while others, staggering about their pens, let out cries that haunted the village. One herdsman, examining his goat, was horrified when the animal's tongue fell out. The stench of burning flesh filled the air for days - a sweet, sickly smell that clung to one's clothes or lingered within each hut. Three large oxen, placed on a pyre, exploded - showering onlookers with globules of boiling fat.

For many weeks thereafter the Shaman - who had manifestly failed to predict these dire consequences - was shunned. Now, on this fateful day, Lumana's reputation - and that of his King - depends upon banishing the Great Shadow, thereby saving the tribe from a lingering death in eternal darkness. To this end he now directs all his skills. His eyes are wild and staring, his face contorted with concentration. Perspiration runs down his chest and arms, glistening in the light of the fire. In his trance he begins to sway from side to side, rocking on his heels and gibbering like an ape.

Suddenly he stands up and from leather bag slung round his neck takes a handful of small bones. For a moment there is silence as everyone watches intently. Then, with a cry, he casts the bones into the embers, whereupon there is an explosion, causing those nearest to the fire to fall back in astonishment.

When the smoke clears they see, in the glow of the fire, their Shaman pointing at the sky. All eyes follow his gaze. Slowly, the black disc obscuring the sun begins to move to one side, bringing light once more. For once Lumana's timing is good and his prompt actions have averted disaster.

The crowd at once lets out a great roar, rises to its feet and begins to leap about, the men waving their spears in triumph. The drums take up the rhythm, the sound spreading like thunder far beyond the perimeter fence then rebounding tenfold from the surrounding hills.

Kofi leaps to his feet, adopts the crouched pose of a monkey and dances the 'Dance of Sorak', his feet pounding the beaten earth in tiny, intricate patterns.

The King, still seated on his throne, watches intently as the light returns to his kingdom, turning his fields the colour of saffron. Although his heart is still beating frantically he can now breathe a sigh of relief. Had his astronomers proved wrong in their predictions or his Shaman ineffectual, then his dynasty might have ended here and now.

Such are the vagaries of history.

***

The celebrations last long into the night but as dawn creeps over the mountains, Kofi's mother wakes her servants and begins preparations for the trek back to their village at the distant, western edge of the tribal lands.

'Thala, prepare Maloa for the journey. Hurry now!'

Thala is Ashtari's principal servant and Kofi's nurse. She is a stout yet formidable woman in her sixties, with long gray hair and skin like parchment stained with beetle-juice. Her eyes are as black as coal.

Maloa now suffers the indignity of being lifted from her wooden cart and held by two attendants, one on each side. Thus suspended, she is like a thin, leather puppet. Thala removes the old woman's soiled clothing and washes her. She is then swaddled in a fresh cloth and eased back gently onto the cushioned floor of her cart. Ashtari finally gives her a crust of bread to suck - to fortify the old woman for the long journey ahead.

Kofi, meanwhile, scampers about the huts like a mad thing, getting in everyone's way - much to the annoyance of his mother's servants, frantically trying to pack. Thala too is becoming increasingly angry with the boy.

'Kofi! Stop that, you little monkey! Go and pack your belongings yourself - or we will leave without you!'

After several further altercations, Thala finally loses patience and boxes the boy's ears, unceremoniously pushing him out of the hut in the process.

'Very well, if you will not help then out you must go, you wicked child! Out! Out! Go on, get out of my way!'

Her shrill imprecations hang on the morning air - accompanied by the giggles of Ashtari's three young Nubian slaves busily packing Ashtari's belongings into great bundles to be carried on their heads.

Kofi, not used to such treatment from mere slaves, squats on the ground outside his mother's quarters and sulks in silence.

When all is ready and Ashtari has made her farewells to the King and the tribal elders, the royal party leave the palace and head east, moving between the fields of maize and on into the rolling hills that separate Kumasi from the outer regions of the tribal lands. To their left the great lake glistens in the early morning sunlight.

Kofi looks back, shading his eyes from the sun. Through his lashes, reflected light from the lake splinters into a thousand shards. Kofi already misses the vast lake's cool depths, its countless fish and secret, subterranean caverns of green, undulating weed. It will be a long time before he will swim in its clear waters again.

***

It is now midday and the suns beats down unmercifully on the small band of travellers heading east towards Ashtari's village.

Here the maize fields - scratched from unforgiving rock - are beginning to sprout. Some women, weeding these cultivated strips, pause respectfully in their work as the royal party passes. Those that are close to the track rush forward and kiss Ashtari's hand or touch the hem of her red cloak. The cloak shows that she is still in mourning for her dead husband.

'Blessings on you, Princess. May your children prosper and your great sorrow diminish and vanish for ever!'

Some of the older women, also recognising the frail figure in the tiny cart, kneel at the roadside as a mark of respect.

'Blessings too on our ancient 'Mother' before whose infinite wisdom we kneel.'

Maloa's reputation as a philosopher and sage is widespread, even amongst these humble farmers. Despite her frailty, she still exerts over these people a fascination that is part respect, part fear.

Her father had been a great leader of the Ashanti and a man of exceptional cruelty. He had won many battles against the Dahomy and had enslaved thousands. His reign had been steeped in blood, including that of his three brothers whom he had murdered on his way to the throne.

***

Ashanti and her retinue have now reached the Bad Lands, some twenty kilometres southeast of Kumasi.

The hills now are salmon pink and the track is covered with shards of black basalt. Little grows here except cactus and dusty, green scrub. The sandstone rocks, weathered into bizarre shapes, stand like sentinels guarding their path.

Kofi takes little comfort from this. To him these rocks are monsters carved by some demonic sculptor. High above their heads - in a blazing, azure sky - a lone vulture idles on the thermal currents, barely moving its great wings.

Kofi has fallen behind the others, lost in his own thoughts.

In a dried-up river to his left lie the bleached bones of a gazelle, its head only partly consumed. One remaining eye, sunken deep in its dry socket, stares resolutely skywards. Suddenly a snake slithers onto the path. Kofi grabs a rock and hurls it at the creature. The mamba slithers off into the bushes with a petulant flick of its sleek, black body. Kofi does not like snakes. Here there are many. He will need to watch his step. His cousin was bitten by such a snake. It had taken the boy five days to die.

Kofi shudders at the memory of his cousin's excruciatingly painful death and hastily rejoins the others further down the path.

***

Kumo, the most experienced of the bodyguards accompanying the royal party, is anxious; he knows how dangerous these parts can be.

'Princess, take care! This is bandit territory. You and Kofi stay close together with me. Ralu, protect Thala and the girls. Yatenga, you watch our backs. Stay alert, both of you.'

They now leave the dry riverbed and move into open scrubland, following a dusty animal track that winds its way between cacti. To the east, far beyond distant hills of grey granite, lies their village - and safety.

It is now early evening. They have just three hours left before darkness falls.

Moreover, Ashtari's elderly servant Thala and the three Nubian slaves are beginning to tire, burdened as they are with great bundles of clothing, gifts from the king and personal possessions. Kofi, pulling Maloa's little wooden cart, is also tired and thirsty and has begun to complain.

'Kofi, be quiet! We will drink when Kumo tells us it is safe to do so... or do you want Thala to box your ears again?'

7

Kofi says nothing but staggers on, pulling Maloa's little cart across rough ground, unmindful of the discomfort this long journey must cause the frail, elderly woman it contains. Kofi is a sensitive child but spoilt, more concerned with his own needs rather than those of others.

They have now entered a narrow gorge. The path here winds its way between steep rocks, which tower above their heads. It is decided to carry the old woman. Kumo is a giant of a man yet he cradles Maloa in his arms as if she were his child. Kofi, still in charge of the cart, follows behind, lost in his own thoughts.

Suddenly two horsemen appear before them, arriving in a cloud of dust, the sun behind them.

'Bandits!' cries Kumo.

The two riders stop, some twenty meters away, and stare at the Ashanti, sizing up the opposition. From Ashtari's proud stance and fine clothing it is immediately clear to them that they are facing a party far more valuable than mere farmers.

Meanwhile, Ralu and Yatenga have rushed forward and now stand between Ashtari and the horsemen, their spears raised. Kumo quickly places the old woman back in her wooden cart, draws his long knife and moves to the head of the column to join the other two bodyguards. Ashtari, her eyes fixed on the two riders, pulls Kofi closer to her side. Thala, together with Ashtari's young attendants - their faces now covered - drop their bundles and stand on either side of their mistress. Maloa, lying in her little wooden cart, begins to pray - the first sounds any of them have heard from her since they left Kumasi, many hours ago.

Three other horsemen now appear, emerging from behind a huge rock to their left. Kumo, glancing to his right, also spots a sixth man, now crouching on a rock above their heads.

The royal party have stumbled into a trap for they are now surrounded and outnumbered within this narrow gorge and with no obvious means of escape. From their face-paint, weapons and clothing it is clear that these bandits are Dahomey - savages infamous for their cruelty and avarice.

For a moment both sides stand and stare, each daring the other to make the first move. Kofi, his heart pounding, wishes he had a knife or some weapon but he has nothing. Instead, he takes his mother's hand and squeezes it - to comfort her while Ashtari herself gathers Thala and the Nubian girls even closer to her.

Suddenly Kumo spins on his heels and throws his knife at the man crouched on the rock above him. The blade spins in the air then strikes the Dahomy bandit full in the face. He falls backwards with a scream and disappears behind his rock.

Now all five horsemen are galloping towards them, brandishing their spears and shouting.

Ralu thrusts at the first rider with his spear. The man, struck full in the chest, topples off his horse backwards onto the track. As Ralu moves in for the kill he is himself struck from behind by the second horseman, wielding a wooden club. Ralu crashes to the ground, his skull crushed.

Kumo now leaps forward, pulls Ralu's spear from the dying horseman's chest, then turns and flings the weapon with all his might at the rider wielding the club. As the man is struggling to turn his horse, the spear strikes him in the back whereupon he slides forward across his horse's neck and falls to the ground. Kumo, drawing a second knife from his belt, leaps forward, grabs the wounded Dahomey by the hair and slits his throat.

Meanwhile, the other horsemen have rounded on Yatenga who is trying to protect the royal party's right flank.

The bandits spur their horses forward, their battle cries echoing from rock to rock. Yatenga flings his spear at the foremost rider but it is brushed aside. He then draws his knife but three Dahomey spears immediately crash into his chest, killing him instantly. He falls to the ground, blood spurting from his shattered rib cage. The women and Kofi, still huddled together at one side of the track, scream - their arms and faces now splattered with Yatanga's warm blood. Thala, hurling abuse at the Dahomy, grabs stones and rocks from the path and flings them at the bandits - to little effect, other than to unnerve their horses.

Kumo is now surrounded and fighting for his life and that of his Princess. He runs at the nearest rider, knife in hand.

The man's horse rises on its hind legs, its hooves flashing inches from Kama's face. Momentarily startled, Kumo tries to leap to one side but is fatally struck on the side of the head by the second horseman, wielding a fearsome ebony club. Kumo, his skull crushed, falls to the ground, his body now twitching convulsively. Within moments he is dead.

The battle is over - or so Ashtari and her companions think. But there is more.

The Dahomey rider, who has just killed Kumo now leans down from his saddle, seizes the handle of the old woman's wooden cart and swings it, and its frail contents, round and round his head. Ashtari watches in horror until, with a final whoop of triumph, the horseman lets go.

When it lands, the little wooden cart containing the old woman splinters into a thousand fragments.

Ashtari lets out a scream of horror and runs to where the old woman's body now lies in a crumpled heap. She picks up a rock and hurls it with all her strength at the bandit who has just committed this sacrilege. It strikes his horse on the neck, causing it to veer to one side and unseat its rider.

Kofi, still crouching amongst the servants, watches in horror as two other Dahomey edge their horses closer to his distraught mother. Ashtari, in her grief, is now tearing at her clothes and hair, her cries and sobs cascading about their ears. Kofi at once rushes forward, ducking under the flank of the nearest horse, and reaches his mother in a swirl of dust. He grabs her hand, pulls her to her feet and drags her off as fast as he can towards a patch of scrub several meters to their left.

Suddenly, the sunlight splits apart as another horse emerges from a cloud of dust before them and rears up, its front hooves pounding the air inches from their faces. Kofi and Ashtari fall back, blinded by daggers of light. The horse rises even higher on its hind legs and paws the air while its rider, wielding his club in great circles above his head, lets out a terrible cry. Ashtari, now crouching on the ground, gathers Kofi into her arms and smothers him with her body, waiting for that final spear thrust or crushing blow. She can feel Kofi trembling and therefore hugs him even closer. Her only concern now is that the two young Dahomey warriors who have dismounted and who are now standing triumphantly above her will dispatch them both quickly.

But the killing thrusts do not come.

Instead, rough hands pull mother and child to their feet. Manacles are fastened to their wrists and attached to a long chain secured to the saddle of one of the horsemen. Thala, who had been clubbed to the ground and now has blood pouring from her head, is dragged to her feet and manacled - as are the three Nubian slaves

The Ashanti prisoners, shocked and disorientated, are then dragged off down the track. Behind them, lying in darkening pools of blood, are the bodies of their three bodyguards. The crumpled, rag-doll remains of Maloa - a venerated figure in whom resides the ancient history of the Ashanti tribe - also lies to one side of the track, her mangled body already crawling with ants.

***

It took only an hour or so for the Dahomey and their captives to quit the rocky canyon and enter a desolate region of scrubland. They are now travelling due south, towards the equatorial forests of what today we call Guiana. Soon they will be in Dahomey territory, west of the river Volta.

Once, when Kofi stumbled and fell to the ground, the leading horseman leant down from his saddle and pulled the boy to his feet - by his hair. Kofi staggers on - supported still by his mother - but his eyes are full of tears of pain and anger.

'Was he not, after all, the nephew of a king? How dare these scum treat him and his family thus? What would his uncle say? How terrible his uncle's revenge, he thought.'

Two hours later the Dahomey pitch camp in a clearing at the edge of the forest. It is now almost dark.

Still manacled together, the Ashanti captives fall exhausted to the ground while the Dahomy feed and water their horses. One of them lights a fire and prepares a meal. The captives are thrown scraps of dried fish and fruit plucked from the forest. A leather pouch of water is passed from one to the other, although they are only allowed one or two swallows each.

Thala, too tired to eat, grieves in silence for those killed earlier that day - not least Manola. The young Nubian girls huddle together and whisper, encouraging each other in their own language with thoughts of rescue and revenge. Ashtari does her best to keep up the spirits of Kofi and her four servants but they are all too tired and frightened to take any real comfort from her words.

'Kofi, rest now. Try and sleep.'

Kofi snuggles closer to her. He is trembling with fear and exhaustion and soon falls asleep. The heavy iron manacles binding Ashtari's hands cut into her wrists but that is nothing to the mental pain that overwhelms her. She is three months pregnant and knows now that this innocent child growing in her belly will be born into abject slavery.

It is a thought that chills her to the marrow.

***

The Ashanti - like many of the great tribes of Africa - were not unfamiliar with the terrors of slavery. They themselves had slaves, captured in battle or demanded as tribute - like the three young Nubian girls huddled together just a few yards from where Ashtari, Thala and Kofi lie sleeping. For centuries, black men and women have been abducted, taken on camel trains north across the Sahara by Arab merchants and sold. Women and girls from Kumasi itself, the tribal capital of the Ashanti in what is today called Ghana, have ended up in the brothels and harems of Alexandria or Aleppo.

Slavery is endemic, woven into the very fabric of Africa. Now, as the Atlantic trade expands, bringing new wealth to ruthless tribal chiefs, once proud nations - like the Dahomey - are being drawn deeper and deeper into the darkness and cruelty of this ancient trade.

Later that night three of the slavers - enflamed with rum - select one of the Nubian girls and drag her into the bushes where she is raped. None of the captives, including Ashtari, protest. None dare. All remain silent, trying to close their ears to the girl's screams that fill the night, reverberating with the cries of alarmed animals deep in the forest.

When her dreadful screams finally stop and the men stagger back into the clearing with blood on their hands and knives, a desperate silence falls over the camp.

***

Dawn came, filling the forest with its thin, baleful light. Within the canopy mists hang like swathes of finely spun cloth, gossamer thin and undulating gently.

Then, as more light penetrates the darker recesses of the forest, other men emerge - like ghosts. They too are Dahomey but from the coastal region. They greet their companions and examine the captives. Ashtari is stripped of her clothes and ceremonial finery, leaving only her beaded pubic cloth. The men leer and prod, touching both Ashtari and the younger women with lascivious hands. When Thala or Kofi try to intervene, they are beaten into silence with sticks or clubs.

After a meal together - at which money and Ashtari's looted possessions change hands - the horsemen take leave of their Dahomey companions and depart, returning north.

The three men to whom they have been sold have the appearance of Dahomey warriors but are dressed in a mixture of native and European costume. One old man, who appears to be their leader, has a black patch over one eye and sports a battered metal helmet - like that of a sixteenth-century Spanish conquistador. This he wears at a rakish angle, tied onto his head with a length of hemp, the absurdly large knot beneath his chin. Another sports an ancient sword that is almost as tall as him. It hangs from an elaborately decorated belt and drags along in the mud wherever he walks. He is, moreover, bandy legged and sways from side to side, rather like a drunken sailor.

The sun is now up and shafts of light filter down through the canopy. Here lianas, like a thousand boa constrictors, wind themselves about their hosts, forming a mass of dense, hairy foliage high above the path. Ashtari and the others, unused to such a dark, green environment, tremble as each step takes them deeper into this vast, primeval forest.

Kofi, mindful of the ghosts that are said to haunt this place, remains watchful and alert.

After several hours they leave the forest path and plunge into thick foliage, the leading Dahomey cutting their way through with his machete.

Suddenly, opening up before them, they come upon a river of fetid, dark-brown water. Here mango groves cluster on the banks and trees on stilts, as it were, rise out of swamps teeming with snakes. For a mile or so they move downstream, clinging to the bank of the river wherever possible. Sometimes water snakes slither past them, skimming across the surface of the river on some dark, impetuous mission. Sometimes they disturb an unseen bird or flying creature, its ghoulish screams echoing about them like some lost soul in torment.

Kofi now began to chant under his breath whatever spells came into his head. He wished now that he had listened more attentively to their Shaman back in his village. Ashtari, faint with exhaustion, concentrates on helping Thala and the two Nubian girls stagger on through rotting vegetation, all four holding their hands over their faces to try and block out the fetid odours that hang about the place like a plague.

Eventually they reach four dugout canoes, hidden beneath palm leaves on a bank near a bend in the river. Nearby, other captives - some Ashanti but some of unknown origin - squat on the bank, their hands and feet also manacled. There are seven in all, mostly men. They have had been waiting for two days. They stare at Kofi, Ashtari and the three other women but their looks are blank, desolate. No words are exchanged for none can adequately describe their mutual despair.

***

For an hour or so all twelve captives are allowed to rest. Their guards share food amongst themselves and light clay pipes, the fumes of which keep the mosquitoes away and help banish the overwhelming stench of rotting vegetation.

Kofi, now cradled in his mother's arms, sleeps fitfully - dreaming of the enormous, black anaconda that legend says lives in these evil waters.

He is awoken with a kick and dragged to his feet by a fierce tug on the chain. Ashtari and her women also scramble to their feet and follow the others down to the water's edge where they are persuaded to clamber aboard the canoes. Kofi, crouching low in the boat, tries hard not to imagine what lurks beneath his canoe's thin, wooden hull.

Ashtari's Nubian slaves are particularly frightened, never having been in a boat before. They whimper and wail and cling to the nearest adult who tries, unsuccessfully, to silence them - fearful of the Dahomey slaver now seated in the stern.

'Kofi', cried Ashtari, 'Help Thala. Girls - silence!'

Their guard is the old man with one eye and battered metal helmet. He is armed with a whip made of animal hide that sits coiled in his lap - like a sleeping snake.

The Dahomey skilfully steer their canoes away from the bank. At first the current is sluggish but then, as they draw closer to the centre it gains momentum, propelling them faster and faster downstream. The river, punctuated now with small islands, teems with wildlife - strange birds and crocodiles and the occasional hippopotamus. Most of the Ashanti had never seen such monsters.

'Surely', they thought, 'these are creatures of the dead and this fearful river the Pathway to Hell!'

***

They travelled downstream for two days, occasionally coming ashore for food and sleep. On the third morning they turned a bend in the river, whereupon the stream broadened dramatically. The canopy overhanging the river now disappeared, revealing sluggish skies portending rain. Instead of muddy banks and thick forest there are broad expanses of water between islands of rich, dark silt. Lurid white trees, their roots immersed in water and asphyxiated by lack of oxygen, perch precariously on tiny mud banks.

Kofi, in the leading boat, was perhaps the first to smell the sea towards which they are now moving. There, stretched before him, is a vast estuary and far beyond that, an expanse of open, dark-blue water.

'Mother, look!'

Kofi knew nothing of oceans or distant seas. He assumed that what he now saw was a large lake, like the one back home at Kumasi. But what is that strange taste? Can it be salt? He ran his tongue over his parched lips, tasting the tang of wind-born sea-salt that cut like a knife through the fetid stink of this muddy estuary

Although none of the Ashanti knew it at the time, they have now reached the mouth of the river Volta, opening into the Atlantic Ocean. To the west, further along the coast, lay Accra - a desolate shantytown that deals exclusively in slaves.

Accra is situated on what foreigners then called the Gold Coast - a region of bare hills and rocky outcrops celebrated for its trade in human misery. Here, for nearly two hundred years, the Portuguese first and now the British, had sold men and women - 'black gold' as they called it in the coffee houses of London or Lexington. Other blacks supplied these slaves, the inevitable product of internal tribal wars. By 1760, several million men, women and children had already been taken from their villages inland and shipped to South America, the Caribbean islands of Jamaica, Barbados or Trinidad or even further north, to North America.

For the prisoners, still squatting forlornly on the floor of their boats, this dreadful journey has already acquired a metaphysical force, transporting them from security and contentment with their loved ones to the deepest despair imaginable. Some, spiritually at least, 'died' there and then but it is in Accra itself that their nightmare will really begin.

2. 'Gin Lane', London
1758 to September, 1762

'The Life and Times of Kitty Fisher'
A Cautionary Tale

London's 'Gin Lane' is an imaginary place - the creation of writers and popular engravers. However, for those who find themselves living in it, even metaphorically, it is real enough.

See in your mind's eye a lane, cobbled in parts, stretching from Charring Cross northwards, passed Covent Garden and Piccadilly to the parish of St. Giles - an area of slums, filthy courts and squalid alleys teeming prostitutes, thieves and beggars. St. Martins Lane - for that is the street we have just taken - leads inexorably to 'Gin Lane.' Here many of the most wretched inhabitants of London struggle to survive amidst mud, horse-dung and discarded oyster shells. This is a place of brothels, seedy taverns and small booths resolutely dedicated to the dispensation of gin - known locally as 'kill-grief.'

In 1758 Jack Fisher was seven years old when it first dawned on him that he and his mother now lived in 'Gin Lane.'

At about the same time it also dawned on him that his mother was not the loving, supportive creature he had always assumed but a drunken whore. Why Jack should have taken the larger part of seven years to realise this is difficult to comprehend for he had been born in a brothel to a woman who, by all accounts, cared neither for him nor the countless clients she serviced in 'Mother' Bishop's celebrated establishment. Kitty Fisher's primary concern was to acquire enough money - by theft, if necessary - to purchase her next flagon of gin.

But it had not always been like this for when Kitty first came to London she was a beguiling, exceptionally pretty fifteen-year-old.

She was, however, no virgin - having willingly given herself to a livery boy called Harry Swan at the Crown Inn, Faversham. Thereafter, she had enjoyed a string of passionate affairs, few lasting more than a day or so. What she lacked in sexual finesse she made up for by youthful enthusiasm and soon acquired a reputation that spread from Faversham itself to Ramsgate and beyond. In 1754, having 'exhausted' Kent - or so she imagined - she came to London, seeking fame and fortune. London welcomed her with open arms, not least those of the young gallants she picked up in the taverns and 'two-penny' houses off Charring Cross.

While she found comfort and support with these young men, some of whom might have even loved her, the real love of Kitty's life at this time was one Lewis Filander.

Lewis Filander was an actor whose incompetence was matched only by his arrogance - which was limitless. He was tall, thin and rather good looking, in an angular way. His skin was the colour of tallow - as used in church candles - thereby giving him a somewhat ecclesiastical pallor. His hair, once a pale yellow, was now so thin that he was obliged to wear a wig cunningly designed to represent his own, natural hair.

In an age when most gentlemen of substance wore wigs all the time, regular theatregoers regarded this as mere affectation. For his fans - and there were many, including the lovelorn Kitty - it was the height of fashion. Unfortunately, Filander's wig was not a good one. It was small, with five curls on each side and a tendency to slide off the side of his head at the slightest provocation. In fact, he had difficulty keeping it on his head at all. This was partly due to its inadequate construction and to the fact that he refused to use any theatrical glue to keep it in place. Instead, he had developed a technique whereby, by hardly moving at all on stage, he could *balance* it on his head.

This gave his acting, which was wooden at the best of times, even less animation.

For his fans and enemies alike, each performance therefore acquired a certain dramatic tension that had nothing to do with the play itself - with half the audience *longing* for his wig to fall off and the other half desperately *praying* that it would not!

Filander's other claim to fame was his unbridled sexuality, coupled with a stamina that a dray-horse might envy. This was most evident in those dreary, five-act plays, which David Garrick and the management at Drury Lane favoured. With so many scene changes and intervals, Filander was able to copulate backstage or in his dressing room many times in one evening. His record to date was seven - but not with the same woman. His ambition was to beat this record. This was an unlikely possibility - unless someone, in a moment of managerial ineptitude, offered him the substantial part of Hamlet.

Kitty, however, saw none of Lewis Filander's frailties - blinded as she was by her passionate infatuation. She had first seen him on stage in the leading role of Captain Plume in George Farquhar's *The Recruiting Officer*. In his red tunic, tight breeches and military boots he had cut a dashing figure. It had been love at first sight. Kitty herself had always longed to be an actress. She was by now an attractive sixteen-year-old but quite without theatrical talent. Determined, however, to try her luck as an actress she had taken to hanging about the stage doors at Drury Lane or Covent Garden, thereby hoping to ingratiate herself with casts and management alike.

Kitty's chance to actually consummate her new but so far imaginary relationship came some weeks later when she was asked to play the part of Ariel in Filander's adaptation of *The Tempest*. This English classic, first introduced to Drury Lane by Garrick in 1747, was now part of the theatre's extensive Shakespearean repertoire. Garrick, otherwise indisposed himself, had asked Filander to play the part of Prospero - the deposed Duke of Milan who ends up stranded on a remote desert island.

There is only one other woman's part in *The Tempest* and that is Miranda, Prospero's young daughter. On the eve of their first rehearsal, Kitty discovered that this part had been given to a jumped-up trollop by the name of Fanny Hardwick whom Kitty had often seen plying her wares in The Strand. Kitty was insanely jealous for she knew for a fact that Fanny's 'audition' had taken place the previous night in Filander's lodgings off Leicester Square. To be beaten at the bedpost, as it were, was something of a setback in her lovelorn pursuit of her dashing 'Captain Plume.'

Rehearsals took place the following day.

These were simple enough since in each performance, whatever the play, Filander always occupied the well-lit, down-stage-centre position close to the newly installed footlights. Here he would remain (unless otherwise occupied back stage or in his dressing room) for most of the evening - with the rest of the subordinate cast hovering about him like moths round a candle.

Since Filander (like Garrick, his guide and mentor) was in the habit of cutting all but his own part to a minimum, Kitty, in the role of Ariel, ended up with very little to say. This pleased her as she was illiterate and learning lines without the help of someone else was almost impossible. Kitty took some consolation in discovering that Miranda's lines had also been cut to ribbons, largely because Fanny - while exceptional in bed - turned out to have something of a speech impediment on stage.

Kitty's challenge (as Ariel) was to fly - with the help of an elaborate harness and a wire suspended on a series of pulleys in the flies high above the stage. Drury Lane, with its *penchant* for elaborately staged pantomimes and extravagant Shakespearean tragedies, was rather good at these effects and so it was with a mixture of trepidation and ill-contained excitement that Kitty prepared for her theatrical debut as a flying, acrobatic Ariel.

Filander himself had designed her costume - a simple tunic which concealed the harness yet showed off her neat figure and pretty legs. Kitty's first air-borne rehearsals had therefore afforded the largely male cast a great deal of salacious pleasure.

Kitty herself, totally unaware of her somewhat exposed position high above their heads, merely concentrated on swinging as gracefully as possible from one side of the stage to the other while wriggling her legs and flapping her arms up and down like a demented seagull.

Their first night was not a great success. Indeed, it turned out to be something of a farce, largely due to the drunken incompetence of one Stan Jobworthy. He was chief stagehand at Drury Lane and therefore responsible for controlling the wire from which Kitty hung. Her first entrance required that she retreat far into the wings stage left then, on cue, run as fast as she could onstage, whereupon Jobworthy would pull on the wire and launch her into the air.

That, anyway, was the plan.

Unfortunately, Jobworthy's powers of co-ordination were bad enough when sober but the added complication of seven pints of porter consumed earlier that evening was to prove his, and Kitty's, undoing. His first mighty yank on the wire was indeed sufficient to launch Kitty skywards but instead of merely disappearing up into the wings stage right she curved outwards, in an elliptical arc, high above the fore-stage and out into the auditorium. While Jobworthy, in the wings stage right, may have momentarily lost sight of his protégé, the spectators in the pit and beyond had an exceptional view of Kitty's pretty legs and pert bottom. Their response was first one of open-mouthed astonishment, immediately followed by rapturous applause, cheers and raucous catcalls.

It was at this point that Jobworthy, un-sighted and in something of a panic, momentarily let go of the wire, causing Kitty - now at the zenith of her elevation - to plunge back stage-wards at an alarming rate. Filander, whom she had narrowly missed on the way up, was still trying to retrieve his wig when Kitty struck him on the way down - sending him sprawling once more across the stage. For a moment there was stunned silence but as Filander struggled to extricate himself from the tangle of arms and legs in which he now found himself, the audience broke out into rapturous applause - loud enough to rattle the chandeliers.

Normally, such a disaster would have prompted instant dismissal but Filander, against his better judgement perhaps, kept Kitty on the payroll. Thereafter, when not on stage, 'Prospero' and 'Ariel' could be found most days in the greenroom or Filander's dressing room in a passionate embrace - but with one hand firmly clasped to his head.

Thus it was that Jack Fisher was conceived - back stage at Drury Lane.

Sadly, Kitty's theatrical career ended soon afterwards. Naturally, Filander denied paternity and refused to give 'the slut' another penny, dismissing her on some pretence just days after she announced that she was 'late.'

Cruelly abandoned, newly pregnant and without a penny to her name, Kitty took to the streets.

Jack was born, not in the gutter as his father had predicted, but in a sumptuous four-poster bed - the property of 'Mother' Bishop, owner and hostess of one of London's most successful brothels, situated in Little Russell Street and not far from Drury Lane itself.

'Mother' Bishop had discovered Kitty 'drunk and disorderly' in Covent Garden late one night - and in danger of being arrested by the officers of Bow Street Magistrate's Court and thrown into the stocks. Taking pity on the young thing, she had given her board and lodging in return for some light work about the house. Although Kitty was now five months pregnant, 'Mother' Bishop saw this pretty young girl as a sound 'investment' for the future. Eleanor Bishop was, if nothing else, a businesswoman whose commercial flair had already made her exceedingly rich.

Throughout his mother's cloistered confinement, Jack himself clung to life like a cat on a steeply sloping roof.

Even in Kitty's womb he shook off a suicidal infusion of laudanum (for toothache), a crippling dose of mercury boiled in water (for worms) and a highly dangerous attempt at an illegal abortion. Indeed, he even overcame the large and increasingly frequent infusions of neat gin by which his mother surreptitiously eased her memories of Lewis Filander - the man she still loved but who had so cruelly abandoned her in her hour of need.

When Jack finally popped out he was some five weeks premature. His first few moments in the real world were touch and go but the swift application of a spoonful of neat mustard to his mouth soon jerked him into life. Although he only weighed five pounds he was pretty enough, sufficient anyway for the women of the establishment to take him to their hearts and thoroughly spoil him. Kitty was less enamoured of her new brat. She was still only seventeen and to be lumbered with a child this early in her career was not part of her plan for herself. Still, she fed him when required and sort of loved him in her slovenly and frequently inebriated way.

It took very little on the part of 'Mother' Bishop to eventually persuade Kitty to relinquish her job as house chambermaid. Indeed, Kitty embraced her new and relatively secure employment as one of Eleanor's regular prostitutes with an alacrity that astonished even the experienced Eleanor Bishop.

When occupied with a client Kitty would leave baby Jack with one of the other girls. There were other mothers in the brothel so Jack was never short of a willing wet nurse.

Thus, over the next few years, baby Jack Fisher thrived - much to everyone's surprise, especially that of his sluttish mother.

***

East of Leicester Fields, through a maze of lanes and alleys covered in mud and horse dung, is Covent Garden with its bustling markets, shopkeepers' stalls, seedy taverns and smart coffee houses. To the east, Drury Lane itself, stretching north from Round Court to Piccadilly with its smart shops and high-class brothels. In between, there lies a maze of narrow, cobbled alleyways and dark courts.

This was now young Jack's 'patch.'

Here, with countless other bare-arsed children, he would beg or steal, splash in the horse ponds, hurl dung at well-dressed pedestrians, dodge the contents of chamber pots tipped from bedroom windows, snatch hats or wigs, pick countless pockets and generally gad about.

Thus he too prospered but three years later, when Jack was eight, a new man entered his mother's life.

Ned Warren was a highwayman - tall, handsome in a rugged way, with long black hair, a sallow complexion and a face pitted with the scars of a youthful attack of smallpox. He arrived one dark night, banging on the door in the early hours of the morning demanding admittance and bleeding from a gunshot wound in his right thigh. Eleanor Bishop at once let him in, re-locked the door and hid him in a secret room at the back of the house. Kitty was given the task of fetching hot water and a cloth and bathing his gunshot wound.

During those first few days, while Ned fought to survive, an unexpected spark of love ignited Kitty's young heart. All memories of her beloved Filander now vanished in a swoon of girlish adulation for a man whose reputation as a thief and murderer had preceded his dramatic arrival into her mundane life. To her duties as nurse she eagerly added those of cook, chambermaid and, inevitably, lover. At night she would curl up in his arms. Sometimes, after their lovemaking, he would tell her thrilling tales of his adventures as a highwayman. Some of these tales were even true!

'Oh Ned,' cooed Kitty. 'What an exciting life you have led. Tell me that story again, my darling.'

Jack of course was told nothing of his mother's new lover. He knew that a famous fugitive was in hiding with them - most of the parish knew that - but he was never shown where Ned was hidden nor told of his mother's part in the highwayman's gradual recuperation.

One night Bow Street runners arrived unexpectedly with a warrant for Ned's arrest. Since Ned's bedroom was at the back of the house and only entered through a secret door behind a large mirror, it took a while before he was discovered. This delay gave Ned time to pull on his breeches and boots, pocket his gold, cock his pistols and shove an hysterical Kitty under the bed - just as the Bowstreet runners kicked in the bedroom door.

Two men died, shot between the eyes at close range, before Ned was clubbed to the floor and dragged into the street. He was taken, unconscious and bleeding badly, to Bow Street where, still unconscious, he was charged. 'Mother' Bishop was also arrested for harbouring a known fugitive and thrown into Brixton prison to await trial.

It was some hours later that day that the girls eventually discovered Kitty still under the bed. She was semi-conscious and lying in a pool of urine. Her face, now a deathly white, showed no emotion. They cleaned her up and eased her back into Ned's bed where she became hysterical. Only by giving her copious amounts of gin were they able to calm her. Eventually she fell asleep in a drunken stupor and it was in this inebriated state that she remained for the next week or so.

***

Ned's 'show-case' trial took place seven weeks later. It was a short, brutal affair but interesting in that the actual circumstances leading to his unexpected arrival at Eleanor's whorehouse now became public knowledge.

He had attacked a man in broad daylight in Hyde Park. On discovering that his victim was only carrying fourteen shillings, Ned had beaten him senseless then mutilated his body, nailing his genitals to a tree. In the chase that followed, Ned had also killed a constable and taken a bullet in his thigh. Despite his wounds, he eluded capture by disappearing into the darkened alleyways off Curzon Street. With the cheers of encouragement from the stall keepers of nearby Shepherds Market ringing in his ears, Ned had then made his way to Covent Garden and the safety of Eleanor Bishop's brothel.

The trial itself was something of a foregone conclusion yet when it ended and the inevitable sentence of death was passed by the Magistrate, a cry of genuine despair went up from the crowded courtroom - including Kitty, who fainted.

Jack first realised the enormity of what had happened when, only a few weeks after Ned's dramatic arrest, 'Mother' Bishop's brothel was closed down by the Bow Street authorities. She herself, after several months languishing in Newgate prison, was tried, found guilty and deported to 'Parts beyond the Seas', meaning the British colony of Carolina in north America.

Kitty and the other girls, having ransacked the house and removed anything worth stealing, went their separate ways - mostly back onto the streets, leaving Jack to fend for himself. Although Kitty had managed to visit her Ned in Newgate Prison once or twice, he had showed little interest in her, surrounded as he now was by numerous female admirers - many of whom were wealthy aristocrats or rich courtesans drawn to an infamous, charismatic condemned highwayman.

Thus spurned yet again, Kitty took to drink, selling her body to anyone for the price of a glass or two of cheap wine or a flagon of gin.

Throughout all this Jack grew more and more scared, realising for the first time perhaps the precariousness of his situation. He was now nine years old, with a mother who showed no interest in his welfare and who was herself deteriorating rapidly. He and Kitty now lived in a series of decrepit boarding houses, each one worse than the next. Sometimes, unable to pay even the modest rent, they would climb out of the window and, clutching their few belongings, sneak off into the night. Jack, still only a child, now found himself increasingly supporting his ailing mother - by begging in the streets or petty theft. Their future now looked increasingly bleak.

**

The day of Ned Warren's execution dawned, bright and cheerful. By noon the crowd of people at Tyburn, near what today we call Marble Arch, was running into thousands, jostling each other for the best view.

Ned's three-mile journey by cart from Newgate Prison, via Holborn and Oxford Street, took about an hour. The cart consisted of a railed platform to which Ned was chained in a standing position. Behind him, on the cart, lay his cheap, wooden coffin. By all accounts he was in good humour, waving to the crowds lining Oxford Street and blowing kisses at any pretty girl he spotted. Many female members of the crowd threw tiny bouquets so that the floor of his cart was soon covered with flowers. The street vendors and sellers of hastily written ballads highlighting Ned's more celebrated achievements - most of them invented - did a brisk trade, as did the numerous pickpockets mingling with the crowd.

There were, however, no fine speeches for Ned's characteristic bravado deserted him the moment they tied the noose round his neck. In fact, he shit himself - much to the satisfaction of the hangman whom he had failed to tip adequately.

The horses, whipped into motion, hoisted Ned aloft until he hung, high above the crowds. For three full minutes he danced at the end of his rope - his legs performing a macabre jig. This gave his fans something else to shout about, many providing an impromptu chorus to accompany his 'dance.' Others, mostly women, burst into tears or fainted. Indeed, so popular was this highwayman that a great lamentation filled the park until Ned's macabre dance finally stopped and the hangman moved closer with his knife.

By the time they had taken him down and slit open his stomach, plunged hooks and hands into the bloody cavity and withdrawn a length of his guts, Ned Warren was probably dead.

**

23

Kitty and Jack were now living in a sordid tenement in the parish of St. Giles. They had neither money nor hope. The year is 1762 and Jack is now ten years old.

Kitty, who was now generally too drunk to even know the time of day, had finally succumbed to the pox. Salivation - a 'cure' for venereal disease that involved 'sweating' it out of the system - had not worked. Dosed with mercury, Kitty's saliva turned black and her gums swelled, causing her teeth, already rotten, to fall out one by one.

Jack, who had himself aged somewhat these last few months, was equally morose. He was at a loss to know what to do. On the day that Ned Warren 'shuffled off this mortal coil', he could be found slumped at the end of his mother's soiled bed, chewing a crust of bread and staring into a bleak, unpromising future.

After the glamour and excitement of Drury Lane, Kitty Fisher and her luckless son had finally reached 'Gin Lane.'

3. The Middle Passage
November, 1762

The 'Cerberus', a brigantine sailing under Captain George Gibson of Lancaster, lay at anchor some distance offshore - conveniently beyond the range of the six rusty cannons guarding the fort at Accra (West Africa).

She had begun life ferrying coal up and down the west coast of England, working out of the small, relatively new port of Whitehaven. In 1752 her holds had been changed to accommodate another, more sinister black 'cargo.' Since then, nine years plying the Gold Coast had turned her pristine sails into a tatty patchwork quilt of rotting, off-white canvas. Her planks, alternately expanded and shrunk by the tropical heat of West Africa and the icy waves of the Atlantic, were now as leaky as a sieve and riddled with teredo worm. In her wake she trailed long strands of seaweed.

Her crew, as verminous a collection of riff-raff as could be found even in these waters, were as bent and twisted as the planks on which they stood.

This particular morning Captain Gibson came ashore in his longboat, surfing in on the Atlantic rollers that pound these coasts. It was an exhilarating, if dangerous, procedure but nothing compared to the dangers of dealing with the Dahomy slavers that inhabit Accra itself. After an exchange of gifts, Gibson sat down in the worm-eaten hut that served as their mess-hall and began the business of the day -

a mixture of intense barter and bribery, washed down with vast quantities of indifferent French brandy.

Later that same morning Gibson visits the barracoon to inspect the sorry collection of men, women and children for sale.

For seven weeks now these slaves in Accra have squatted in their own excrement, with little protection from the blistering sun or the sudden squalls of rain that constantly batter this coastline. Imprisoned in this stinking compound, Kofi and his mother have 'survived' on a diet of boiled horse beans and yam gruel. However, mother and child are now showing signs of profound physical and mental debilitation.

Many in the barracoon have by now grown so weak that they simply squat in the mud, waiting for death. This included Thala - despite the comfort and support that Ashtari had tried to give her throughout their ordeal thus far. Not long after their incarceration, Thala simply lay down and died. Grief for Ashtari and Kofi's captivity and the murder of Maloa had clearly proved too much for this loyal Ashanti servant. Slavers took her body away later that day and threw it into a large pit; an open grave already filled with the naked bodies of those who had prematurely died in captivity.

Perhaps they were the 'lucky' ones.

Thereafter, Ashtari missed Thala terribly. She often thought also of her dead bodyguards and the young Nubian slave, gang-raped and murdered in the bush. No one knew what had happened to the other two girls. Being young and pretty they probably ended up in one of the many brothels along the Gold Coast that serviced those foreign sailors - British, Dutch, Portuguese - who manned the many slave ships that regularly visited Accra.

Some captives in the compound itself became mad, crouching in a corner of the stockade and gibbering to themselves like demented monkeys. Surrounded by such horrors, it is as much as Ashtari can do to preserve her own equilibrium. She does so by focusing all her loving care and attention on her son and by being as positive as she can - even though in her heart she knows that they can not survive much longer.

Gibson, peering over the wall of the barracoon, can see that these abject creatures have suffered terribly. Many, he realised, were unlikely to survive the journey to Jamaica. However, anxious to first line his own pockets, Gibson selects five of the better-preserved blacks for his own use - including Kofi and his mother - and seventy-three others (men and women) for his wealthy clients back in Whitehaven.

'The tall woman is clearly pregnant. Two for the price of one', reasons Captain Gibson. 'As for the others, God knows what will become of them! We shall see, no doubt!'

Later that morning Gibson's slaves are taken from the barracoon and placed in canoes by Dahomey slavers. Some can barely walk after weeks of captivity in the barracoon yet all somehow scramble into the fragile boats, 'encouraged' by frequent lashes from the slaver's whips. Kofi, revived somewhat by the fresh sea air that now fills his lungs, gazes seaward in wonder at the huge ship lying at anchor, its sails already unfurling.

***

The short but choppy journey over the reef that guards the sea entrance to Accra proves something of a nightmare so that by the time Ashtari and the others reach the towering hulk of the 'Cerberus' they are in no fit state to clamber up the ship's ladders. The crew, therefore, manhandle them, boat by boat, into a great net and hoist them aloft like cattle.

Unceremoniously released from the coarse netting, they now lie on the deck in a confused heap of abject humanity - exhausted and frightened.

Kofi found himself crushed beneath the arms and legs of four men. For a moment he panicked, fearing suffocation, but slowly they rolled apart and he was able to extricate himself. His mother, lying close by, is clutching her stomach. After the vile stench of the barracoon, the deck of the ship smells very strange to him - a mixture of tar, coal and brimstone.

Sailors, manning water pumps, then begin to hose the slaves down. The fierce jets of salt water send those who have managed to stagger to their feet sprawling once more - much to the amusement of the British sailors manning the hoses.

As the wind fills her sails, the great ship now begins to move, slowly turning to confront the Atlantic rollers thundering in towards them. For the slaves, many now chained below decks, this sudden, violent motion is absolutely terrifying and a great cry of lamentation fills the darkness of their new prison.

Those still on deck are now herded towards the main hatch leading to the wooden dungeons. Kofi, at the back of the crowd and clinging to his mother's arm, watches as his companions disappear down this black hole. The stench that meets Kofi as he and Ashtari step down into the blackness is indescribable.

***

The 'Cerberus' is now well underway, her sails straining in the brisk, offshore breeze and her prow cutting through the Atlantic waves with a speed that ran contrary to her dilapidated appearance. In still waters she appears sluggish and squat but at sea, helped by the favourable Guinea current and a good wind, she is almost graceful.

Gibson has set his course due east, for the Portuguese island of San Tomas. This volcanic outcrop is rich in fruit, vegetables and fresh meat. Here he will pick up the provisions he needs for the long journey to Jamaica.

Although the overall quality of the batch of slaves he purchased in Accra is poor, Gibson now has sufficient numbers to allow him to quit the Gold Coast and head for the Caribbean - then home to England. With First Lieutenant Bellamy Tait in charge of the short trip to San Tomas, Gibson is now free to return to his cabin on the quarter-deck and pour himself a large, well-earned brandy.

'Lucy! Where are you, girl? Bring me brandy, you little black trollop. And my pipe, while you are at it!'

Apart from Tait, Gibson's only real companion on board the 'Cerberus' is Lucy. She is a young, black slave he acquired on a previous trip to the Gold Coast. Lucy is now fourteen. Since Gibson treats her well - having first wooed her into his bed with a few, small gifts - she quickly fell under his spell, thereafter appointing herself cook, cleaner and ship's 'wife' to the tall, handsome, blond-haired captain of the 'Cerberus'.

Lucy's most precious possession is a little mirror. She has a pronounced squint in one eye but 'hides' this by closing her bad eye, as if winking at you, and looking sideways with the other. This shy, somewhat provocative look proves curiously attractive but sometimes, coming in upon her unexpectedly, Gibson invariably catches her staring forlornly into her little mirror, clearly wishing her squint would vanish - as if by magic.

There are of course other women on board the 'Cerberus' - apart from those now stowed below. These are the official 'wives' of the crew. They are made up of professional white prostitutes or willing black slaves - the latter preferring an active sexual life in the forecastle or tweendeck to a slow death in the holds below. These women move freely about the boat, attending to their domestic duties and drinking with the sailors between watches.

The Master-at-Arms on board the 'Cerberus' is Nathaniel Wilson. He is the oldest man on the ship and has skin that is so wrinkled and weather-beaten that he resembles a pickled walnut. His hair is grey and very short, so that it has the look of a worn scrubbing brush.

Wilson has knocked about the Caribbean for the larger part of his fifty-three years and there is little he does not know about man's inhumanity to man. He is a brilliant shot and very handy with a cutlass but his speciality is the branding iron. Once each new slave has boarded the 'Cerberus' he goes below and deftly applies his red hot iron, throwing a bucket of water over the victim when they faint with the pain. Sometimes, if one dies on him, he attaches a line to its feet and drags the body behind the ship as shark bait. Grilled shark-meat is a nourishing alternative to salt pork or ship's biscuit.

For some reason - much to Wilson's annoyance - Gibson had forbidden him to brand certain of the women and children imprisoned below - those the captain had selected for his own use. This meant that 'favoured' slaves - like Ashtari and Kofi - and eleven others have been spared this barbaric indignity.

Nathaniel Wilson himself lives in the orlop.

His cabin - more a cupboard than a room - is next to the powder magazine in the lowest part of the ship. Because of its proximity to the filthy bilge slopping about inches beneath his feet, the smell here is actually worse than that of the slaves' quarters above but Wilson thinks nothing of it, so accustomed is he to its evil stench.

It is here too that he 'entertains' his 'black beauties.'

Nathaniel Wilson has never had a regular 'wife' on board ship, preferring instead to take his pick most nights from the many women or young girls incarcerated in the ship's hold. Each night he would drag his chosen 'companion' to his cabin in the orlop.

Down there, in the very bowels of the 'Cerberus', her screams could not be heard.

***

Kofi, gaining strength from his mother's fortitude, has survived these first days at sea better than most. Indeed, he has begun to recover some of his former spirit, despite the dreadful conditions in which he now finds himself. At night, however, it is a different story. For Kofi, their capture by the Dahomey had been the most frightening experience of his short life. The suddenness and brutality of the attack, the murder of their bodyguards and the callous way the slavers had killed Maloa, had made a profound impression on him.

In his dreams Kofi relives those moments, night after night.

For Ashtari, Maloa's murder had also been a defining moment - not only in her life but in that of the tribe. Maloa had been a living link with their past; an oracle to whom they could turn and a repository of all that gave the Ashanti their identity. Now she was gone and her descendants, including Ashtari herself, are cut adrift in a sea of violence and confusion, with neither past nor future.

There were, however, some consolations.

Although neither Ashtari nor Kofi fully understood their relation to Captain Gibson, it soon became clear that somehow they were under this white man's protection. Occasionally Gibson would descend below and examine his 'property.' With a sponge doused with attar-of-roses clamped to his face against the foul stench, he would edge his way along the gangplanks and into the smaller hold at the front of the ship. Here Ashtari and some eleven other women and children were housed. Although still very confined, their quarters at least offered some privacy - something not possible in the main holds where the majority of men and women lived cheek-by-jowl and in total, terrifying darkness.

Although Gibson never spoke directly to his slaves, he smiled and nodded at them - from which they took a crumb of comfort. Later, when the buckets of gruel came round, there would be extra portions of horse beans fried in lard, with occasional lumps of salt-beef, pork or shark for the captain's 'favoured' slaves, including Ashtari and her son.

Favoured or not, it was the sanitary arrangements on the 'Cerberus' which traumatised most of her captives - especially Ashtari, who had always been fastidious in matters of personal hygiene. Large barrels had been placed at intervals the length of the ship, including the small hold in which she and Kofi lived. Into these the slaves could defecate.

For those who subsequently developed dysentery - including two women and a child in Ashtari's quarters - or who became too weak to reach the barrels, the squalor was indescribable. This in turn led to further outbreaks of diarrhoea, until parts of the slaves' quarters were awash with liquid manure. Once a week the sailors came below with hosepipes to wash down the floor of the hold and its ailing cargo but it was never enough to mitigate the horrors of life below decks.

***

Gibson is feeling good. Two weeks have now passed and the 'Cerberus' is in mid-Atlantic and with the southeast Trade Winds now filling her sails. To the north lie the Cape Verde Islands and to the west - Jamaica. He is thoroughly glad too have quit the Gold Coast with its pirates, treacherous slavers of all colours and the Bight of Benin with its disease-ridden coastal swamps. Moreover, only a handful of slaves have died thus far. At this rate he might just make a good return on his and the company's investments.

'What will be, will be!' he reasoned. 'Lucy, more rum!'

Conditions for the slaves below have also improved. Each day, in rotation, a group of slaves are allowed on deck for an hour or so - to take the air and to exercise. Those strong enough for work are set to scrub the decks and rinse them with vinegar. The women also help with the cooking or with grinding corn. This corn is then added to the slaves' regular diet of bean soup, together with a little rice or peppers.

Although material conditions have improved somewhat, the *mental* state of the slaves is deteriorating rapidly.

For Ashtari, the last few weeks have been particularly hard. Surrounded by women and children, she feels it is her responsibility as one of royal blood to set an example to her fellow sufferers, many of whom are also Ashanti. Although her primary concern is with Kofi's welfare, she has taken it upon herself to look after as many of the others as she can. This proves a constant strain on her own mental and physical strength, not least because she is now nineteen weeks pregnant.

In her heart, despite all her maternal instincts, she now knows that she does not want her child to be born into such a terrible world as that in which she and Kofi now find themselves.

***

In the southern Atlantic Ocean violent squalls, storms and even hurricanes are common but so far their voyage has been without incident. Now, however, the 'Cerberus' has entered the Doldrums - a region of low-pressure midway between the Trade Winds to the north and those of the south. Here the sea is flat and glassy, the lack of any breeze causing the ship's sails to flap listlessly. The ship's motion, such as it is, is now is extremely uncomfortable - to mariner and slave alike

For the crew it is a particularly busy time - endlessly trimming the sails to catch the slightest breath of wind, first from one quarter and then from another. The men at the sheets come off their watch exhausted and demoralised and with little encouragement or support from Nathaniel Wilson whose constant commands and abuse ring in their ears, hour on hour.

For the slaves imprisoned below it is even worse.

The heat there is now intense and the humidity intolerable, so much so that pitch between the planks has begun to melt, some of it dripping down into the holds. Dehydration is a serious problem and although Gibson has increased the slaves' water rations it is not enough to counter excessive sweating in cramped, airless conditions. To add to their discomfort, refuse from the 'Cerberus' - largely human excrement from the vats emptied into the sea - has formed a stinking pool of effluent surrounding the ship. Thunderous showers occasionally eased their suffering but the cooling water soon steams away, leaving the cramped holds hot and airless.

While regular exercise on the upper decks has improved morale, malnutrition and enforced inactivity the rest of the time has reduced most of the captives to a weakened state. Lethargy, foul breath and extreme tenderness of the gums indicates scurvy, a debilitating condition caused by a lack of fresh fruit. The slaves themselves have become alarmed as livid blotches appear on their arms and legs while teeth loosen and gums turn to fungus. Although they are occasionally given a mouthwash of limejuice, this does little to improve their overall condition.

Each day another one or two die. Each day Ashtari, mindful of the child within her, fears for her little family.

For these captive men, women and children there is simply no conceivable future. Some therefore slide into a profound depression from which there is no return - until death comes and 'saves' them. While Gibson and his white savages might call it suicide, the blacks on board the 'Cerberus' see it as a natural solution to the horrors in which they now find themselves. Several of the Ashanti slaves died in this manner - willing it upon themselves by way of escape from the horrors below decks.

***

Gibson himself has no interest in the mental state of his slaves. Even if he could understand their anguish, it is unlikely that he would have cared either way. For him they are little more than 'goods and chattels' - to be bought and sold. Feelings for these abject, Godless creatures - pathetic descendants of Ham the Cursed - did not really enter into it. That Lucy was also such a creature did not, however, seem to occur to him either. She was his willing mistress and somehow that set her apart from her 'cursed' brethren - souls lost for ever in God's exclusively Aryan universe.

Gibson had once been an officer in the Royal Navy, learning his seamanship the hard way. By 1756 he had had enough of its peculiar brand of brutality and that year had persuaded his father to give him the money to relinquish his commission. Although The Reverend Thomas Gibson had coughed up, Gibson junior jumped ship in Tobago and promptly used his father's money to buy a share in the

'Cerberus', thereby becoming a slave trader at the age of forty-two - and a Royal Navy deserter, the punishment for which was death by rope from the yard arm.

Captain George Gibson had been a slaver now for four, lucrative years. Soon he will have made enough money to retire and live the life of a country gentleman on his estates in Lancashire. He would ride to hounds, get gout and generally lead a dissolute life appropriate to his status as local squire. Many of those currently in Parliament had done just that, creating fortunes out of the misery and labour of countless blacks. Indeed, many had been knighted for their troubles. Of course, Lucy would have to go. His devoted black 'wife' had served him well for two years now. When the time came he would simply sell her at the slave market in Trinidad - for a handsome profit.

A loud knock at his cabin door wakes Gibson from this reverie. It is the Master-at-Arms, a man of few words. The word he spoke now was 'cholera.'

'How many?'
'About ten, maybe a dozen.'

Wilson left, closing the cabin door behind him.

Far below, in the stench and blackness of the ship's hold, news of an outbreak of cholera has already spread like wildfire. The sick men and women are situated near the stern, the most cramped quarter in the ship. While they do not know it as cholera, some are already familiar with its symptoms since in times of famine or flood many villages in the Ashanti lowlands had been wiped out by this mysterious yet dreadful disease.

Suddenly the hatches open and a gang of sailors, their faces covered with kerchiefs, descend the stairway. They unchain the dozen or so sick men and women lying there and drag them back towards the stairs. At first, in the gloom, it is not clear what is happening but soon a great cry goes up from the other captives in the adjacent holds. The sick themselves fight and struggle but most are too weak and can only scream and shake with terror as they are manhandled up the steps and out into the blinding light. The sailors, working in pairs, then begin to lift the sick men and women off the deck and throw them overboard. Wilson, armed with a cutlass, struts up and down the quarterdeck, supervising the massacre - with undeniable relish.

'Step lively, lads. You don't want to be catching 'nuffing from these buggers. Chuck 'em over - quick now!'

Wilson is in his element. He already has a fearsome reputation for cruelty, having once on a previous trip on the 'Cerberus' punished a black mutineer by personally chopping off both the man's hands and hanging him by his feet from the rigging - to bleed to death. Three others, thought to have been involved in this attempted mutiny, had had their ears cut off before being flung to the sharks.

'Come on now, me darling boys. Step lively! Davy Jones is already a'callin' them filthy blackies!'

When the other sick slaves see what is happening they stagger to their feet and run about the deck in an attempt to escape, whereupon they are knocked to the floor by sailors wielding cudgels or belaying pins and then thrown into the sea. This is accompanied by jeers and catcalls from the off-duty crew and their 'wives' who have gathered on the forecastle or who hang from the shrouds in order to obtain a better view.

From his cabin window at the stern, Gibson watches his sick slaves littering the ship's wake. When eventually the sharks move in, the sea beneath his window is a cauldron of activity, turning the sea a lurid crimson

Gibson, who has watched all this with some interest, now opens the casement window of his wardroom for Lucy to obtain a better view but she refuses to look and withdraws instead to her little galley where she busies herself with her pots and pans.

***

The brutal murder of those dozen slaves with cholera had a profound effect on all the others in the dark holds of the 'Cerberus'. Feelings of guilt were paramount, especially amongst those who had known the victims and who somehow blamed themselves, merely for surviving thus far. Close relatives or members of the same tribe plunged into terminal grief - never to recover. Many became deranged, tossing and turning in their narrow spaces, rolling their eyes and muttering strange, incomprehensible words - reminding Gibson of the lunatics he had once seen in The Bedlam back in London.

For Ashtari and her ailing son it was a terrible time.

For hours on end Kofi lay on the wooden floor staring at the planks a few feet above his head. When Ashtari tried to tell him a story or recall happier times he would turn away and bury his head in his hands. He never cried but for Ashtari his silence was far more heartrending even than sobs of anguish.

There were now one-hundred-and-eighteen prisoners left of the two-hundred-and-thirty that had left Accra. That night Gibson opened another bottle of brandy.

With shaking hands he poured himself a generous measure and over the next three days sank into a drunken stupor.

4. London, England
January, 1763

The Cruel Apprenticeship
The continuing tale of Jack Fisher - abandoned son of Kitty Fisher, sometime actress, whore and professional drunk

Jeremiah Blagg left Tyburn Road and pointed his flea-bitten donkey south, towards Golden Square. It is not yet dawn and the night-men's carts are heading for the fields of Mary-le-Bon and Tottenham Court to dump barrels of excrement from a thousand privies. Even Blagg, who is not exactly fastidious in matters of personal hygiene, clamps a large, hairy hand to his nose and gives his donkey a sharp dig in its ribs with both hob-nailed boots.

The very small boy walking at his side is completely black - with soot. So black is he that it is difficult to see where he begins and where the muddy streets leave off. Moreover, he is finding it very hard to keep up with Blagg, largely because of his own battle with a sack from which an exceedingly angry goose is struggling to escape.

'Step lively, young Scab', growls Blagg. 'We ain't got all day.'

It is light by the time they reach Golden Square and find the house requiring their services. Blagg had to knock several times before a maid, emerging sleepily from the basement, lets them in.

The grimy urchin, having deposited sooty footprints on the stairs all the way up to the attic, then scrambles through the skylight and up onto the roof. Clinging to a chimney pot, Scab unexpectedly lets out a great cry - like a triumphant rooster.

'Get on wiv it, you little bugger!' yells Blagg from the safety of the attic.

Balancing precariously on slippery slates, the boy next reaches into his sack and extracts the goose - which would have flown off immediately had not the child held it resolutely by the throat. Despite a flapping of wings and enough strangled squawks to wake the neighbourhood, the goose is then shoved down the nearest chimney pot, head first.

Blagg promptly quits the attic and races downstairs, his boots clattering on the wooden treads. He arrives in the drawing room just in time to see his goose land on the carpet in a shower of soot. The bird immediately shakes its wings and takes flight, straight into the shutters which it hits with a resounding 'thump.' It lies on the floor momentarily stunned - long enough for Blagg to pop it back into its sack.

'That will be thruppence!' says the sweep to a startled housekeeper.

***

Some hours later, behind Hungerford Market, Blagg is accosted by a young woman holding an empty bottle in one hand and a small child in the other. The sweep had often seen her previously, usually drunk and slumped in the gutter. Today she is really quite coherent.

'Ow much, then?'
'Ow much? Wot do yer mean, ow much?'
'For 'im. Ow much?'

Blagg looked at the grubby child hiding behind its mother's skirts.

'Two shillin'!'
'Three!'
'Two shillin' and that's final!'
'Sold! Giv us yer money!'

Blagg hands the woman two coins and grabs the startled boy by the collar, dragging him away before his mother can change her mind. Without so much as a wave, she then turns and staggers off - heading towards the nearest gin shop in Villiers Street.

Thus was Jack Fisher, aged ten years and two months, abandoned and apprenticed in one swift, brutal transaction.

A brief account of the life and times of Jeremiah Bragg

Jeremiah Blagg, now fifty-seven, has been a sweep most of his life. Indeed, he began climbing chimneys when he was six years old.

'In learning a child', he often claimed, 'you can't never be soft wiv 'im. You must always use wiolence.'

That he himself had been abused and exploited at an early age was, it seems, justification enough for the cruelty he now lavishes on each young sweep that falls into his clutches.

'When I was a climbing boy', he would boast, 'we slept five or six together in a kind of cellar, with straw for our beds and our soot bags for cover. Me father was a silk-weaver and he did all he knew to keep me from being a sweep but I niver thought of anyfink but climbing and look at me now - Master Sweep, and proud of it!'

This little speech, which most of his cronies had heard many times before, cut no ice in London's Chick Lane. It was generally felt among the murderers, pickpockets, body-snatchers and 'tarts' who made up his neighbours that a sweep - especially a Master Sweep - was little better than a double-poxed, long-arsed son-of-a-bitch and, therefore, best avoided.

Which they did - unless they could persuade him that it was his turn to buy another round of ale.

***

Blagg held Jack captive for three days, locked in a freezing cupboard under the stairs in Blagg's 'gaff' and fed only on bread and water. 'Soften them up first, then train 'em.' That was his 'method.' It had worked on countless boys before Jack and would, no doubt, work on him - even if he were proving to be a spirited little bastard.

For Jack, the cupboard was unmitigated torture. He spent hours squatting in his own excrement. Night was the worst for then he became cold and hungry. At such times he thought of his mother, Kitty. He had always suspected that one day she would abandon him. Now it had finally happened. For as long as he could remember he had been living on his wits, fighting for survival from one day to the next in the streets of London. He was still only a child but his life had been one long struggle, apart from the first few years in 'Mother' Bishop's brothel when he and Kitty had lived like 'pigs in shit.' But that was then and this is now.

The last year had been particularly difficult. Kitty, for reasons Jack could not discover, had unexpectedly left the brothel one day and taken to the streets again. Her drinking thereafter increased dramatically, until the larger part of each day was spent in a drunken, gin-soaked haze. But Blagg was different. He was dangerous. Even Jack could see that and it made him shake with fear. While he had, in his short life, encountered many violent characters, Jeremiah Blagg was turning out to be one of the worst. If he were to get through this new period of his life, Jack knew that he would have to draw upon both his experience and his natural flair for survival.

On the morning of the third day Blagg pulled him from his dark prison beneath the stairs and out through the front door.

'Well now, Jack', said Blagg with an evil grin, 'it's time you earned your bed and lodging'!'

'No it aint!' yelled Jack, his eyes blazing with three days of pent-up anger. 'Go to hell, you filthy old bugger!'

Although weak from his stay in the cupboard, Jack struggled and kicked as Blagg dragged him further into the street.

'Let me go, you evil, pock-faced son of a doxy!'

Blagg silenced him with a thump round the ear that sent Jack sprawling into the gutter where he lay, stunned. Blagg then lifted him up by the collar of his tattered jacket and dragged him screaming down Chick Lane and then on to a large house in nearby Ludgate. Here Jack was stripped to his breeches, given a peaked, canvas cap and a small brush and shoved, headfirst, up a still-warm chimney.

At first Jack was so startled that he could say nothing but then a wave of panic, claustrophobia and anger overwhelmed him and he let out a shout that reverberated up the chimney - causing a sudden shower of soot to cover his eyes and mouth. Coughing and spluttering, he tried to withdraw - only to receive a kick from Blagg standing in the hearth below. Jack cried out in pain and kicked back but it was no use, there was no escape. Another sharp blow followed, sending him even further up the narrow flue. Clawing with his free hand and pressing hard with his knees against the rough interior of the chimney, Jack eventually scrambled clear of the grate - and Blagg's lethal, hob-nailed boots.

After several minutes of climbing Jack reached a slight bend in the chimney. Here he could pause for breath. He spat the filth from his mouth, shook his head like a spaniel and peered upwards - towards the light. In the warm currents of air still circulating in the chimney, minute flakes of soot hung above him like black moths Although the sky was not yet visible, enough light spilled down the shaft to stop him from feeling entirely claustrophobic. His elbows and knees were already cut and bruised. He felt blood trickling down his arms from his grazed knuckles.

Another shout from Blagg below persuaded him to scramble further up the chimney. Each movement of his arms and legs now sent a stab of pain through his body. He began to cry. His tears - a mixture of anger and pain - formed thin, white streaks down his sooty cheeks. For an hour he scrambled up - then down - that chimney, bringing with him quantities of soot. When he eventually landed in the grate, coughing and spluttering, his hands and knees were covered in blood. Much later, resting on a crude bed in the verminous room he now shared with two other climbing boys, Jack thought only of the pain - and escape. That night he cried himself to sleep.

***

Chick Lane - a ramshackle collection of houses and filthy courts, ankle-deep in mud and grimy snow.

Blagg's 'gaff' is a modest terraced house at one end of this rat-infested street. Even though it is too close for comfort to the open sewer that is Fleet Ditch, it is home to Jeremiah Blagg. He liked Chick Lane.

Inside this hovel Blagg and his lads are as snug as bugs in a rug. Since the boys 'slept black' the house is as sooty as they are. They never wash. Scab, who is eleven, cannot remember when he last saw soap and water - unless it was at the Foundling Hospital once when he was three. Jem, the eldest apprentice, had once fallen in the Serpentine but that didn't count.

The boy's room is very small. It contains a rough table, a chair or two and three greasy, wooden cots set into the wall. The boys sleep on sacks filled with straw and cover themselves with the bags they used for carrying soot.

The next morning Jack is woken with a thump in the ribs. It is Blagg, leering down at him. It is dawn and sleet is scudding against the tiny window in fitful bursts, causing the grime to run down the panes in inky rivulets.

'Wake up! Its time you was brined.'

Jack turns away and buries his face in the sack that served as his blanket. Blagg promptly snatches the sack from Jack's cot just as Scab enters the room. The sooty urchin, who is very small, is struggling with a bucket of thick, brown liquid which he then plonks in front of the boy.

'Brine!' says Blagg - with relish. 'You rubs it on yer wounds. It will stop 'em bleedin' and 'arden yer scabs!'

He then grabs Jack from behind and holds him in a vice-like grip, whereupon the sooty urchin dips a rag in the liquid and slaps it onto each bloodstained knee. Jack lets out a scream of agony as the salt enters his wounds. Blagg tightens his grip as Jack twists and turns and lashes out with his legs. Scab, skipping neatly to one side, applies another quick dab to Jack's elbows - whereupon Jack faints - much to the amusement of his two torturers.

Jack came to in the cupboard, some hours later. He could barely move. The scabs on his knees and elbows were still sticky. When he put his fingers to his lips he could taste blood - and brine.

A brief account of Jem,
Principal Apprentice to Jeremiah Bragg, Master Sweep

Dawn broke, creeping like a thief through the cracks in the door of his prison. At first Jack refused to leave his cupboard, preferring its filth to that of another terrifying scramble up some dark, sinister chimney. Blagg, wise in the ways of reluctant young sweeps, seized him by one ear and pulled him screaming into the hallway.

'Well now, Jack', said Blagg pleasantly. 'That 'aint no way to treat yer Master, anxious as I am to learn you the secrets of our ancient craft. Why, Jem 'ere was just like you - once. Now look at im. What a fine, upstanding sweep he's become - and all because I nurtured and trained 'im proper!'

Before them lounged a thin youth covered in soot from head to toe. He was seventeen years old and stood with his hips tilted at a very strange angle while his hands, knees and elbows pointed in every other direction - north, south, east and west. The only colour visible was his eyes, which were pink like an albino rabbit's.

In the climbing fraternity Jem was famous - not least because his thin, etiolated limbs often ended up in the most unexpected places. On one occasion, descending the stairs in Lord Chesterfield's house off Curzon Street, Jem got his left elbow and right leg inexplicitly stuck in the banisters. It took two footmen and a chambermaid to extricate him. He was, however, much admired by other 'climbing boys' on account of him being, so Blagg claimed, 'entirely double jinted.'

'Now Jack', said Blagg, 'I want you to accompany Jem to a very agreeable chimney near Puddle Dock. But don't get no ideas of runnin' away! Jem may look soft in 'is head but really he's as 'ard as nails and likely to skin you alive before I can save yer! Aint that the gospel truth, Jem?'

Jem grinned but said nothing. Jack noticed that the youth's teeth were a greenish yellow.

***

Jem led Jack out of the house and down Chick Lane, then south towards Newgate Street. It had begun to rain.

At first Jack found it difficult to walk, partly because of his night in the cupboard and because the wounds on his elbows and knees were particularly painful. Jem, sensing Jack's discomfort, took him by the arm and helped him down the street. Although neither spoke, Jack felt that in the midst of Blagg's terrifying world he had unexpectedly found a new, if somewhat strange, friend.

At the start of Ludgate Street they passed a sedan chair hurrying west and a lamplighter extinguishing his oil lamps. Carts, filled with hay, climbed the hill while a solitary herdsman prodded three skinny cows towards Smithfield Market. An elderly night-watchman stepped out of his hut and stretched his bones. He shivered, peered skywards, and then retreated into his sentry box.

Jem hurried on, leading Jack through the alleys and passageways that burrowed through the city like wasps in a windblown apple. This was the domain of rogues, cloak-twitchers and catamites.

As if on cue, a group of young 'blades' suddenly rounded a corner and staggered towards them. They were drunk and clung to each other, giggling. Their faces were heavily rouged and their lopsided wigs decorated with girlish ribbons. They greeted the two boys with open arms and lascivious winks. One youth, dressed in pea-green breeches and ruffled shirt, detached himself from his leery companions and advanced towards Jack - wagging his tongue up and down in an obscene manner.

'Why, look what we have here!', he cooed. 'A little black cherub just ripe for plucking!'

The youth was now blocking their path, grinning and swaying his hips from side to side in a provocative manner. Suddenly he leapt forward and made a lecherous grab at Jack but with a well-aimed shove Jem swiftly sent him sprawling into the gutter.

'Buggerantoes', whispered Jem, as he led Jack into the darkness of a nearby alleyway. 'You don't want nuffin' to do with them cherries.'

Suddenly, looming above them, there appeared the huge shape of St. Paul's Cathedral. It hung for a moment but then, like a great storm cloud, vanished behind tall, elegant buildings. Turning south they now crossed Carter Lane and headed downhill towards the Thames. Here the houses were ramshackle affairs, made of worm-eaten wood and crumbling brick. The alleyways that criss-crossed this part of London were thick with excrement thrown from bedroom windows. The lanes were still empty but soon beggars, drunks, prostitutes and children of the streets would swarm like rats in every direction. The stench from the open sewers that meandered sluggishly down each lane towards the river made the air thick with contagion.

When they reached Puddle Dock they turned east and followed the river towards the Tower of London.

They eventually found the house in Thames Street. It was a tall, terraced building in the Palladian style belonging to some rich merchant. The scullery maid let them in and showed them to the drawing room on the second floor. Sheets had already been spread in front of the fireplace. Larger linen cloths protected the expensive furniture. Jack stripped to his breeches and began his second, painful ascent.

'Hold yer brush above yer 'ed wiv one hand...', said Jem, as Jack's feet disappeared up the narrow flue, '...and use yer 'uvver hand for leverage.'

Jack did as he was told, coughing and spluttering as a shower of soot fell on his head and shoulders.

'Press hard wiv yer back and feet behind yer and wiv yer knees in front', added Jem, now kneeling in the hearth and watching Jack's painful ascent from below.

Jack felt a sharp pain as his knees and elbows made contact with the rough, un-plastered walls of the flue. He forced back his tears of pain and carried on climbing.

'Now bring yer knees up to yer chest and push like buggery!'

At first Jack clawed frantically at the walls of the flue. Already his fingers and knuckles were covered in blood. Soon though, following Jem's advice, he found himself moving more easily up the chimney - like a caterpillar. He at once felt a surge of excitement and began to climb even faster, his rapid movements dislodging a great deal of soot - more by chance than design. Far below, still squatting in the grate and peering up the chimney, Jem watched Jack's progress then let out a whoop of excitement as clouds of soot fell about his ears like black confetti.

Jack now reached a slight bend in the flue, which he negotiated with difficulty. Although the chimney itself was still pitch black, higher up a thin pall of greyish sunlight slid down towards him.

Sensing victory, Jack climbed even faster.

It had stopped raining by the time Jack's head emerged from the chimney pot. Although the pot itself was too narrow for him to get his shoulders through, by pushing hard he could just about peep over its rim.

There before him, spread like a great map, was the City of London bathed in sunlight. Countless church steeples rose above the rooftops as if to greet him while the river, far below, sparkled like an enormous serpent, its sinuous back encrusted with diamonds.

Jack let out a great cry of triumph - a cry that spread out across the city, rippling and expanding like water, until it reached the very brink of London's smoky horizon.

5. Montego Bay, Jamaica
February 1763

He leant back in his chair, rested his riding boots on the veranda rail and stared out across the bay.

A Caribbean sunset, stretched like the painted cloth of a second-rate, theatrical melodrama, filled the horizon. Far below the great house, beyond the plantations reaching to the beach, the sea shone - like a sequined costume from a Drury lane extravaganza. He lit a cigar and drew on it contentedly, watching the smoke drift across the veranda in elegant spirals

Sir Charles Fitzallen, youngest son of a wealthy tea merchant, had been dispatched to Jamaica for having impregnated three of his father's kitchen maids. For a young man, educated at Eton and Wadham College, Oxford, one seduction was considered normal by the corrupt standards of the 18th Century. But *three,* and in rapid succession? Well, that was too much! Even Charles' father, himself acknowledged by his peers as a cad of the first order, had found that unacceptable.

Despite his initial misgivings at such harsh punishment, Charles readily took to the plantation way of life, finding consolation in a string of largely compliant black females. For the last fifteen years he had prospered, using the profits from his sugar plantations to buy land and a stately home back in England - and a knighthood.

Charles left the actual day-to-day running of the plantation to his Manager, James Grundy. Grundy was very efficient at his job, making Sir Charles' plantation one of the most successful on the island. In the Caribbean the profits from rum, raw sugar and coffee were staggering - creating, in effect, a new generation of rich, politically powerful, colonial barons. Greed was good and Sir

Charles and the other plantation owners on the islands were greedier than most.

***

It was two months ago now that the 'Cerberus', under the command of Captain George Gibson, had limped into Montego Bay and discharged its cargo of slaves onto the wooden jetty. Gibson had heard that Kingston was already full of slave ships. He had, therefore, extended his journey by a day or so to drop anchor in the large, natural harbour at Montego - on the northwest corner of the island. Here the price for 'black gold' would, he reasoned, be higher than in Kingston, currently awash with fresh slaves. He was right.

However, those blacks that had survived the crossing from Accra were either riddled with disease or so weak from lack of food that many had to be off-loaded in nets. For those still able to walk, the climb to the upper deck had been difficult enough but the walk down the gangplank onto the dockside was agonising. It therefore took some time before the survivors knelt on the dockside, blinking in the fierce, Jamaican sunlight.

Many of those who had died in the Middle Passage did so from malnutrition since Bellamy Tait, charged with buying the ship's provisions in São Tomé, had secretly pocketed the larger part of his budget, leaving crew and slaves alike well short of even their most basic needs. Tait himself did not survive the voyage, having had his throat cut by Nathaniel Wilson one dark night soon after his treachery had been discovered.

As for Captain George Gibson, the last three weeks of the crossing had been spent in a drunken stupor. The 'Cerberus' had eventually escaped the Doldrums and made good progress once she hit the north-east Trade Winds but lack of food had hastened the demise of the weaker slaves, causing a rapid increase in the normal, expected death rate of fifteen percent. For Gibson this meant near disaster since the condition of his slaves was such that they would not sell easily. He might still make a profit but his share was now considerably less than anticipated. It was, moreover, imperative that Tait's treachery be kept secret, especially from the other shareholders. Nathaniel Wilson, who alone knew what Tait had done, had been silenced with a handsome bribe - or so Gibson hoped.

***

They were met at the dockside by a number of agents from the numerous plantations on the island, including Grundy.

The sale of the majority of slaves on the 'Cerberus' would take place later that day at a public auction in the town square but the personal property of Gibson, including Ashtari and her son, was privately disposed of - over a flagon of rum in the Customs House. Although Gibson himself was in no fit state to cope with a protracted bargaining session - much as he enjoyed Grundy's genial company - he staggered back to his ship two hours later well satisfied with the manager's final offer.

Ashtari, now five months pregnant, had survived only because she and her son were amongst Gibson's favoured slaves. He had protected his 'investment' by giving them extra provisions - even when others, including his own crew, were beginning to starve. Kofi, to whom Ashtari had clung with the tenacity of a threatened she-lion, was similarly treated. Both, therefore - although in a deplorable state - were able to walk ashore unaided.

Grundy, who always had an eye for a bargain, had spotted the tall figure of Ashtari almost before she stepped onto the jetty. The boy, morose and clearly debilitated, was also something of a bargain. As for the others, most were in a sorry condition. Still, it was common practice in Jamaica to buy blacks at the very end of their physical tether then fatten them up and put them to work or sell them on to another plantation. Time alone would tell if they survived to turn an even bigger profit. Thus Grundy, after some vigorous bargaining, had purchased mother and child and eleven other black men and women for a mere £37, four shillings and tuppence.

***

The journey from Montego Bay to Sir Charles' plantation, some fifteen miles to the northwest, took the rest of that day. The slaves were in no condition to walk any distance so Grundy and two trusted black drivers threw them into the back of a couple of large, horse-drawn wagons. Here they lay, exhausted and disorientated, for the duration of the journey.

The shantytown that had sprung up close to the harbour was a sorry place, consisting of a few stone buildings and numerous wooden huts. The streets, although cobbled in places, were open sewers and littered with soiled straw, rotting fruit and vegetables. The town itself was crowded but with very few whites in evidence. Most of the men wore European clothes while the women were dressed in brightly patterned 'crinolines', their heads covered with colourful scarves or turbans. Ashtari and the other black women, clinging to the rails of the cart, were therefore acutely aware of their almost complete nakedness - especially when men in the streets stared and pointed at them or made lewd remarks. They were glad when the carts left the town and reached the comparative privacy of open countryside.

Their journey took them along the west coast for some miles then northeast, towards Mahoe Bay. Here the sea, visible from the track, was an azure blue flecked with white foam. Soon, however, the beaches were replaced by dense mango groves that stretched into the coastal plain - causing the track to wind its way inland. In this expanse of turgid water and rotting vegetation there lurked snakes and deadly alligators.

Soon the wagons left the coastal track and moved to higher ground consisting of gentle, rolling hills with mountains beyond. This mountainous region to the south, just visible from the track, was 'Maroon' country - a land of bandits, runaway slaves and other black 'savages.' On the coastal plain itself, the swamps were now replaced by open fields full of cattle or dense with maize or sugar cane. Men and women, dressed only in rags, could be seen working in the fields - watched over by other blacks yielding whips.

Few of the workers looked up as the wagons passed. If any did it was with a listless, faraway look.

The great plantation house itself appeared round a fold in the hills with the suddenness of an unexpected scene change in a Drury lane melodrama. Hyde House stood, three stories high, on a bluff of rock, dramatic and imposing - as was its architect's intention. The slave quarters were situated to one side of the great house. They consisted of rickety wooden huts roofed with palm leaves. In the yard between these hovels several young children were playing, surrounded by scrawny chickens foraging for food. Mangy, emaciated dogs covered in ticks lay snoring in whatever shade they could find.

The wagons stopped and the slaves clambered down as best they could, closely watched by Grundy's guards. A number of black women, who had emerged from their respective huts, stared in silence at the newcomers.

'Mary, where are you, woman? Run cum yah, quick!' - yelled Grundy.

Mary immediately emerged from the biggest hut, mopping her brow with a large white kerchief. She was enormously fat. She first stared at Grundy then at the new slaves now gathered before her.

'Mercy Lawd, massa Grundy, what am dis yuh got der, eh? Rotten fish? 'Cos dat's what dem smell like!'

Grundy grinned.

'Maybe, but them's what we got. I'll go and tell Sir Charles. They need food. See to it, woman.'

Grundy turned on his heels and strode off towards the stone steps at the side of the great house.

The fat woman - known as 'Queen Mary' - led the new slaves towards two large huts on the far side of the compound. Silently, and without any evident fellow feeling for the bedraggled party of confused prisoners, she led Ashtari and the other women into one hut and the men into another. Here, although there were neither beds nor blankets, merely a mud floor, they were allowed to rest. The men were each given an old pair of linen breeches and a ragged shirt. The four women, including Ashtari, were provided with white shifts and a thin cotton underskirt. They were pleased to cover their nakedness. Although clearly second-hand, their new clothes smelled clean and fresh. Kofi, who was allowed to stay with his mother - he being the only child Grundy had purchased - was given just a shirt. It was far too big for him but at least it covered his thin, emaciated body.

The plantation women, although they spoke in a Jamaican patois that was largely incomprehensible to Ashtari and her companions, appeared friendly enough although Queen Mary herself continued to be aloof - as appropriate to her elevated status as one of Grundy's trusted black servants. Later other women brought bowls of food - thick vegetable soup with rice. After the paucity of provisions on board the 'Cerberus' this first meal was both generous in its portions and rich in sustenance.

At last, after months of hardship and abuse, Ashtari felt a tiny ray of hope. Their miserable lives had finally taken a turn for the better - or so it seemed.

***

Over the next few days Mary looked after her 'chicks' like a conscientious hen. For those with sores or boils caused by malnutrition she provided herbs, picked from the plantation gardens at the rear of the house - such as comfrey, Jamaican dandelion and nettle. For the pregnant Ashtari, Mary found fresh greens to relieve her constipation, herb teas against backache and infusions of barley water to prevent cystitis.

After seven weeks at sea the plantation seemed like a garden paradise, overflowing with fruit, vegetables and herbs.

Although Mary herself appeared to be old she was in fact only thirty-three. She must have weighted at least twenty stones, with great rolls of fat concealing two beady, black eyes. She had worked on this particular plantation since she was seven and had known no other home. Once she had exhausted her usefulness as a worker in the sugar plantations or the kitchens she had been given the task of looking after new slaves. Since the mortality rate of slaves here as elsewhere on the island's plantations was alarmingly high, hers was a full-time job.

She knew it took time for new slaves to recover from the ravages of the Middle Passage so neither she nor Grundy made any particular demands on this new batch of 'niggers' - letting nature and good food takes its course. They were, however, given small tasks - such as cleaning the huts, a little gardening or preparing vegetables for the workers' evening meal. Kofi was given responsibility for gathering eggs, which he found hidden under bushes or in dusty cavities beneath the huts. After a while he became quite good at this and once obtained a grudging smile from an otherwise severe, largely uncommunicative Mary.

This gentle approach was not chosen for humanitarian reasons but out of practical necessity - weak, emaciated slaves were of little use in the fields. The sooner they gained their strength, the sooner they could be put to the backbreaking plantation work intended for them.

While it was clear to Ashtari and the others that they were now fully enslaved, they at least *knew* their fate. Although this knowledge did little to ease their inner torment, it gave their lives some clarity, even purpose. Little consolation, perhaps, for those for whom Africa and home with their families now seemed a distant dream but at least they now had a future - no matter how bleak it might seem.

***

Kofi quickly took to this new life. While there were other children in the compound, he was the oldest. He treated his new responsibilities seriously and was soon popular amongst the men and women he encountered, moving freely about the plantation or the extensive gardens at the back of the house. He also picked up the local Jamaican patois quicker than most. His quick wit and ready smiles endeared him, even to Mary. In short, he appeared to have largely forgotten his experiences on board the 'Cerberus' and to have embraced his new life with a determination and vigour that was frankly astonishing. He even took to his new name - 'Sambo.'

The naming of new slaves was a ritual that every plantation practiced. It was the plantocracy's way of robbing its slaves of any vestige of tribal identity that might have survived after capture, incarceration in the barracoon and the final degradation of the Middle Passage. Ashtari - the proud daughter of a tribal prince and sister to a king - became simply 'Dido.' It was a name she naturally refused to acknowledge, except when used by any of the overseers or Grundy himself. Having witnessed Maloa's brains plastered over some rock, she was in no mind to readily surrender the one thing she still cherished - her former dignity and status back home in Africa; an Africa that she now knew she would never see again.

***

Ashtari is now nearly six months pregnant. During her first few weeks on the plantation Mary had taken her under her wing, feeding her portions of raw mango and a tonic of dried kola nuts. Soon her skin acquired its original tautness and gloss. Her nails and hair grew once more and her large, beautiful eyes shone with a brightness that had been extinguished since the moment she had stepped down into the black hold of the 'Cerberus'. In short, under Mary's expert supervision, Grundy's latest prime 'breeder' was now well on the way to recovery and would soon give birth to another member of Sir Charles' growing 'family' of slaves and their hapless dependents.

Meanwhile, Ashtari herself is given light work as a maid in the great house, polishing the silver and dusting the rich furnishings. At first this was done under the watchful gaze of one or other of the established housemaids but after a few weeks she is now allowed to work alone, without supervision.

While Sir Charles' palatial mansion was vastly different from her brother's palace back in Kumasi, the richness of its tapestries and other hangings often reminded Ashtari of Africa.

In her own village she was celebrated for her creative skill in the design and manufacture of elaborate necklaces or pubic aprons, using colourful *millefiore* and powder-glass beads in the Ashanti style. While nothing in the great house resembled such tribal artefacts, Ashtari appreciated the quality of the European work she encountered - marvelling at the delicacy of the embroideries, for example, in Sir Charles' extensive collection. Sometimes, when there was no one about, she stole a moment or two to examine the pictures, caress the gold and silver ornaments scattered throughout the house and even sit on a mahogany chair or Chesterfield. Once, she pressed the keys of the piano in the drawing room and was startled by the sudden noise it made. Fortunately no one heard and thereafter she was careful not to touch its ivory keyboard, even when dusting.

Few of the regular slaves on the plantation ever came into direct contact with the master of Hyde House. Sir Charles, now in his early forties, preferred the company of rich planters and their wives - or the three or four black women in his service he regularly persuaded into his bed. Often, though, he was away, spending his fortune in the gaming houses of Kingston or the brothels of Falmouth - a large, fashionable, stone-built town further up the coast. It was here, in Falmouth, that some years ago, Charles had first met Annie Palmer - a rich widow whose plantation at Rose Hall was adjacent to his own. Her first husband had died in suspicious circumstances - that was why she was known locally as the 'White Witch' of Rose Hall.

Annie was a beautiful young woman and for a while Charles assiduously courted her. However, their brief, passionate relationship came to nothing. The following year she married someone else. Within weeks he too was dead. That was enough to persuade Charles that further pursuit was not only pointless but also possibly dangerous!

When not in Falmouth Charles wandered about the large, elegantly decorated rooms at Hyde Hall, smoking his cigars or lolling on the veranda with a bottle or two of brandy. Here, in the splendour of his palatial home, he appeared a moody, solitary figure and not the witty, elegantly dressed bachelor hugely admired by the fashionable white women of Falmouth. No one who knew Sir Charles could explain why his beautiful mansion filled him with such melancholy but at Hyde Hall he was someone else - a man for whom its sumptuous interiors and valuable collections meant absolutely nothing.

One day Ashtari walked into his study to dust, only to find Sir Charles seated at his desk. He looked up, stared at the tall, handsome figure before him and smiled. Somewhat flustered, Ashtari quickly turned on her heels and fled the room.

Some days later she was polishing the casement window in the Long Room when she caught his reflection in the glass. He was standing behind her, motionless, in a doorway and clearly staring at her. She did not dare turn round. Instead, she pretended she had not seen him and continued her polishing until he was gone. Other such incidents followed and from then on Ashtari had the uneasy feeling that Sir Charles was following her. She was not comfortable with this idea and began to worry, even dreaming once of him watching her as she slept at night in her hut with the other women and children

***

Some weeks after this first, somewhat troubling encounter with Sir Charles something happened that had a profound effect on Ashtari and the slaves newly arrived at Hyde Hall.

'Gustavus', whose real name was Opoku, had been a slave on the plantation for over year but had recently fallen foul of one of the black overseers. For weeks now this man had brutalised him, finding fault with everything he did and using his whip liberally. One day Gustavus snapped and struck the man so hard that he knocked him into a ditch, breaking the man's jaw in the process.

After that Gustavus had no choice but to run.

However, instead of heading up into the mountains behind the great house he struck out for the coast. In the confusion of the chase he missed the track and ended up in the extensive mango swamps lying between the plantation fields and the sea.

For two nights he eluded capture, hiding in the swamp itself. Eventually the dogs found him - lying exhausted on a mud bank and covered in leeches. They brought him back to the camp in Grundy's carriage then threw him to the ground. His fellow slaves, who had quickly gathered round to watch, saw at once that his arms and legs were terribly lacerated. It would seem that Grundy's dogs had mauled him horribly - until Grundy had eventually called them off.

Instead of tending to his wounds, Grundy's men nailed Gustavus to a tamarind tree by one ear. There he remained for three days. No one gave him food or water; no one dared. Some of the older women or those that knew him well, averted their eyes every time they passed him nailed to his tree. Even the children in the compound ignored him, playing in the dust within feet of the dying man. Stray dogs licked his wounds, now covered in flies, but otherwise he was assiduously ignored.

They finally cut him down - by severing his ear. He died the following day of his injuries.

For the new slaves it was a painful lesson in the futility of escape. Since that was surely the intention of Grundy and his savage overseers, it was a lesson well learned. Thereafter, a sombre mood pervaded the huts, accompanied by feelings of guilt amongst the new slaves - as if Gustavus had somehow died merely as an object lesson to them; as if it were entirely *their* fault.

For Ashtari - who could now feel her baby moving within her - it was a turning point. She resolved there and then to destroy her new child rather than let it be born into such a barbaric world. That night, holding Kofi in her arms, she secretly wept for both Gustavus and her unborn child.

***

One night, not long after Gustavus had been buried in a shallow grave at the back of the house, Ashtari slipped out of her hut. Hugging the shadows, she crossed the compound to a wooden shed in which lived an old woman they called Coobah. Coobah was the compound's unofficial midwife. She was also responsible for arranging the occasional abortion, since Ashtari was not the only mother on the plantation who had trembled at the thought that her unborn child was destined for a life of poverty and subjugation.

Coobah's 'cure' was a terrifying mixture of ground foxgloves, molasses and gunpowder. Ashtari, who had arranged this secret meeting just days after Gustavus had been flung into his grave, swallowed the evil concoction with beating heart - then squatted in a corner of Coobah's hut to await results. Other women arrived and settled down in silence to watch the proceedings.

Ashtari, frightened and as yet unable to talk 'plantation', simply stared back - increasingly aware of the enormity of what she was doing.

At first the pain was bearable but after an hour or so Ashtari had to be restrained and a gag forced between her teeth. She had now broken into a feverish sweat, the moisture dampening her hair and causing her shift to cling to her body. Waves of excruciating pain cascaded through her, starting between her breasts and descending to her groin, then beginning again. Two of the women lifted her to her feet and held her by the arms, suspended above a battered iron bowl. Others fussed about her, mopping her brow with a damp cloth or making encouraging sounds in the darkened hut.

Eventually Ashtari's waters broke. Coobah massaged her stomach with thin, bony fingers and soon afterwards Ashtari's stillborn child fell into the bowl, closely followed by the afterbirth. The dead child's cord was then cut and the bowl and its bloody contents taken outside and thrown into a drainage ditch at the back of Coobah's hut. Ashtari's gag was then removed, a wad of raw cotton placed between her legs and her bloodstained dress replaced. She was then placed on an old blanket on the floor and allowed to sleep.

No one told her what they had done with her dead child, nor did she ever ask. It was as if it had never happened. Kofi, ignorant of all that had taken place that night, was later told only that his mother had been ill but that now she was better.

The next morning Mary entered Coobah's hut, grabbed Ashtari by her hair and began to beat her about the arms and face. Frightened and still partly drugged, Ashtari was too confused to defend herself and simply hung there until Mary had vented her fury, leaving Ashtari battered and bruised.

The following day Ashtari was set to work in the sugar plantation. Her job was to gather the cut lengths of sugar cane, remove any remaining leaves and stack them onto the back of an ox-drawn cart. Soon her hands and arms were covered in bloody lacerations and her shoulders red-raw from the sun. There were other women nearby who helped her with encouraging words and smiles, for news had quickly spread as to why the new housemaid had suddenly turned field-worker. For her part, Ashtari worked as hard as she could - if only to avoid another beating or the attention of the black overseers with their long bullwhips.

***

Two weeks later Sir Charles visited the field where Ashtari was working. He was on horseback. He stopped at the side of the track and spoke to one of the black overseers. Ashtari watched him out of the corner of her eye. He appeared to be pointing towards her, since she was the only one in that part of the field. When she next looked he had vanished in a swirl of dust, spurring his horse back up the track towards the great house. That evening Ashtari found herself again working in Hyde Hall as a housemaid. She was glad to be back in its cool interiors. Polishing floors on her hands and knees was clearly preferable to stacking cane in the blistering sun.

It was in that position that Sir Charles found her later that afternoon. She first heard his footsteps behind her. She at once stopped polishing but dared not look back at him. Then silence - except for her beating heart. When eventually she looked up he was standing above her, hands on his hips and gazing down at her.

At first she was not sure what to do but before she could make any decision for herself he leant down, took her gently by both hands and raised her until she was standing in front of him. He did not let go of her hands but instead examined them carefully, turning both her wrists upwards to expose the cuts and scratches she had sustained on her lower arms. Then he kissed her, first on one arm then the next, his tongue following the lines of the deep scratches and cuts that crisscrossed her arms and wrists.

Ashtari began to struggle but he would not let go. He was laughing now, teasing her but she was too frightened to respond. She broke free, turned and ran out of the room and down the corridor towards the kitchens - and the safety of the women's hut in the yard beyond.

It was now night but a large moon, rising sedately above the great house, turned its white, stucco facade a sickly yellow. Fireflies danced between the trees, forming intricate patterns of light while the dogs howled at the moon.

Ashtari was eating her evening meal with Kofi in her hut when Mary abruptly entered, grabbed Ashtari by the wrist and pulled her outside into the yard. Ashtari thought she was about to be beaten again and cowered in anticipation, trying to protect her head. Instead, Mary took her firmly by one arm and led her across the yard towards the house. Ashtari was too frightened to ask Mary what was to happen to her. Only two days before one of the scullery maids had been caught stealing a knife. She had been tied to a tree, stripped to the waist and whipped until her back was covered in blood. Was that to be her fate too, Ashtari wondered?

Just as they were about to leave the compound Ashtari looked back at her hut on the far side of the yard. The other women, clutching a distraught Kofi, were standing in the doorway staring at her. No one spoke - except Kofi. His screams, like a startled screech owl, filled the night air.

Suddenly Ashtari realised that something dreadful was about to happen. She began to scream and shout in Ashanti and to struggle, dragging her bare feet in the dust and trying to wrench free from Mary's grip. It took all of Mary's considerable strength to drag her up the stone steps and into the kitchen where Grundy was waiting. He seized Ashtari by the wrist and dragged her into the great marble hall at the front of the house. She resisted, sliding on the polished stone floors in her bare feet, but Grundy's grip was even stronger than Mary's so escape was impossible.

In this darkened house, alone and unprotected, she was more frightened than she had ever been in her entire life.

Now the great curved staircase rose up before them. The hall itself was in darkness but moonlight poured through the windows, turning the stairs a leprous white. Grundy proceeded to pull Ashtari up them by her long, black hair. Several times she stumbled, falling to her knees but each time he wrenched her to her feet and continued until they reached the landing. The passageway at the top of the stairs was lit by candelabra placed at intervals along the corridor. Portraits of Sir Charles' family stared down at them, the gilded frames shining eerily in flickering candlelight reflected in a dozen, antique mirrors.

At the end of this corridor Grundy kicked open a door and shoved Ashtari into a large bedroom. The mahogany furniture, highly polished, glowed in the darkness. Silver ornaments, table mirrors and glass decanters glinted and shone - like the eyes of forest animals. The heavy, exotic scent of Jamaican lilies pervaded the room. Grundy then locked the door behind her, leaving Ashtari lying on the carpet at the foot of the great bed, breathless and trembling with fear.

***

Sir Charles, leant back in his chair, rested his riding boots on the rail of his veranda and stared out across the bay.

The sea, bathed in moonlight, was the colour of polished pewter, flecked with splashes of yellow foam as waves broke upon a distant, coral reef. He lit a cigar and drew on it contentedly, watching the blue smoke drift slowly across the veranda in elegant spirals. Grundy then appeared, shuffling his feet and grinning lewdly.

'Dido's in your room but what do you want me to do with Sambo?'
'When does your ship sail?'
'Tuesday morning, Sir Charles.'
'Take him to Storrs Hall. You can deliver the other two boys as well. I'm told Thirkell already has them in the jail at Kingston, ready for your departure. My sister will know how to dispose of all three.'

Sir Charles stood up, kicked his chair to one side and threw his cigar butt into the bushes.

'Now go. Dido and I have business to attend to upstairs.'

***

Later that night Grundy enters Kofi's hut and seizes the boy by the scruff of his neck and drags him screaming into the yard. There, already loaded with luggage, is Sir Charles' ornate carriage. Startled by Kofi's screams, the four horses tug at their traces, causing the carriage wheels to clatter back and forth over the cobbles. It is as much as the driver can do to control his increasingly startled horses.

With his hands now bound behind his back, Kofi is thrown onto the floor of the carriage. He lies there, too terrified to move. Grundy then steps into the carriage, sits down and places a boot firmly on the boy's neck, forcing his face into the straw on the floor of the carriage.

Then, with a crack of the whip the driver sets off, the great carriage clattering across the yard and out onto the gravel road in front of the house.

Their abrupt departure is watched by Sir Charles from the bedroom window on the second floor.

In front of him stands Ashtari, clearly distraught. She is naked, her hands bound behind her back. Grasping her long, black hair, Sir Charles crushes her face against the glass of the bedroom window, thereby forcing her to watch in mute horror as her beloved Kofi disappeared into the night.

6. Chick Lane, London
12th April, 1763

Life and Death
The continuing Adventures of the ill-fated Climbing Boy,
Jack Fisher

Spring in Chick Lane is very little different from any other time of the year, except perhaps that a bedraggled flower or two might occasionally force itself skyward in Jeremiah Blagg's filthy back yard - whereupon his under-nourished donkey finds it and gobbles it up.

It has been a miserable few months, during which Jack has climbed more chimneys than he cares to remember. Often he was accompanied by Jem or Scab but increasingly he now ascends alone. As his confidence grew so too did his self-esteem. For the first time in his short, brutal life he is a success. He still longs to escape but as he has nowhere to go his desire for freedom imperceptibly diminishes, day by day.

Besides, he has grown to like his fellow sweep, Jem. He senses that, despite his greater age and experience, Jem is clearly the more vulnerable of the two. This gives their friendship a depth that Jack has never experienced before. At night they curl up together in each other's arms beneath their filthy sacks - like two orphaned brothers.

Jack now thinks less and less about his mother, whose 'treachery' first put him in this predicament. She might be dead for all he knew - or cared. Occasionally, as he and Blagg tramp the streets of London towards some horrendous chimney, Jack imagines he sees her in the figure of some drunk slumped in the gutter. Since he is not even sure any more if he would recognise her, these brief 'sightings' remain just that - imaginary encounters.

***

'Well now, Jack' - said Blagg one morning - 'Jem 'ere says you done well. Well enough, by all accounts, to try somethin' special!'

He grins his evil grin, his face close to Jack's. His breath stinks of onions and stale beer. Jack flinches, turns away and continues the painful process of rubbing brine into his knees and elbows. Scab, his bucket at the ready, looks on approvingly.

'How do yer fancy Buckingham Palace? Big enough for yer? Jem knows Buckingham Palace, don't yer Jem?'

Jem grins his foolish grin but otherwise says nothing. Jack knows that behind his grin Jem is as frightened as he is most of the time.

'Right! Finish that rubbin' and we'll be orf. Jem, you stay 'ere wiv Scab and guard the fort. Scab' - here Blagg kicked the sooty urchin holding the bucket of brine - 'fetch the donkey.'

Scab drops his bucket with a clatter and scuttles across the room, a slight case of rickets causing the sooty urchin to roll like a miniature, bandy-legged sailor. With the dexterity of an acrobat, Scab then dives through the open window and into the yard where Blagg's decrepit donkey is tethered. Blagg then winks at Jack, lights his pipe, takes a few puffs and looks out into the yard where Scab is now trying to coax a reluctant donkey back into the land of the living - by boxing its ears with a violence that is truly staggering for one so small.

'And don't take all day, you little bugger!'

Blagg turns back into the room, moves to Jack's bed and sits beside him, placing one arm around the boy's shoulders.

'We can't keep 'is Majesty waitin', can we Jack?'

***

Heading west, they cross the Fleet Ditch by a rickety wooden bridge that shakes alarmingly. Below them is the river Fleet itself, now little more than a slow-moving sewer. The stench, which is palpable, derives from a mixture of liquid manure, rotting vegetables and the occasional dead animal. Jack, who is leading the donkey by its rope across this fragile bridge, is relieved when they get to the other side.

Blagg sits astride his donkey like a black potentate dreaming of sherbet. He puffs contentedly on his pipe. Clouds of thick, black smoke drift back over his shoulders towards the stream, where - unable to compete with the Fleet's evil smells - they curl up and died. A huddle of rag pickers, mostly children, squat by the roadside, oblivious to the Fleet's poisonous vapours. They are still squabbling over their pile of rags and soiled garments when Jack, Jeremiah and donkey eventually reach The Strand.

Although it is still early, numerous carts and carriages clatter up and down The Strand, many heading east towards Smithfield Market. Sedan chairs, carried by liveried car-men, dive in and out of the traffic, brushing pedestrians aside each time they veer across the pavements. Street merchants and beggars, pickpockets and housemaids jostle, cheek-by-jowl, as London once more rubs its eyes and crawls from its bed.

After the squalor of Chick Lane, The Strand is like another world. Here the houses are tall and elegant and the streets clean and cobbled.

Blagg's donkey is less impressed.

It holds its ears in a very peculiar way - as if somehow they wished to be disassociated from the rest of the animal's flea-bitten body. Moreover, it curls its lips constantly, smiling secretly to itself as if at some obscure joke. Every other part of its dilapidated carcass exudes disdain. Jack noticed also that it seemed completely oblivious to the horse-drawn traffic which now swirled past them on all sides. Picking its way fastidiously between potholes in the road, the donkey simply plods on - regardless.

Once, when a sleek, black carriage suddenly bore down upon them, the donkey lifted its head and gave the chestnut mare a look that would have pole-axed a rhinoceros. The carriage abruptly swerved aside, balancing precariously on one wheel before careering off up the street. The driver's curse hung in the air long after he had disappeared into the London traffic.

Eventually they reach Charring Cross where The Strand, Whitehall, and Cockspur Street collide. Here the traffic is even greater, with stagecoaches adding to the confusion. They pass below the statue of Charles I - gazing pointedly towards the site where that king's execution had taken place - and pop into the Golden Cross so Blagg can 'whet his whistle'. Jack remains outside and shares a bucket of water with the donkey.

After these crowded streets, the parkland surrounding Buckingham House was a refreshing change. Trees, patches of grass and broad, gravel walks stretched in all directions. The donkey kept wanting to stop to eat the lush grass but Blagg was having none of it and beat the poor animal about the ears with the back of his brush. The donkey stopped anyway, eventually deciding that boxed ears were a small price to pay for an occasional Spring buttercup.

During the day, St. James' Park is a fashionable resort for rich women in smart carriages and swell 'bucks' on horseback. At night, though, it becomes the haunt of murderers and thieves. Even highwaymen are sometimes found in these parts, lying in wait for unwary travellers. Jack knew all about highwaymen and although he could not read he had learned about their daring adventures from newspaper accounts and popular ballad sheets others had read. In Preston, for example, one Joshua Bloom had become the 'Terror of the North' while here in London Jack Rann, George and Joseph Weston and Richard 'Galloping Dick' Fergussen were household names.

***

Blagg, Jack and the donkey now enter St. James Park and the avenue of lime trees leading to Buckingham Palace. An ornamental canal runs the length of this avenue, extending from the Whitehall entrance to the palace itself. It is as much as Jack can do to stop their donkey from swerving off the path towards this canal every few yards.

'Give over!', says Blagg angrily, as Jack tries to pull the donkey back on course. 'Or I'll give *you* a taste of me brush!'

Blagg had never fathomed why, of all the donkeys in London, his should be drawn to water. 'Aint natural", he said to no one in particular. 'There is definitely somefink' wrong with that stupid creature!' He gave the donkey another sharp blow on its head with the end of his brush and dug both heels into its belly. To his surprise the donkey immediately took off at a gallop, towards the palace. As Blagg had never managed to persuade this particular donkey to go faster than a dignified trot, it was something of a surprise now to find it charging up the avenue towards Buckingham Palace at such an alarming rate.

After a gallop of some fifty yards the donkey, now wheezing like a blacksmith's bellows, reached the palace railings and abruptly stopped - causing Blagg to slide over its neck and land heavily on the gravel.

'You bugger!', yelled Blagg. 'You...you...donkey!'

Before them stood the palace itself, an elegant confection of red brick and white stucco curves and columns but there, in the middle of its stone-flagged courtyard, was the reason for their donkey's excitement - an ornamental pond with statues spouting water. Jack watched, fascinated, as Blagg's donkey stuck its nose through the railings and sniffed at this miraculous, watery vision.

But if Blagg's donkey had thought it had found Paradise its rapture was short-lived. Blagg - his face now a livid puce - picked himself up and staggered towards the bewitched animal and, to the amusement of the small crowd that had now gathered, gave the poor animal a resounding kick on its very bony rump.

'There! That'll lern yer, you poxy bitch! Don't *ever* do that agin or it's the knackers yard for you, and no mistake!'

His donkey said nothing but smiled its secret smile.

Still muttering angrily to himself, Blagg now turns and leads Jack into the servant's entrance to the palace where a liveried footman conducts them to the drying room next to the laundry.

Stripped to his shirt and breeches, Jack then steps up into the most elaborate chimney any climbing boy might expect to encounter in a long and dangerous career.

'Don't get lost up there, will yer Jack! We aint got Scab or Jem 'ere to fetch you out if you gets stuck'.

Blagg's words floated up the chimney like a bad dream but Jack kept climbing. After some fifteen feet the chimney turned sharp left and Jack is able to crawl along on his hands and knees. Here the tunnel is narrow but level. Suddenly, the floor of this narrow passage disappears and for a terrifying moment Jack hangs suspended in mid air. Only by spreading his arms and legs like a startled cat is he able to stop himself plunging headfirst down into absolute darkness. Blagg's voice again reverberates through the long, twisting tunnel - as if from the far side of the world.

While he could not make out what he was saying, Jack knew that he had to press on. He takes another deep breath and cautiously lowers himself down into the shaft. He climbs down and down, pressing his back to one side of the descending flue and his feet against the other. After a while he finds he can virtually 'walk' down but only by scraping his back against the wall. He is glad he kept his shirt on. Eventually he lands in a pile of soot at the bottom of the shaft and sits there, resting.

Back in the drying room Blagg is sipping tea and chatting amicably to a young footman. It would be some time before Jack would reach the far end of the chimney and begin sweeping. Blagg therefore leant back in his chair and belched sonorously, much to the amusement of several young laundry maids folding fluffy towels or ironing crisp, white sheets at the far end of the steamy, tiled room.

High above their heads, in a remote part of the huge chimney, Jack sticks his brush in his belt and feels his way round the bottom of the shaft with tentative, outstretched fingers. He eventually finds the exit tunnel and moves forward slowly, crawling on his hands and knees. When he bumps his head he realises that he has come to the end of the tunnel. Feeling a sudden movement of stale air above his head he now knows that he is getting close to the end of this convoluted flue.

He begins once more to climb with swift, easy movements.

This vertical shaft proved to be about twelve feet long, at which point it turned sharp right and then levelled out once more. Again Jack was able to shuffle forward on his hands and knees. The flue here is encrusted with soot, causing him to cough and splutter. The air feels thick and putrid. At the far end of this level section the chimney again dropped down suddenly. Jack is prepared this time for such an abrupt change of direction and negotiates the drop confidently. After this descent he rests on the mound of filth that has accumulated at the foot of this shaft.

It clear now that there is no way he can remove all this soot. What he has to do is sweep each section separately. It seems a daunting task.

He sat there, despondently, listening to the sound of his own breathing. In the relative silence of the tunnel it seemed very loud. He had never been afraid of rats, not least because he had seen too many of them in the sordid tenements he and his mother had occupied from time to time. But here, in these narrow, twisting tunnels he could hear the scrabble of clawed feet getting nearer and nearer. Sometimes he even heard people talking, audible through the walls of this endless chimney. At other times he thought he heard Blagg's voice, rising in anger and drifting through this elongated dungeon like a poisonous vapour.

Two more abrupt turns and another vertical shaft brings him to a section that is like a ramp. Without light, all Jack can do is feel with his outstretched hands as he cautiously moves up this steep slope. Occasionally he loses his grip and slides a few feet back down the tunnel.

Here now the flue is very narrow. With his back pressed against its roof he feels, in his imagination, the entire weight of Buckingham House pressing down upon his shoulders.

***

Meanwhile, in the drying room far below, Blagg is in a foul mood and quite happy for all-and-sundry to know it. Jack has now been in the chimney for two hours. That is far too long. Jem had taken half that time when he had first climbed this infamous chimney.

'Wot is he up to? Wot is his little game? Eh!? '

When not pacing up and down Blagg is now screaming abuse at anyone in sight, punching the air with his fists and waving his arms about like a Bedlam lunatic. Every now and then he would crouch down in the hearth and peer up into the chimney. His threats reverberated up the flue and vanished, unanswered, into sooty blackness. His foul language caused some of the younger housemaids to blush and hold their hands to their mouths and giggle with embarrassment.

Blagg was convinced that the little bastard was deliberately hiding up there. He also knew there was no way out, except back down the way he had gone - Jem had said as much. It followed, as night follows day, that Jack was playing silly buggers! Trying to trick him! Trying to make a fool of him! A fool of Jeremiah Blagg, Master Sweep? One of the most respected, and feared, members of his profession? Yes, he was doing it to spite him! The evil, little bastard! Son of a drunken whore! Traitor!

'Fetch me hay! We'll *smoke* 'im out!'

***

Far above them, in some obscure part of the palace and in darkness that was thicker than pitch, Jack begins his final ascent.

He has now reached the top of the ramp. Pausing for breath, he looks up at the vertical shaft that towers high above his head. At the top he can see, or so he thinks, light sliding down towards him - like a damp stain on a crumbling wall. After so much blackness that light is like a breath of fresh air. He begins to climb, slowly and painfully at first but then much faster as the light grows stronger.

He is about twenty feet up this vertical shaft when he first senses danger. He looks down quickly. There, at the foot of the shaft, a frail wisp of smoke is curling slowly up towards him. Wraith-like, it glides and sways in the gloom, moving ominously closer and closer to where he now hangs, suspended by his nails. Jack at once begins to climb as fast as he can, away from the rising smoke, clawing at the rough walls with fingers now covered in blood.

Soon the smoke is thicker and Jack can smell its acrid fumes. His eyes begin to smart and his mouth and throat feel as if he has swallowed something hot and caustic. Large motes of soot detach themselves from the walls and float towards him on currents of hot, stifling air. In obscure cracks and crannies of this vast chimney, stagnant pools of poisonous vapours stir sluggishly. Soon the rising heat from Blagg's fire will suck them upwards - like putrid marsh gas at dawn.

Jack is now completely enveloped in clouds of hot, acrid smoke. His head begins to swim. Visions of open fields, apple orchards and sunlight swirl before him. He makes one last, desperate effort to reach the light above. He fails and instead plunges, feet first, down the smoke-filled shaft.

By the time he strikes the ramp, some thirty feet below, Jack is unconscious. His limp body slides down the slope and finally stops in a cushion of soot. He lies there unmoving as smoke swirls past, drawn faster and faster towards a small vent in the roof of the palace.

Jack Fisher has finally stopped breathing.

Far below, in the drying room, Blagg watches the fire in silence until all the hay has been burnt and its smoke has vanished. He stirs the ashes with his boot, morosely. He knows now that Jack is dead.

Without a word to the servants standing in stunned silence around him, Blagg leaves Buckingham Palace and heads back home to Chick Lane, loudly cursing his luck.

7. Sunderland Point, Lancashire, England
13th April, 1763

The ship emerged from the morning fog - like a tall, elegant ghost. Its cargo, some twelve-hundred-and-fifty hogsheads of Virginia tobacco, was destined for Liverpool and the snuff mills of Kendal. After the long journey from Jamaica, the brigantine's wooden hulk is now encrusted with barnacles and trails behind her long strands of rubbery seaweed.

Kofi clambered down the side of the ship and into the longboat, followed by Grundy. A piratical old man with a matted black beard steadied the boat until, with a push of his oar, they quit the shadow of the ship and set off for the shore. Kofi lay in the bottom of the boat, wrapped in a sack. Grundy gazed wistfully out to sea as the ship, now heading for Liverpool, disappeared into the mists as silently as it had come.

For a while Kofi listened to the squeak of the fisherman's oars then, lifting himself up on one elbow, peeped over the side.

After the constant rolling of the brigantine, the motion of the rowing boat, although slight, felt strange. His teeth chattered. He was very cold. Through gaps in the sea fog he could make out long, flat stretches of mud glistening in the early morning sunlight. The fishermen's, cottages clustered together on the shore, were dark silhouettes against a flat, grey sky. Long, black whammel boats were drawn up on the beach. Bushes and small trees, bent double by the prevailing winds, dotted the horizon. A smell of mud and decaying seaweed filled Kofi's nostrils. He sank back onto the floor of the boat and curled up - like a dog that has been beaten.

They landed on the beach, close to the row of squat, black cottages. Here the margins of the Lune estuary are a mixture of wet grass, smoothed flat by the ebbing tide and pools of water crawling with minute, slimy creatures. Kofi picks his way across this beach, attached to Grundy by a short length of rope. He felt like a goat being led to market. Their arrival is watched by fishermen at work on nets slung between poles. Their women, who stand at the door of each cottage, are silent and un-welcoming. They wear shawls over their heads and thick wooden clogs. When they saw Kofi some withdrew into their houses, as if afraid of this small, black stranger.

Grundy paid the oarsman and led the boy up a steep bank and onto the track. Kofi stumbled, unused to walking on dry land after weeks at sea but Grundy quickly pulled him to his feet and, with a curse, dragged him towards the waiting cart. They passed beneath a tree with a gnarled trunk and small, dark leaves.

Some believed that this tree had grown from seed fallen from a bale of cotton landed many years before. Kofi recognised the shape at once.

Suddenly, memories of his mother came rushing back - their brutal separation; Ashtari's cries as Mary dragged her towards the great house and his own abrupt departure from Kingston harbour a few days later. This cotton tree, here of all places, was an ill omen.

They left the village and headed across the estuary towards the mainland. Kofi lay in the back of the cart, curled up under his sack. He began to cry.

The journey from Jamaica had taken nearly five weeks. He had been well treated on board but for the first few weeks at sea he had languished in a deep melancholy. Later, with the help of both the Captain and a young midshipman who took pity on him, he recovered some of his former self. He helped the cook in the galley, ran errands for the officers and generally made himself useful. He had even learned a few words of English and now spoke in a babble that was part Ashanti, part 'plantation' and part English.

There had been two other black boys on the ship. Grundy had bought them aboard just before their ship left the harbour at Kingston. From their language Kofi suspected that they were Dahomey - or from some tribe further to the east. He had watched them clamber up the ship's ladder then disappear into the forecastle,

63

where they remained under lock-and-key for most of the Atlantic crossing. Kofi never saw them again.

***

At high tide Sunderland Point is cut off from the mainland - an island in a waste of mud and twisting channels. Twice a day visitors risk being cut off by fast-flowing tides or stuck up to their axles in the slimy ooze. To the northeast, across a dangerous, three-mile channel, is the city of Lancaster with its castle, handsome Georgian townhouses and imposing Customs House on the southern bank of the river Lune. Though the tide now ebbing, the track is still covered with fast-moving, muddy-brown water. The car-man, a young fellow with a pale face and sullen disposition, picked his way through the streams of tidal water. The horse, its head bowed, obeyed each tug of its reins or painful twitch of its master's whip. Their route is marked by blackened wooden posts, stuck at intervals in the mud.

Kofi, peeping from beneath his sack, stared at the fishermen's cottages, now just a wet smudge on a damp skyline. Far beyond, in his mind's eye, lay Africa and home. On the plantation in Jamaica he had begun to forget his tribal lands and its great lake, partly as a way of coping with enslavement and partly because even he knew that escape from that Caribbean island was impossible. But now, having reached another foreign land even further away from his loved ones, Kofi felt a great longing for Africa. Frightened and alone in the back of this rickety cart, he promised himself that one day he would return to this place. From here he would begin his great trek back to his village and the shimmering lake at Kumasi.

***

Two hours later they arrived at Hest Bank - a cluster of mean cottages at the edge of Lancaster Sands, known today as Morecambe Bay. Here they waited for the stagecoach to take them north - across the bay. Grundy tethered the boy to a tree and threw him a crust of bread. Other travellers, resting at the inn close by, watched Kofi with curiosity. The boy stared back - wide-eyed and resentful, gnawing like a rat at his crust. The strangers hastily looked away, discomforted by Kofi's proud stare.

When the stagecoach arrived with a clatter of horse's hooves on the stone track, Kofi watched the entry of this black beast with a mixture of alarm and excitement. The coachman stepped down and stretched. The landlord hastened from the inn and handed him a flagon of ale that he promptly demolished. Two more flagons followed in quick succession. Grundy untied Kofi and led him to the carriage and took his seat opposite a thin cleric and his wife, a mealy-mouthed woman in her late fifties. They both stared in horror as Kofi crawled under Grundy's seat and crouched on the straw-covered floor of the stagecoach.

'What, sir, is that?' asked the cleric, pointing at the small, black boy at his feet.
'That, sir', replied Grundy, 'is me blackamoor.'
'Why can he not travel on top, with the rest of the baggage?'
'Because, sir, blacks is wont to run away. Here I can keep me eye on 'im!'

The Reverend Crabtree is about to protest further when the stagecoach lurches off, whereupon the cleric's tall, black hat is knocked to the floor and his wig tips over one eye. His wife clings to her husband's arm and lets out a screech, like a wounded cat.

Kofi, from the safety of his 'kennel' beneath Grundy's seat, watches all this with growing alarm. The last time he had been in a coach with Grundy it had taken him away from his mother. Now he is once more on the move, observed by strange white people - as if he were some kind of market produce or historical curiosity. This is not only humiliating but a disturbing new development. He has endured so much cruelty since his capture some eight months ago that he is almost used to physical violence but the cold, malevolent scrutiny of strangers is something for which he is ill-prepared.

The stagecoach, chased briefly by a handful of ragged children throwing stones, moves off down the lane towards the coast. After a while The Reverend Crabtree delicately prods Kofi with his ecclesiastical boot, as if the boy were some kind of weird, anthropological specimen.

'A great number of blacks come daily to Lancaster. T'is thought that if they be not suppressed, the place will soon swarm with 'em!.' This is said with great feeling, with Mrs. Crabtree nodding approvingly. 'They are the most ignorant and unpolished people in the world.'

They have now reached the end of the lane and before them lay Lancaster Sands. When the tide is out this bay becomes a desolate waste of mud, stretching west as far as the eye can see. To the north lie the hills of Cartmel and behind them, the distant mountains of Cumberland, purple in the afternoon sun. After following the coast for a mile or two the stagecoach suddenly plunges down a steep bank, throwing its occupants into further confusion. Then, with a shout from the driver and a resounding crack of his whip, the four horses set off across the sands at breakneck speed.

A silence now fell on the adult occupants of the coach for it was well known that the bay was full of quicksand. Many had disappeared, sucked into the mud - foolish travellers, perhaps, ignorant of the few safe paths across the bay. One man had been found buried still astride his horse. Although clearly treacherous, the route across these sands cut many miles off the journey north and was therefore frequently used by travellers. Kofi, however, is now beginning to enjoy this new and exciting experience. He moves to the other side of the carriage and looks out through the open window. Stagnant pools of water lie scattered like mercury on a plain of mud. Here and there a solitary figure, gathering cockles, stands out against a limpid sky.

Kofi's excitement abruptly vanished. Feeling suddenly very lonely he slumped back onto the floor of the carriage and closed his eyes. After the rich, tropical colours of Jamaica this strange, cold country - consisting largely of mud and sand - has the cold pallor of death.

'How ugly he is!' said Mrs. Crabtree. 'Look at him!'
'They are, my dear,' said her husband, 'as mischievous as monkeys but infinitely more dangerous!'
'Maybe,' said Grundy, keen to add his pennyworth, 'but there aint nothin' else wrong wiv 'im. Why, look at his teeth!'

Grundy grabs Kofi's face and twists it towards his fellow passengers. With his other hand he forces the boy's thick lips apart - as if examining a horse.

'Sound in wind and limb!' he adds, reassuringly. 'He'll make someone an 'ansome servant, wont yer Sambo?'

Kofi wriggled free and withdrew to his corner of the carriage where he sulked, much to Grundy's amusement.

***

Carefully following a line of 'brobs' - branches stuck in the mud to define the safest route - the stagecoach now drew near to a colourful band of travellers, crossing the bay in the opposite direction. They are gypsies, some thirty in number. Most are on foot, some on horseback. The women wear colourful shawls and long skirts that trail in the wet sand. The men are dark-skinned with black hair falling to their shoulders in oily curls. The younger men wear velveteen coats with elaborate silver buckles. Some carry children on their backs. Others struggle beneath cloth bundles. Pots and pans dangle from the necks of several donkeys. A wild-looking dog charges back and forth across the mud, chasing some imaginary rabbit. Kofi noticed that its paw-prints disappeared in the wet sand almost as soon as the animal made them.

The stagecoach now slowed to walking pace in order to pass this ragged band. The coachman made no greeting but watched them carefully out of the corner of one bleary eye. Tinkers are not welcome in these parts. They are feared for their dark looks and violent tempers, together with a well-known tendency, according to local legend, to abduct village children. Kofi, however, watched these strange people pass by with great interest. They were not black like him but they were certainly unlike any white men or women he had ever seen. One small girl, perched precariously on a donkey piled high with baggage, smiled at Kofi and gave him a friendly wave as she passed. Kofi is so taken aback by this unexpected gesture that at first he does not know what to do. He is just about to return her wave when Grundy grabs him by the collar and pulls him back in from the window.

'Don't 'av nuthin' to do wiv them tinkers, me lad. Thieves, murderers, every jackass one of 'em!'

The Reverend Crabtree nods approvingly at Grundy's wise words. Kofi crouched once more in his corner and covered his head with his arms and elbows. For one as deprived of affection as he was, a friendly wave was something to cherish. Now he had been denied even a chance to return the girl's greeting. He suddenly felt very lonely and began to cry, burying his face in a corner of the carriage away from the disapproving looks of both Crabtrees and Grundy's sardonic grin.

Once clear of the travellers, the stagecoach quickly gathers speed. Shafts of sunlight strike the bay, illuminating patches of wet sand and pools of evil-smelling water on both sides of the track. Curlews dive between the remains of a derelict boat, its wooden ribs stuck in the mud like rotten teeth. Herring gulls swoop low in menacing arcs above the horses' heads, screaming their own unique abuse.

What happened next was inexplicable, even to Kofi. Suddenly, he scrambled to his feet and leaps, head-first, through the open window of the moving coach, landing on the soft, wet sand and rolling over and over until he comes to a stop in a pool of stagnant water. Before Grundy fully realises what has happened, Kofi has picked himself up and is running off across the mud.

'Stop!' cried Grundy, with a great scream of anger. 'Stop the coach!'

The driver responded immediately but even before the stagecoach stopped Grundy leaps to the ground, falling heavily. He lies there winded for a moment but then staggers to his feet and limps off in pursuit of his runaway slave.

Kofi runs on blindly, aware only of a desperate need to escape. His heart pounds as he careers across the quaking sands. The rope, still attached to his wrist, trails in the ooze, leaving snake-like marks behind him. He can hear the incomprehensible shouts of the gypsies and, above their warning cries, the distant sound of Grundy's bloodcurdling threats.

Suddenly Kofi plunges into deep, wet sand - sinking up to his waist within seconds. It is quicksand!

At first he does not realise what has happened - even as he sinks deeper and deeper. All he can hear now is blood coursing through his veins and the rasp of his breath as he fights wildly to pull himself from the mire. Then, with only his head, arms and shoulders still clear of the mud, he suddenly stops struggling and closes his eyes, calm now and unafraid. Visions of Kumasi swim tantalisingly before his eyes and from the swirling mists there appears the beautiful face of his mother, beckoning him towards her with outstretched arms.

'Catch this rope! Quickly now. Catch the rope - before it is too late!'

Kofi opens his eyes - to see not his mother but a gypsy kneeling on the sand close by and frantically gesticulating. In one outstretched hand he holds a length of rope. Kofi snaps out of his trance, panic returning with the speed of a tidal wave. He opens his mouth to scream but nothing comes out. He watches in mute horror as the gypsy swings the rope slowly above his head. Other Romanies now join the man with the rope, anxiously watching or urging Kofi to respond. They speak in a language Kofi cannot understand but their meaning is clear enough.

Kofi tries to move but with each movement sinks deeper and deeper into the quick- sands. After several attempts the rope eventually lands inches from the boy's outstretched fingers. With a final, desperate effort Kofi grabs the rope, twists it about his wrist and pulls as hard as he can. The man takes the strain, helped by others. At first there is no discernible movement but then slowly they pull the boy from the mud, dragging him across the green ooze to safety. Immediately a cheer goes up from the crowd. Even the animals sense that something dramatic has happened and all the donkeys began braying loudly - more or less in unison.

The men squat on the sand, exhausted by their efforts while Kofi lies at their feet, a bedraggled bundle of wet, filthy rags. A Romany woman kneels beside the boy, dips her kerchief in a pool of water and wipes the mud from his mouth. Suddenly, a breathless and angry Grundy shoulders his way through the crowd. He is limping and his face is purple with exertion. He grabs Kofi by the hair and pulls him to his feet.

'You degenerate! I'll teach you to run from me, you son of a black whore!'

He raises his arm as if to strike the boy but is at once stopped by a man with dark, wild-looking features. He is also holding a very long knife.

'What!? Get out of my way, you, you…!'

Grundy's words die on his lips as others, muttering sinister Romany oaths, surround. Grundy looks round at the menacing faces and lowers his arm. He lifts

Kofi, cradles him in his arms and walks back towards the stagecoach. The crowd parts before him but he can feel their eyes burning into the back of his neck. He then lowers Kofi into the carriage, steps up and closes the door. The Reverend Crabtree and wife stare in silent horror as Kofi, wet and stinking, collapses onto the floor in a crumpled heap.

The Romanies watch the stagecoach move off towards Cartmel, on the far side of the bay, and then resume their tramp across the vast sands. When the little gypsy girl on her donkey looks back over her shoulder for the last time, the stagecoach is but a faint blur on the rim of the sky.

8. Storrs Hall, Windermere, Cumberland
14th April, 1763

Seven miles north of Lancaster Sands lay the mountains and lakes of what today we call the Lake District. It was there, on the shores of Lake Windermere, that Lord Fitzallen had built his stately home - in 1663. Today, exactly one hundred years later, his direct descendent, Lady Sarah Fitzallen, stood before the great window at Storrs Hall and stared into the gathering gloom. She had inherited this house from her father who had died leaving neither her nor her elder brother a penny of his once considerable fortune - other than this elegant, rambling villa. With Charles in Jamaica generating his own fortune, Sarah Fitzallen had been obliged to live on her wits. Since she was intelligent, ruthless and excessively ambitious, she too had prospered.

Sarah is a striking young woman. Her hair, which she wears long, is black. Today she is wearing a sack-back gown of exquisite yellow and white woven silk. The lights from a nearby *girandole* show her face to be handsome yet pale, her eyes dark and intense. She bears a striking resemblance to her brother, Charles Fitzallen of Hyde Hall, Jamaica.

She loves Charles as a sister but in recent years has grown distant towards him. He has changed from the wild young man she remembered to someone who, on his frequent visits to London, she no longer recognised. At Eton he had hunted and fished and gambled with the rest of his wealthy cronies but he had done so with an abandon that she had found, as a young girl in awe of her elder brother, utterly beguiling. Now, after years on his plantation, he seems far more introspective - as if the brutality of his trade in human misery has permanently soured him.

At Oxford he had done his fair share of womanising but for a year or so had actually taken his studies seriously, reading law at Wadham College with a view to a career as a fashionable lawyer. Some minor indiscretion or two with his father's maids, coupled with Charles' escalating gambling debts, had ended all that. His irascible father, with whom he had never really got on, promptly withdrew his financial support and banished his son to Jamaica - and to a life dedicated to the acquisition and exploitation of 'Black Gold.'

By now the sun has set and darkness envelopes the ornate garden and lawns stretching down to the lake. A few lights from the hamlet on the far side of the lake pierce the darkness, the black water gleaming fitfully. Lady Fitzallen rang a bell, summoning servants. They quickly brought more candles and prodded smouldering logs in the grate into fiery animation. With a thin, wax taper Sarah lit her clay pipe, drew smoke up its length and savoured the acrid taste. Exhaling, she returned to the unshuttered windows and peered into the darkness, expectantly.

***

Thanks to Sarah Fitzallen's industry and far-sightedness, Storrs Hall had acquired a reputation for the importation and distribution of black children, popularly known as 'blackamoors.' Wealthy women would pay Sarah extravagant amounts of money for the purchase of such a child - to act as something between a servant and a pet. These children would be trained to wait at table and carry their owner's fan or smelling salts. They would be dressed in extravagant costumes and adorned with jewels or have an expensive silver collar riveted about their young necks. They occupied a social position in these aristocratic households somewhere between a scullery-maid and a pampered lapdog.

Sarah never considered the ethics of this dubious trade. Someone, after all, had to pander to the needs of the wealthy, indulgent and socially ambitious women of her class so why not her? Besides, she had a limitless supply of blacks to choose from her brother's plantation and moreover, the contacts in England to create an economically viable distribution network. For a number of years now black children, thanks to Sarah Fitzallen, had been shipped to Sunderland Point, cleaned up and sold on - a process of mutual satisfaction to both distributor and client alike.

Suddenly, deep within the vast house, bells rang and doors slammed. Servants, armed with flambeaux, hastened across the lawn and down to the lake. Behind a cluster of trees at the water's edge is a landing stage, curiously disguised as a small, Greek temple. It is here that a sailing boat now landed, disgorging its precious cargo - a thin, bedraggled boy wrapped in a sack. One servant conducted Grundy, now limping badly, off towards the house while another, holding his flambeau in one hand and Kofi's rope in the other, dragged the boy towards a side entrance leading to the servants' quarters. Kofi, who had lost his shoes in the quicksand, felt the gravel bite into his bare feet.

As they followed the path from the landing stage to this entrance, with lawns stretching off into the darkness on either side, the great stone house loomed above them. Kofi had never seen anything so big - or so frightening. The servant's torch cast lurid shadows onto the walls and windows. For Kofi, these shimmering patterns of light were devils, dancing some macabre dance of death.

The journey up the lake had taken two hours. Kofi had been very cold and frightened, not least because the mountains that surrounded Lake Windermere were for him places of indescribable terror. Kofi knew that ghosts remained close to where the living beings had died and his senses had told him that these bleak hillsides and chill waters were thick with such creatures. Although he had never actually seen a ghost he knew that they were white - like dried bones. He knew also that for the purpose of carving man-meat, ghosts had a huge thumbnail - like an enormous, butcher's knife.

Kofi and the servant entered the house. After walking the length of a stone-flagged corridor, they turned into a large room full of cauldrons of boiling water. The walls of this room were covered with white tiles. Large sheets and towels billowed from the ceiling. There were pools of warm water on the stone floor. Numerous instruments of torture - with handles, hooks, cogs and wheels - stood on long tables of scrubbed pine. The whole room was shrouded in warm mists that spiralled, like evil spirits, towards a vent in the ceiling. At the far end of this diabolical chamber was a black stove, belching smoke.

A terrifying thought entered Kofi's head. Was this, perhaps, where they first *boiled* their captives?

He was about to snatch the rope from the servant and run out of the room when there appeared before him a short, elderly woman with grey hair and a rough, sunburnt face. She was wearing a coarse linen apron over a black skirt and a broad, white collar across her shoulders. She had pale, watery-blue eyes. She stared for a moment at Kofi, and then smiled. Kofi, somewhat taken aback by this approach, stared back, trying hard to summon what little courage he still possessed.

'Well now', she said kindly, 'what have we here?'

Kofi said nothing but narrowed his eyes and scowled. Other women in white aprons and rolled-up sleeves now entered the room. On their feet they wore wooden clogs. One held a long, sharp knife. Cooks? Kofi's mouth was dry with fear. Such a long journey to end thus - in ignominy! Mrs. Daniels, for that was the name of Lady Fitzallen's housekeeper, dismissed the manservant and cautiously removed Kofi's filthy sack. The boy flinched but held his ground, determined to conceal his fear.

'Why, 'tis a black child, to be sure! And stinking like a rotten kipper. Girls, I think this young man needs our help!'

The girls advanced, their clogs clacking menacingly on the stone floor. Kofi, fearing the worse, tried to run for it but was grabbed by two young 'cooks' and dragged screaming towards the far end of the room. The one with the long knife cut the rope from his wrist while the others swiftly removed his filthy rags. Naked and screaming, Kofi was then flung unceremoniously into a large vat of hot, soapy water. Armed, not with knives but scrubbing brushes, the 'cooks' swiftly removed the filth and grime of six weeks at sea and a close encounter with Lancaster Sands. Kofi, now thoroughly clean, was then lifted from the tub, wrapped in a warm towel that smelt of lavender and deposited - high, dry and breathless - on a chair before the fire.

Confident at last that he was not about to be eaten - at least, not yet - Kofi rewarded his captives with a grin that might have melted the heart of a cannibal.

***

Grundy, still nursing his twisted ankle, did not fare so well. On his arrival at Storrs Hall he had been summoned to attend Lady Fitzallen. She was angry, it seemed. Disappointed, even. At least that was what her servant had intimated when conducting Grundy through the great marble hall, up the stairs and into a long, gloomy corridor. Here he was told to wait. Half an hour had now passed and still no summons. He had walked up and down - or at least as much as his swollen ankle would permit - until he could take no more. Now he sat, somewhat nervously, trying to remove the filth from beneath his broken nails. Large, imposing portraits stared down at him from every wall. Each face, man or woman, had the dark, piercing eyes of Sir Charles Fitzallen - or so it seemed to Grundy.

He suddenly felt homesick for Jamaica. Although he regularly visited England on behalf of his master or on business of his own, he much preferred plantation life to hobnobbing with Sir Charles' business cronies in London, Bristol or Lancaster. He was a simple man with simple tastes. He wished fervently, therefore, that he were back now in Jamaica with a generous plate of mutton chops, a flagon of rum - and a willing black wench to follow.

'Lady Fitzallen will see you now, Mr. Grundy', said a young maid, suddenly appearing from nowhere. Grundy stood up. His ankle was now badly swollen and it was with some difficulty that he followed the girl up the corridor towards Lady Fitzallen's drawing room.

Grundy did not like Sarah Fitzallen. Charles was a sadistic bastard at times but at least you could trust him to do the decent thing when it came to business relationships. Much of the success of the plantation had been down to Grundy's hard work and ruthless exploitation of the 'niggers' under his control. Since Charles was a generous employer, Grundy had also prospered. From his humble origins as 'white trash', Grundy was now a trusted member of the Falmouth community and reasonably wealthy in his own right. With enough black women on tap to serve even his needs, he was like a 'pig-in-shit.' But Sarah Fitzallen, with her extravagant tastes, big house and haughty manners was something else. No, he did *not* like Charles' arrogant sister, that's for sure!

They reached the end of the corridor whereupon Grundy was ushered into an expensively furnished drawing room.

'Mr. Grundy, your Ladyship', said the maid.

Sarah Fitzallen was seated by the fire. She held a small, overweight dog in her lap. She did not look up as Grundy stood, hovering on the edge of an ornate *Savonnerie* carpet and nervously twisting his hat, but continued to stuff the animal with morsels of food from a silver dish.

Since she remained thus resolutely absorbed in her dog, saying nothing, the maid left, closing the door behind her. An awkward silence followed - except for the heavy tick of a bracket clock on the mantle piece. Grundy was not sure if it was up to him to open the conversation or not. In the end he said nothing and merely looked about the room, anxiously.

'Well, Mr Grundy', she said at last, 'I trust your long journey was worthwhile?' This was accompanied by a sidelong, somewhat girlish smile.

Grundy, not expecting such sweetness and light from the formidable Mistress of Storrs Hall, was at first flummoxed but eventually found his tongue.

'Yes, your Ladyship.'

Another long, awkward silence followed.

'Well, not entirely!'
'What do you mean, sir? Are they not even now below stairs?'
'Well, one is. T'others aint!'

Lady Fitzallen looked up at him now for the first time - her eyes fierce, black coals in a deathly white mask.

'What do you mean, Grundy? Explain! Where are the *three* niggers you were contracted to bring to me?'

'Yes, well...er...two didn't make it, your Ladyship.'
'What do you mean, *didn't make it*?'

Grundy took a deep breath then plunged, headfirst, into the speech that he had rehearsed over and over in his mind during the last few weeks of his journey from Kingston.

'Well, your Ladyship, one escaped overboard - off Barbados. I reckon the sharks got 'im! T'other died. Killed himself! One morning he just sat down, closed his eyes and snuffed it. We threw 'im overboard. Aint no use to no one dead, were he?'

Sarah Fitzallen rose, placed her dog carefully on its silk cushion on a nearby chair and crossed to the fireplace. She stared for a moment into the fire then turned back into the room towards Grundy. She spoke now with quiet, measured tones but Grundy could sense her anger.

'Very well. We must make do with what we have. What is it like, this boy?'
'Excellent, your Ladyship', said Grundy. 'And very pretty, if I may make so bold!'
'Does it bite?'
'Yes...and scratch. Just like its mother!'

Lady Fitzallen crossed to the bell-pull at the far end of the room and summoned her maid.

'That will be all, Grundy. I will settle with you tomorrow.'
'Yes. Tomorrow. Thank you, your Ladyship.'

The maid reappeared as Grundy left the room - as fast as his twisted ankle and good manners would permit.

'Beatrice, tell Mrs. Daniels I shall see the new black tomorrow, at ten o'clock.'
'Yes, your Ladyship.'

The maid curtsied and left the room - whereupon Lady Fitzallen picked up her dog's dish and hurled it violently at the door.

Meanwhile Grundy, still limping badly, had reached the cobbled yard at the back of the house. He stuffed his hat on his head and set off towards the servants' quarters where he had been given a room for the night. 'So much for Sarah Fitzallen's 'hospitality', the parsimonious bitch!'

His meeting with her Ladyship had gone rather well, all things considered - or so he thought. Normally, being highly-strung she would have shouted at him. On one celebrated occasion, three years before, she had hurled her book at him, blacking his eye in the process. Today at least she had remained within the bounds of civility. No doubt she would give him a sealed letter to deliver to her brother, secretly disparaging its carrier in no uncertain terms. This she had done once before. Charles had read it, shown it to Grundy and had then torn it up. It would take more than a cross word from his distant sister to sour Charles' relationship with his Manager, *confidante* and pimp.

Sarah, seated now at her desk, finished her letter to her brother Charles, placed it in its envelope and pressed her signet ring into the molten wax, thereby sealing it and - or so she assumed - Nathaniel Gundy's fate.

9. Buckingham House, London
14th April, 1763

It was generally thought at this time that the streets of Georgian London were paved with gold. This was not true.

Gold was the least likely commodity to be found in the grimy streets of London, covered as they were in a rich, glutinous mixture of horse droppings and urine-soaked straw. True, some parts were more commodious than others. These newly constructed squares and paved avenues were swept by small boys with large brushes and closed to the poor inhabitants of Georgian London. It was here that the rich and famous lived.

One such place is what we now call the 'West End' - an area between Leicester Square and Hyde Park, with Cavendish Square at the northern limit and Buckingham House to the south. Buckingham House - now known generally as Buckingham Palace - was built by the first Duke of Buckingham in 1703. Because of its classical Palladian facade it is held to be one of the most beautiful houses in London. It is here that the new king of England and his young, German wife now live.

But not everyone who lives in Buckingham House shares the glories of George III's sumptuous new residence.

Take Charity Bucket, for example. Charity is the latest of several pot-room skivvies employed by His majesty at Buckingham House. She therefore occupies *the* most humble position within the complex community that is the Royal Household. Hardly her fault of course but in every great household someone has to be at the top and someone else at the bottom. Charity is at the bottom. She is the unwanted daughter of a devout Quaker and was, therefore, shoved into service almost as soon as she could talk. She is now seventeen. She is a plain young woman, as ignorant as one could be and almost devoid of personality but she is a good, hardworking girl and always says her prayers before going to bed.

Tonight, as usual, Charity Bucket undresses, brushes her hair with her little brush and kneels in all her ignorance and pious humility on the bare floor of her bedroom; a tiny room that is little more than a cupboard at the very top of the palace. Kneeling in front of the fireplace, she puts her palms together and fervently prays for a sign that someone, somewhere - like her beloved Jesus, for example - really loves her.

Meanwhile, high above her head in an even more remote part of the palace, something stirs.

At first it is but a trickle of soot, barely noticeable in the labyrinthine maze of chimneys within the palace but then, gathering momentum, it plunges faster and faster, transforming itself into a black avalanche until, with an explosive crash, it lands in Charity Bucket's grate. Not content with this dramatic 'entrance' it at once turns into a thick pall of air-born soot, rising like a ghost from the hearth and enveloping the startled girl still kneeling in her white, cotton night-dress.

When the other girls on her landing, hearing Charity's screams, rush to her door and crowd in, all they can see is a black figure, her arms spread wide and her eyes as big as saucers. Only Charity's delicate pink feet and the palms of her little hands are untouched by the black cloud that has covered her in its sooty embrace. It is indeed a sign! Even as tears of joy well from her eyes, forming inky rivulets down Charity's cheeks, the corridor echoes to the hysterical laughter of her fellow servants - until, that is, the Housekeeper shuts them up and sends them back to their beds with a thunderous curse.

***

Over the next few days, some of the other servants on Charity's landing also begin to hear strange noises at night and rapidly convince themselves that ghosts now lurk in every recess. For these palace servants (mostly ignorant young girls) such stories quickly assume alarming proportions, so much so that at night some tiptoe along the bare, wooden corridors and slip into a friend's bed where, sleepless, they cling to each other for comfort.

The real explanation, of course, is much simpler.

Jack the climbing boy - Bragg's incorrigible sweep - is not dead but alive somewhere in the chimney up which he had vanished just a few days before.

76

Despite the poisonous fumes and scorching heat, Jack survived Bragg's attempt to 'smoke him out.' Coming to an hour or so after Bragg had stormed out of the palace, he somehow managed to cling to life by a thread. He knows he is alive because his lungs still hurt, his eyes sting and his hands and feet are blistered - scorched by the heat from Bragg's pile of burning hay that had smoked merrily in the great drying-room hearth, watched at the time with a mixture of horror and fascination by all those present.

It took Jack two days to recover from this ordeal but now hunger and thirst have begun to gnaw at his belly, making him forget the pain of his blistered hands and feet. His coughing has subsided but he is now desperate and knows that without food and drink his days are numbered. Later that evening, having recovered a little of his former strength, he manages to crawl back down the chimney a short distance. Here he finds, tucked to one side of what appears to be a disused shaft, a small recess. He enters it cautiously and finds, to his surprise, that he can almost stand upright. Gingerly, he feels his way round this tiny room until he knows every nook and cranny. Like some proud housewife he then brushes it clear of soot until he reaches bare brick.

Although completely enclosed in the blackness of these labyrinthine chimneys, this tiny space now provides temporary safety and a place for Jack to lick his wounds.

Meanwhile, only a few yards away from where Jack lies, Agnes Millichop - the Housekeeper in this wing of the palace - is preparing her supper. She sees herself as a kindly, benevolent old soul. In truth she is a tyrant, ruling her brood of silly girls with an iron rod. She is fond of smacking her charges with the flat of her hand and once hit Cherry Tucker so hard that she did not wake up until the following Sunday. Thereafter, Cherry spent a large part of her working day staring into space - for which she was eventually dismissed.

Mind you, being Housekeeper in this part of the palace does have its perks. While Agnes is usually able to purloin some morsel of food from the kitchen for her supper, on this occasion she has acquired nothing less than a hand-full of green beans and three potatoes. These she now drops into a pot of boiling water, with a pinch of salt, and sits back in her chair to watch it cook. While her little room is bare - with hardly a stick of furniture other than a chair, her bed and a small chest of drawers - it is very cosy. Once she had been given some scraps of meat, said to be from the King's own plate - at least that is what William the footman had told her. Later that night she had crept up to her room, fried them in a pan of goose fat and had devoured them in a swoon of guilty pleasure. Tonight, though, it is just beans and potatoes.

High in his secret den in some dark corner of the palace chimneys, Jack can now smell Agnes' modest meal. The vapours from her pot sidle up her chimney, ease their way round several bends and insinuate themselves in the myriad tunnels and shafts adjacent to Jack's tiny 'snug'.

***

Dawn rose over London, tingeing the elegant facade of Buckingham House with a delicate pink light. Cocks crew and slowly the palace, rubbing the sleep from its eyes, awoke to the business of another busy day.

The first to arrive later that morning is the sea-coal merchant. Drawing his cart up close to the trap door at the back of the palace kitchens, the coalman's sturdy lad shovels the dray's contents into the bowels of the building. Almost as soon as it strikes the floor of the coal cellar, footmen and chambermaids fill their scuttles and hurry off to far corners of the palace. One by one the fires in a dozen bedrooms are lit, bringing warmth and light to their sleepy incumbents. Slowly, the smoke of a score of newly lit fires rises skyward, meandering through the palace's many convoluted chimneys.

Jack had dreamed that night, not of boiled beans and potatoes, but of a dish of herring his mother had once given him in an uncharacteristic moment of maternal indulgence. He awoke, however, to the smell of the thing he now feared most - a simple bedroom fire. Trapped in his snug, he now withdraws like a frightened animal into a corner. Here he crouches, his nerves tingling and his body tense with fear.

To his surprise, the fumes and dense black smoke drift on past the entrance to his 'den', drawn by some current of air up towards the palace's vast, slate roof. There, liberated from the maze of chimneys in which it too had been trapped, it bursts out into the London sky, turning and twisting in the breezes high above St. James's Park. Somehow, Jack's den has remained untouched by the heat and fumes that had, only three days before, blistered his skin and lungs. Perhaps he might survive up here after all!

Besides, he has nowhere else to go - certainly not back into Jeremiah Blagg's evil clutches, that's for sure!

***

William Appleby, the newly appointed footman in the north wing of Buckingham House, is something of a lady's man. Well, that is how he sees himself. For most of the women within his employ he is an odious, self-opinionated lecher. For some weeks now William had been pursuing a pretty young thing called Phyllis - second chambermaid to the King's new Consort, Charlotte of Mecklenburg-Strelitz. Phyllis is not much younger than the Queen herself, barely eighteen, but is an intelligent girl who has risen rapidly in the affections of her somewhat naïve Mistress.

Strictly speaking, Buckingham House is Charlotte's private home but everyone, including William, can see - now that Charlotte and George are married - that it is now the nation's official royal palace. While the new Queen - having recently given birth to George's second son, Frederick - remains under the dominant influence of George's mother (the redoubtable Augusta of Saxe Gotha) in the relative isolation of Buckingham House Charlotte can at least indulge her passion for cards; an enthusiasm shared by her young yet obliging second chambermaid.

That morning, having lit her Mistress's fire, Phyllis tiptoed from the royal bedroom on the first floor of the north wing, closed the door quietly behind her and hurried off down the corridor towards her pantry where she knew William would be waiting for her.

It was generally understood below stairs that William and Agnes, (the Housekeeper) had an arrangement whereby she would supply him with willing young partners from her maids and skivvies, in exchange for numerous small favours. This was a strictly confidential arrangement but thus far it had worked well enough - to their mutual advantage.

However, not all William's partners were always actually willing. Rose Hedley, for one, had defended her virginity stoutly and had been slapped into temporary oblivion for her trouble. Her dismissal had followed soon after - much to William's relief.

Phyllis, however, is different from the slovenly, somewhat 'dim' Rose. Being an intelligent girl she understands the workings of the palace. She is ambitious and therefore willing, when necessary, to accept the protocols of abuse and exploitation some call 'patronage'. In the social microcosm that is any great house, who sleeps with whom acquires crucial importance - particularly for those wishing to rise within its complex, social hierarchies. In this respect, Buckingham House is no different from England itself, still the most feudal of European nations.

Thus it was that Phyllis allowed William, for the first time, to bend her over the pantry table, lift her skirts and fondle her pert, pink bottom.

***

Meanwhile, back up his chimney, Jack can wait no longer. He knows that unless he gets food and water soon he will become too weak to escape the dark labyrinth in which he is otherwise trapped.

In the blackness it is difficult to tell what time of day it is although the various smells that drift past his snug give some clues. He judges it to be late morning, a most dangerous time for a renegade 'climbing boy' to be abroad, but hunger now drives him on, recklessly. With mounting trepidation, therefore, he twists and squirms down the nearest chimney, clawing at its walls with blistered fingers. After a minute or two light begins to seep up towards him; light that makes his eyes smart. He pauses for breath, pulls his cap down over his face and listens intently.

Silence. The room below is empty.

With one last wriggle Jack is free of the chimney. He drops into the empty hearth, shakes himself like a dog and dives for cover under a small table on the far side of the room.

Peering from beneath his cap, he can see - now that his eyes have adjusted to the daylight - that he is in some kind of stillroom, used by palace staff for warming bedpans and emptying chamber pots. At one end there is a sink with a tap above it. Unable to wait any longer, Jack emerges from beneath the table, turns the tap on and dinks great gulps of cold water - whereupon he collapses onto the floor, coughing and spluttering. It is the first water he has tasted for nearly three days.

It tastes fantastic but even more wonderful to behold is the plate of bread and cheese and a half-empty bottle of wine someone has left on the table beneath which he had, only moments before, been crouching.

Jack immediately scoops the food - pewter plate and all - into his shirt, grabs the bottle with one scrawny hand and is back up that chimney before you can say 'Jack Robinson!'

Later that morning, when William came to rinse His Majesty's royal chamber pot, he did not notice that the food and wine had gone from the table but on examining the palm of his gloved hand some moments later he saw that it was now, inexplicably, covered in soot.

***

At night, in the intense darkness that is now Jack's secret world, the eyes play tricks. Although Jack had never actually seen snakes or alligators he clearly remembered Jem's vivid description of such creatures when, from time to time, Blagg visited a pawnshop off Silkman's Alley, Ludgate to reclaim the 'family jewels.' There Jem had seen these fabulous animals hanging from the ceiling and had later told Jack and Scab all about them. These particular 'monsters' were, of course, stuffed with sawdust but still terrifying to small, ignorant boys.

Jack was now drunk, having consumed half a bottle of Burgundy on a near-empty stomach. He lay, therefore, slumped in his snug, as these very same monsters gyrated before him, sliding and slithering in the darkness and forming intricate patterns inches from his startled face.

***

Thaddeus Pratt is Head Butler at Buckingham House and a more odious individual it would be difficult to find. He is about fifty, tall, thin and has the sallow, pockmarked complexion of a corpse. He fills the many servants beneath him with terror for an uncomplimentary word from Pratt in King George's ear would blight their careers forever - or worse. Indeed, it was Thaddeus Pratt who had recently accused one of Queen Charlotte's chambermaids of stealing jewellery. The luckless girl was tried and sentenced to death. Much to Pratt's annoyance, the Queen herself then intervened and managed to have the girl's sentence reduced to deportation to a sugar plantation somewhere on British Barbados.

Such is Pratt's reputation.

However, what now occupies his thoughts and disturbs him most is the *range* of items that staff had recently reported missing - such as candles, a flintlock, blankets, cushions, cups, plates and all kinds of food and drink. While theft is common in large houses full of underpaid, light-fingered servants, Pratt is the first to see a pattern emerging. While he had been told that Bragg's climbing boy had died up the chimney, he himself - being of a suspicious nature - was never convinced.

If the climbing boy is indeed alive and running loose in the palace at night then he, Thaddeus Pratt, is determined to catch him.

Meanwhile, Jack is beginning to enjoy his life as a renegade sweep. He is now surrounded in his snug by all the creature comforts that he had never known in his short, impoverished life. During the day, when the palace is busy, he sleeps on soft cushions and eats off silver plates by the light of a stolen candle or two. At night, when the palace sleeps, he drops from some chimney and explores the dark rooms and corridors in search of food or anything else that catches his fancy - such as napkin rings, silver-plate or gold goblets. Not even 'Mother' Bishop's brothel had boasted such luxuries.

While not all the palace flues are linked, such is Jack's knowledge now of their inner construction that he can travel about the palace with remarkable ease - emerging in rooms that he knows are unoccupied. Once, however, rounding a corner late at night, Jack literally tripped over Henry Saville, the Duke of Sussex, lying outside his bedroom door. The young libertine was so drunk that he did not even notice the sooty urchin.

Jack promptly turned on his heels and headed for the nearest chimney where he remained, fearful of discovery, for two days.

Thereafter, however, Jack became increasingly careless. Sooty footprints were sometimes left on stone floors. Maids even reported the occasional black handprint on cupboard doors or pantry shelves and lurid accounts of ghosts in remote corners of the palace increased. Even Agnes, whose contempt for the silly notions of her girls knew no bounds, began to grow suspicious. For Pratt, however, all this circumstantial evidence only convinced him even more that the young climbing boy was alive and hiding within the palace.

It was, therefore, only a matter of days now before this dangerous young sweep was captured and strung from the gallows at Tyburn. That, at least, is now Thaddeus Pratt's fervent hope.

***

Two days later Jack became aware that something special was afoot within the palace. All morning servants had been rushing about. It was clearly too dangerous to quit the chimneys so Jack had to be content with listening and trying to make sense of what he could hear.

The State Rooms, designed by William Winde in 1705, are situated on the first floor of Buckingham House. These handsomely proportioned chambers are approached up a fine marble staircase and entered through large, double doors. The Saloon itself is decorated in paintings relating to the Arts and Sciences while the roof bears a painting by Gentileschi, eighteen foot in diameter, representing the Muses playing in consort to Apollo, lying on fluffy clouds. It is here that on state occasions King George sits enthroned with 'Queen Charlotte of 'Muckleberg Strawlitter' - as William and his fellow footmen now secretly call her.

Today, however, King George's primary concern is to rid himself of the bucket of black tea he drank for breakfast. William, who is in attendance that morning, proffers the royal chamber pot into which the King pees with evident relief. This 'heroic' act, in full view of the assembled company of Courtiers of the Bed Chamber, is accompanied by polite applause. At this time George is twenty-four and seems to possess every advantage. Although not exactly handsome, the young king is generally regarded as good looking - in a rather Germanic way. His face, and in particular his prominent eyes, already give some indication of his strong character. He is, moreover, the first monarch since Queen Anne to have been born and educated in England.

Like his young wife, George loves music. Once a month, therefore, he and Charlotte organise a concert. Handel is their preferred composer, for amongst George's most prized possessions is a harpsichord that had once belonged to that great musician. These musical *soirees* are usually accompanied by a sumptuous banquet in an adjoining room. It was this music therefore that Jack, hidden in his secret den, heard later that night.

Much later, when the music and laughter had subsided and the King and his friends had retired to bed, Jack worked his way through a myriad of connecting tunnels and shafts until he reached the large chimney that rose, like a cathedral spire, from the State Rooms on the first floor.

Cautiously, attentive to every sound, he lowered himself down into the hearth, swung (Jem-like) out over the still-smouldering ashes and landed softly on the carpet of the Royal Saloon.

What met his astonished eyes was a scene of gastronomic devastation. Running the length of the room is a great table on which are piled the remains of a state banquet. Jack has never seen so much food and wine and silver plate, all scattered haphazardly across the polished table - as if an earthquake had struck it. Cold meats, salads, vegetables, puddings, cakes, custards and blancmanges - a veritable 'cornucopia' of half-eaten food.

More alarmingly, Jack is not alone.

At one side of the table an elderly courtier lies slumped, head down in a large, pink blancmange. On the other side sits a corpulent woman, bolt upright in her chair and snoring loudly. Her ornate wig hangs precariously to one side - like the leaning tower of Pisa. On the floor, lying in a pool of dried vomit, is a young courtier and close by another, fast asleep but still clutching an exquisite, cut-glass decanter of Portuguese brandy.

Jack, totally disregarding the drunken 'revellers' still present, leaps onto the table and begins to cram into his mouth handfuls of food. These he washes down with swigs of wine, brandy, port or ale - whatever comes to hand.

Overwhelmed by the sheer excitement of his escapade, Jack then dances an uncertain jig on the polished table, waving his arms and legs about like a drunken windmill - until he collapses in a heap on the floor, breathless and intoxicated with both the moment and the large amounts of drink he has rapidly consumed.

Jack then sees, for the first time, the King and Queen's golden thrones at the far end of the room.

He immediately staggers to his feet and walks unsteadily towards the King's throne until he stands in its shadow, the great chair looming high above him. For a moment he stares at it, mesmerized by its ornate splendour of rich carvings and plush red cushions beneath a golden canopy.

Then, trembling with excitement, Jack steps up onto the raised dais, turns and sits down - luxuriating in the forbidden knowledge that His Majesty's most humble, most *wanted* subject, is now actually sitting on the very throne of England!

10. Storrs Hall, Windermere
15th April, 1763

Kofi spent his first night at Storrs Hall, Windermere locked in a cellar beneath the kitchens. Although he was cold and still frightened, it was the best night he had spent for many weeks. Not only was he clean after the long journey from Jamaica and his recent escape from the quicksand but also he had been given fresh clothes and a meal of cold meat and potatoes. True, his wrist still hurt from the rope but so far his captors had neither beaten him nor chopped him up for supper.

One of the girls in white aprons - Flora, they called her - had clearly taken a shine to him. It was she who had given him his supper and a blanket in which to sleep. She had, throughout, spoken to him gently. Although too shy as yet to reply, Kofi had given her of his smiles. That seemed to please her. Later, when she came back to remove his empty plate, she slipped him an apple. Before bolting his iron door on the way out she gave him an encouraging smile and a friendly wink.

Once she had gone and he had eaten his apple, Kofi took a stroll round his cell. It did not take long.

The walls were dry but there was a musty smell that he found very disconcerting. From the ceiling hung several plump birds. They were brown with red neck-feathers. Blood dripped from their beaks to the floor, forming tiny red pools on the flagstones. In one corner, close to a stool, someone had scattered goose feathers.

If this was a torture chamber then these strange people clearly preferred to torture birds rather than children.

Kofi retreated to a corner of his cell, curled up in his blanket and was soon fast asleep. He dreamed he was drowning in a sea of mud until saved by a giant chicken, which plucked him from the mire - like a worm.

The next morning he was woken up by a young girl, not much older than himself. She gave him a bowl of gruel and left, without saying a word. Kofi sniffed the food but, suspecting poison, left it on the stool, uneaten. A little later Flora came and led him by the hand up the stone steps and into the kitchen.

'Don't be frit,' said Flora. We aint going to hurt you. Time though to meet 'er Ladyship!'

They entered the kitchen. Kofi had never seen such a large room, not even in the great house on the plantation back in Jamaica. The walls were lined with huge iron stoves. Against one wall stood a rack, containing pots and pans the colour of lead.

When Mrs. Daniels saw Kofi she sat down on a chair and placed him before her. She looked approvingly at the fresh clothes, which Flora had given him after his bath the previous night.

'There now, aint he the smart one!'

Kofi, not knowing what to do, thought it best to grin.

'Why don't he say somethin'?' asked Flora. 'Don't he speak like us?'
'According to Mr. Grundy,' replied Mrs Daniels, 'he never stops. Once he gets going!'

It was true. Kofi's command of English had much improved on the long journey from Jamaica, encouraged by both the officers for whom he had worked and the young midshipman, Peter Tarleton, with whom he had struck up a somewhat unexpected friendship. Peter had taught him a great deal of naval slang, none of which he had ever dared use. However, his command of basic English was now good enough for him to understand most of what was said to him - even if, as yet, he was still too shy to reply with any confidence.

Flora sat on a stool close to Kofi and took both his hands in hers, drawing him gently towards her.

'Wot's your name? You can tell us! We won't hurt you, will we, Mrs. Daniels?'

'Never! You aint the first black we've had pass through 'ere and you wont be the last if Her Ladyship has her way!'

Kofi looked cautiously from one kind face to the other, still not sure what to do or say.

'Go on, tell us!' urged Flora. 'Wot's your name?'

Kofi felt troubled. He had been called 'Sambo' for so long now that it was sometimes difficult for him to remember his real name - let alone tell it to total strangers. To do so was, in his mind, to relinquish a secret part of his soul. It was an act of trust not to be taken lightly. However, some instinct told him that Mrs. Daniels and Flora could be trusted with such information and thus it was, for the first time since he had been captured, enslaved and transported to no less than two strange lands, that he revealed his true identity.

'My name' - he said, speaking in a quiet, tremulous voice - 'is Kofi and my uncle is Kwasi Obodum, King of the Ashanti!'

The two women looked at each other in astonishment at this unexpected revelation and were struggling to break the awkward silence which followed when Lady Sarah Fitzallen's maid Beatrice stuck her nose round the kitchen door.

'Her Ladyship will see the new black now. I hope he's ready, Mrs. Daniels!'
'He's as ready as he'll ever be, poor lamb!'

Mrs Daniels stood up, took Kofi by the hand and led him to the door. A silence fell on the room. Kofi suddenly became aware that everyone was watching him. He took a deep breath and tried to remember how his grandfather had once told him to stand - as befits one of royal blood.

'Now, young man', said Mrs. Daniels, placing her arm round his thin, bony shoulders and giving him a friendly hug, 'Beatrice will take you upstairs to see her Ladyship. As long as you do what you are told, no one will hurt you. Do you understand?'

Kofi looked into her watery blue eyes and nodded gravely. Turning on his heels he followed the maid out of the kitchen and into the corridor.

'And Sambo, no more stuff-and-nonsense about kings and queens, whatever your real name is!'

Mrs.Daniels' words echoed unheard down the corridor for Beatrice and Kofi had already turned the corner.

***

Lady Fitzallen was seated at her dressing table when Beatrice shoved Kofi into the room and closed the door behind him.

It was a small, exquisitely appointed room with pale-green, panelled walls decorated with scrolling acanthus foliage. The furniture was satinwood, covered with marquetry and ivory inlay. She sat facing a large, ornate mirror.

Sarah Fitzallen's dressing table was covered with the elaborate paraphernalia of a rich woman of quality. What fascinated Kofi were not the silver hair brushes, combs, paints, pastes and powder boxes or even the delicate porcelain figurines that covered its surface, but the heavy perfumes that filled the room, causing his head to swim. Was this woman about to cast a spell - with her magic ingredients and talismanic figures? Was she not like the witch his uncle had once banished for turning the heads of the young men of the village with her exotic perfumes and potions?

If this was Lady Fitzallen's intention then he must resist at all costs - his life clearly depended upon it!

Slowly, and with an air of studied languor, Lady Fitzallen turned towards the boy and stared hard at him. Kofi's fragile resolve to resist vanished almost at once under the cool, unremitting gaze of this beautiful 'witch'. Instead, he studied the carpet and shifted, nervously, from one foot to the other. For the first time he realised that his new shoes were far too big for him.

'Grundy was right. You are a *very* pretty creature! What is your name, boy?'

Kofi looked up and opened his mouth to speak - then thought better of it. He racked his brains for some way to assert a measure of control on the situation. The sweet, seductive perfumes that swirled about the room had begun to make him giddy.

'Well, child!? What do they call you?'
'Sambo.'
'Not very original but it will do until we can think of a better name for you. Now come here, Sambo. I have something very important to tell you.'

She drew the boy towards her with a slight movement of one hand until he was within arm's reach. Kofi saw that her eyes were very dark, almost black and that her skin had the smooth, flawless texture of ivory. When she spoke she did so very quietly but with an intensity that made the hairs on the back of his neck stiffen.

'Sambo, you are to become servant to a very rich lady. Do you understand?'

'No. I....'

'You will. Meanwhile, you must call me and the other ladies 'Your Ladyship', otherwise you will be beaten. If you try to run away a cruel man with a sharp knife will find you - wherever you may be. He will cut off your arms and legs. Do you understand?'

'Yes. Your Ladyship. Me understand.'

Sarah turned back to her dressing table and picked up a tiny glass bell, which she rang.

'Beatrice, take Sambo to my drawing room. Stay with him. I will call you when we are ready. Has Lady Bowers arrived?'

'Yes, your Ladyship. She's waiting in the library.'

With an abrupt wave of the hand, Kofi and the maid were dismissed. Beatrice, seizing Kofi by the sleeve, pulled him from the room and closed the door behind them. Holding the boy's arm in a grip of steel for one so slight, she dragged him off up a corridor containing, as Kofi noticed with horror, other replicas of the beautiful witch under whose influence he had fallen and in whose enormous palace he was now a prisoner.

***

In the great, white marble hall below, servants ran hither and thither, opening doors. There was much commotion - orchestrated by the imposing figure of Lady Fitzallen's butler in his green and gold uniform.

Lady Evelyn Lowther, whose carriage had just drawn up on the gravel outside, swept in like a galleon in full sail. Her long, satin cloak floated slowly to the marbled floor as she slipped it from her shoulders. It was at once gathered up by two servants and born off, like a trophy of war, to some adjacent closet. The butler, standing at the foot of the marble staircase, bowed deeply then turned on his heels and led the way up the stairs towards the library. Lady Lowther followed, trailing an elegant hand up the stone banister. As soon as she and the butler had disappeared from view and the other servants had scuttled off to obscure corners of the house, calm descended once more - like autumnal leaves slowly settling after a sudden gust of wind.

***

Lady Jane Bowers - who had arrived at Storrs Hall a few minutes before Evelyn Lowther - had already been conducted to the library by a footman. Although offered a chair she had elected to stand at the great window and gaze out at the lake below. A few moments later Sarah entered the room, joined her at the window and shook hands.

'Evelyn will be with us shortly. I trust you are well, Lady Bowers?'
'Perfectly well, thank you.'

Lady Bowers was the moderately rich wife of a banker from Lancaster and known within the county and beyond for her exceptional lack of taste.

'What charming *muffetees,* my dear Jane. Did you choose the feathers yourself?'

The objects in question were wristlets of lurid parrot feathers, one worn on each of Lady Bower's chubby wrists. To compliment these she had chosen that day a bright red hat in the shape of a turban, balanced precariously on an enormous, pink wig. The extravagant peacock feathers topping off this creation gave her the look of a startled cockatoo.

'Yes. Yes, I did, Sarah. Quite.'

Jane Bowers, who was short and corpulent, had never liked either Sarah Fitzallen or the Lowthers of Rigmorden - especially the willowy Evelyn with her fine airs and graces. Some said Evelyn Lowther was related to the King but only on the distaff side. Anyway, Jane's own family was much older than both the Fitzallens *and* the Lowthers, even if her family no longer had quite so much money. Arrogant bitch! Yes! That described Evelyn Lowther perfectly. Rich, arrogant bitch!

At that moment Lady Lowther herself was ushered into the room by the butler. She entered with a flourish, her fan fluttering in her hand like the wings of an exotic hummingbird.

'Evelyn, my dear!' said Sarah. 'Welcome to Storrs Hall. So kind of you to come all this way.'

The two women kissed. They were like two male peacocks, studiously eyeing each other with a view to ruthlessly eliminating what they perceived to be a natural rival.

'You know Lady Jane Bowers of Barbon?'
'Of course.'

Evelyn did not so much as glance at the little, fat 'cockatoo' standing at the window but swept across the room and seated herself on a chair close to the fire - where she spent the next minute or two spreading her hooped skirts about her with all the fussy finesse of a swan settling on its nest.

'What a delightful room, Sarah. How clever of you to choose *such* an original colour. So bold. So *pink*!'
'Thank you', replied Sarah, somewhat coldly.

The butler, still hovering at the library entrance, was dismissed, closing the large mahogany doors behind him.

'Ladies, will you partake of a dish or two of tea first or shall we see the boy at once?'

Lady Bowers, still staring resolutely out across the lake, took a moment or two to register the significance of Sarah's use of the singular 'boy' but when the penny eventually dropped she turned, crossed the room and sat down heavily on a chair beside Evelyn.

It should be noted at this point that Lady Bowers had recently shaved off her eyebrows and had replaced them with two tiny semi-circles of mouse skin. These narrow strips of fur, silhouetted against the lurid matt-white *ceruse* of her face, gave her the appearance of one who is perpetually startled, as if questioning the metaphysical existence of everything upon which her gaze falls - such as her coal scuttle or even her long-suffering husband. Here though, they are for once appropriate.

'Boy? Did you say boy?' she asked, staring hard at Sarah. 'But I thought there were *three* nigger's to be presented. Three, not one!'

Lady Fitzallan, who was now seated, shuffled slightly on her cushions and smiled sweetly at the fat, petulant woman opposite.

'Well, there *were* three but two did not, unfortunately, survive the journey.'

Jane Bowers and Evelyn Lowther, both now distinctly uneasy, glowered at each other and then at Sarah.

'How then', asked Lady Lowther after a moment's angry silence, 'are we to resolve this dilemma? You are surely not proposing that we participate in some kind of Dutch auction? Hardly appropriate, I would have thought, for women of our position!'
'Of course not, my dear Evelyn. I have a much better idea!'

Sarah rose, crossed to a small desk at the far end of the room, opened a drawer and returned with a pack of playing cards. She then positioned a small table between her two guests and placed the cards on it.

'I propose that we solve our 'little problem' with a game of Hazard. Whoever wins, gets the black. His price? Well, in view of the current scarcity in the market, the winner must pay me seventy-five guineas if they are to call Sambo their very own!'

In the silence that followed this proposal, Lady Fitzallen picked up her glass bell and shook it gently. Its tiny sound was at once born, like a delicate butterfly on a warm current of air, into the corridor and beyond.

'But first', she added, smiling sweetly, 'I think you both should inspect the goods, *n'est pas?'*

Kofi arrived, a few moments later, escorted by Beatrice. He was led across the room and told to sit on a small, wooden stool near the fireplace.

All three women stared at him - as one might when deciding to purchase a new poodle or some other unnecessary luxury. Kofi stared back. His first thought was that this was some kind of tribal meeting for these women, surely, were the tribal elders dressed in all their finery.

'He may be pretty, Evelyn, but I prefer something lighter. Why, this creature is as black as this ace of spades!'

At first Kofi tried to sit up straight but as soon as the elders became absorbed in their divinations - for that is what he assumed they were doing - he lost interest. Besides, the heat from the fire was beginning to make him sleepy.

Lady Bowers placed a black card upon the table, giving her opponent opposite a look as if to say 'Follow that, you arrogant bitch!'

'Although we call the Negro complexion black, from it being many degrees darker than that of the darkest European, yet it is far from being of one uniform blackness.'

As she spoke Lady Fitzallen glanced at Kofi squatting on his stool. Much to her annoyance he had began to pick his nose.

'Sambo's tint, though less varied, has a richness which, in a painter's eye, may compensate for its comparative monotony.'

Lady Lowther, who had followed her opponent's card with an ace, looked at Kofi and then smiled sweetly at her hostess.

'I once saw a nigger who was developing white spots on his body. Tis probable, if it lives, he may in time become white all over!'

All three women laughed at this but Kofi, who had long since lost interest in the proceedings, stretched, yawned and wriggled on his stool. Since, moreover, none appeared to wish to speak to *him*, he leant back against the warm marble on one side of the fireplace and closed his eyes.

'I accept that variety, gradation and a combination of tints are among the highest pleasures of vision but black is absolute monotony!'

Here Lady Bowers turned to Kofi and waved her cards, held like a fan, at the little boy slumped against the wall.

'Why, look at the child! Such creatures are so black and with such flat noses that they can scarcely be pitied!'

Kofi, who had fallen asleep, began to snore loudly.

'Tis impossible to believe that God, who is such a wise Being, should place a soul in such an ugly black body.'

Kofi, now fast asleep, slid slowly off his stool - ending up in a crumpled heap on the carpet in front of the fire.

Ignoring this breach of manners from their bewitched 'prize', the two women resumed their game - interrupted only by Kofi's loud snores. As the game progressed over the next fifteen minutes or so Lady Jane Bowers became more and more agitated. Finally, having lost the game, she threw her cards onto the table and flounced out of the room in a flurry of muslin and quivering peacock feathers.

'I always knew she was a bad loser', said Evelyn with some relish. 'Besides, you are right, Sarah. Even though rather dark for my taste, the child *is* exceptionally pretty.'

Lady Evelyn rose, smoothed down her rumpled skirts with an elegant, gloved hand then crossed to Sarah's *escritoire* at the far end of the room and sat down. Taking pen and paper she began to write.

'Some say', added Sarah, 'that Lady Bower's husband is so disenchanted with his 'plain Jane' that he has secretly taken a second wife in Bristol. Perhaps next time you see her, my dear Evelyn, you should tell her of this development. I'm sure the poor man is far too busy to tell her himself!'

Evelyn laughed, rose from the *escritoire* and moved back to the fireplace beside which Kofi was now snoring even louder.

'Thank you, Sarah. I am very pleased with my purchase.'

She handed her promissory note to the value of seventy-five guineas to a grateful Sarah.

'Provided, of course, that I can teach it some manners!'

Kofi, ignorant of the transaction that was about to change his life, merely dreamt of Africa. Sarah Fitzallen then rang her bell, summoning Beatrice.

'Let us, my dear Evelyn, be eternally thankful that, unlike this poor boy here, you and I were born with the colour of Innocence and in the livery of Freedom!'

***

A few minutes later Kofi was awoken with a kick from Beatrice and quickly bundled downstairs - to await Lady Lowther's departure.

Several servants - including Flora and the housekeeper, Mrs Daniels - gathered in the kitchen to see him off. As they waited for Lady Lowther to leave, Flora helped Kofi into a woollen jacket several sizes too large for him while Mrs.Daniels brushed his hair and wiped his face with one corner of her apron. Neither woman could speak and Kofi, not at all sure what was happening, did not dare ask either of them.

Flora, whose eyes were now filled with tears, gave the boy a final hug and led him by the hand into the great, marbled hallway.

Outside, Lady Lowther's carriage was already in position, its two horses pawing impatiently at the gravel. Her footman stood in readiness by the open door, a travelling rug folded across one arm while her driver, in top hat, livery and cloak, sat in his seat, whip in hand.

After a moment or two Lady Lowther herself swept down the marble stairs and across the hall, gathering Kofi by the hand as she passed. The group of female servants who had assembled by the door curtsied and watched as Kofi was led out of Storrs Hall and into the carriage of his new owner. As the black brougham moved off down the driveway, Flora ran on to the steps at the front of the house and waved at Kofi whose frightened face was still visible, pressed against the glass of the carriage window.

Flora remained staring across the parkland of Storrs Hall long after Lady Evelyn Lowther's carriage had disappeared into the Cumberland mists.

11. Buckingham Palace, London
27th April, 1763

Thaddeus Pratt was now dedicating a large part of his time towards the capture of the small boy hiding somewhere within the palace chimneys. While food continued to disappear, the thief had now stopped taking candles, flintlocks and other essentials. Instead, he had shifted his interest to small but valuable objects. This Pratt found very worrying, not least because if it were to continue he would have no choice but to report such thefts to the Lord Steward of the Royal Household.

It was proving very difficult to obtain actual evidence, not least because the aristocracy were notoriously careless with their possessions and because the palace was already riddled with light-fingered servants determined, given half a chance, to line their pockets.

Jack, meanwhile, was getting restless. He was, if the truth be told, bored with his life in Buckingham House. Worse, he was getting fat.

After months of near starvation under Blagg's tutelage, the rich food and drink now available to him most nights was beginning to turn his emaciated body into something more approaching that of a healthy eleven-year-old. Jack did not want to get stuck up some chimney but as the weeks passed and he put on weight, that was becoming a distinct possibility.

Pratt, for his part, was equally troubled - but for different reasons. When Blagg's boy had disappeared up the drying-room chimney some five weeks ago Thaddeus Pratt had taken it upon himself to hush up the event, threatening those who had witnessed the 'smoking out' with dismissal if they even mentioned it. It had worked and only a few people inside the palace knew that there was a dead child up His Majesty's chimney. Now that there was a chance that the child was alive - and robbing the place blind - it could prove very difficult to keep a lid on the situation. So far, Pratt had kept his enquiries to himself and a small band of trusted servants within his employ but if it were to 'go public' then all hell would let lose and his own position would become untenable.

For the last few nights, therefore, Thaddeus Pratt had taken to wandering the darkened corridors of the palace - like a ghost. Twice he had surprised some servant girl sneaking out of the bedroom of one of His Majesty's equerries and once, in the early hours of the morning, he had thoroughly alarmed one of Queen Charlotte's attendants surreptitiously emptying Her Majesty's chamber pot into a fire bucket.

But so far nothing of the renegade climbing boy.

Nothing, that is, until early one morning Pratt found himself in the King's Library. The room was empty but just as he was about to close the door after him he was startled by a sudden fall of soot in the fireplace. He darted forward, fell to his knees and peered up the chimney. For a fleeting second he was sure that he saw movement - a bare foot perhaps - but then a great shower of soot fell upon his bald head and shoulders. He staggered backwards and fell onto the hearthrug, spitting and coughing and fighting for breath.

It was in that undignified position that two footmen, about to begin their morning shift, found him.

***

Jack, acutely aware of just how close he had been to discovery that morning, lay low for a day or two. He knew he was getting careless but part of him no longer really cared. Perhaps it was, after all, time to quit the palace? But there was a problem. Although he had now accumulated a number of valuable objects - including silver three napkin rings, several spoons, a fine signet ring and three gold candlesticks - it was hardly enough 'loot' to set himself up as a gentleman of quality. Each night, as he roamed the palace corridors or landed softly in the hearth of some aristocrat's bedroom, there were rich pickings to be had. Why stop now that when untold riches were his for the taking?

Then there was the little matter of escape.

While he was now very good at moving about the palace at night it was quite another thing to leave the building completely. He couldn't simply walk out the back door! The house and grounds were swarming with palace guards and it was clear from s close encounter two days before that they were now probably on to him.

What he really needed was an audacious escape plan!

Meanwhile - despite all of Prattt's efforts to the contrary - word spread rapidly amongst the palace staff that the sweep had been discovered, living in the chimney above the King's Library.

'Why, what did I tell yer', said Agnes Millichop immediately on hearing the latest gossip. 'I knew that little bugger was up there. Did I not say so at the time? Did I not tell yer?'

Since it was Agnes who had steadfastly ridiculed the strange events her skivvies had reported - ghosts, phantoms and other such nonsense - the Housekeeper's certitude now was considered somewhat rich. Still, it did explain a number of mysterious events, not least the loss of an under-butler's keys only the day before.

Jack had taken to exploring the servants' wing at the back of the palace. He had considered escaping this way but the garden walls there were extremely high and guarded at night. While he was always on the lookout for valuables, of which there were plenty in the royal chambers or those suites of rooms reserved for visitors, what he was *really* after were keys. Keys gave him access to all manner of interesting nooks and crannies, not least pantries full of food and drink. For weeks now he had been unsuccessful in this search but then one night he stumbled on a set of keys in the butler's pantry.

Unfortunately, these particular keys were still attached to the under-butler in question!

Jack was a natural thief. Having been neglected by his drunken mother, thrown onto the streets of St. Giles to fend for himself almost as soon as he could walk, it was inevitable that he should quickly acquire the requisite skills. Mixing with older children already accomplished in the surreptitious removal of pocket watches and silk handkerchiefs, Jack was a professional thief by the time he was five. It was easy, therefore, for him to prise the keys off the dozing under-butler's belt and tiptoe from the room, undetected.

During the next few days Jack tried a number of likely doors, thereby stumbling on a drawing-room cabinet containing enough silverware for a king's banquet (literally), a pantry full of succulent hams and numerous other useful places previously unknown to him. Since it was considered a crime of Tyburn proportions to lose one's keys, the under-butler, on discovering his loss the next morning, told no one - until Prattt's 'discovery' provided him with the opportunity to blame someone else other than his own carelessness.

Thaddeus Prattt's determination to capture the sweep was matched only by his increasing anxiety about the consequences of failure.

Although Pratt was not a man to be trifled with and of some standing within the Royal Household, his handling of the situation thus far was well short of exemplary. Moreover, it was one thing to keep the Royal Household staff reasonably quiet but if any of the numerous officials associated with the actual Court of St. James discovered what was really going on it would only be a matter of time before His Majesty was told and then all hell would break loose.

True, it had taken Pratt a while to recover from the indignity he had recently suffered in the King's Library but now he was more determined than ever to catch Jack - for that, he discovered, having made some discreet enquiries in the vicinity of Chick Lane - was the boy's name. His brain, more used to the intricacies of seating protocols and the order of cutlery at banquets, had now to be applied to plots, plans and stratagems to catch a thief. Traps had to be laid, snares set - if the rascal was to be apprehended. It was a challenge now occupying most of Prattt's waking hours.

***

Jack's original snug was now rather cramped - filled as it was with the products of several weeks of indiscriminate yet determined pilfering. It was clearly time to move. Jack therefore took to sleeping in a small void high in the west wing, immediately beneath the roof slates, retaining his snug as his 'Aladdin's Cave' in which to keep his 'treasure.' He had stumbled on this obscure roof void some weeks ago by accidentally putting his foot through a lathe-and-plaster wall whilst negotiating a particularly narrow flue. As far as he could tell this 'unofficial' entrance was the only one, they're being neither a trap door nor any other means of access. It was, in short, perfect and for the first time in weeks Jack luxuriated in the space this new, secret 'attic' gave him.

Three days later Pratt came up with a bold plan that required the assistance of selected members of the royal household, all (hopefully) sworn to secrecy. He would, as Blagg had tried to do that first fatal day, *smoke* him out!

The following day, at precisely twelve noon, fires were simultaneously lit throughout the palace. Hay was applied and a veritable storm of smoke spiralled higher and higher, writhing its way throughout the flues and tunnels that, like the holes in a barrel of Ementhal cheese, riddled the palace. Pratt, sporting an enormous shillelagh lent to him by an Irish publican of his acquaintance, ran from room to room like a demented fireman while footmen, grooms and stable-lads, positioned at strategic fireplaces and armed with an assortment of sticks, cudgels and pokers, waited for Jack to emerge, coughing and spluttering.

Nothing happened. The fires died away and the smoke vanished into clear skies above London. But still no Jack.

Perhaps this time he actually was dead? Or perhaps, after all, he really *was* a mere figment of Prattt's lurid imagination? So thought many of the palace servants as they returned to their normal duties. Pratt himself, thoroughly demoralised by yet another failure, was last seen sat on the floor in the corner of one of His Majesty's water closets, with his head in his hands and sobbing loudly.

Jack, blissfully unaware of Prattt's 'Great Plan', had slept most of that day in his new attic, dreaming of life as a rich, man-about-town. Provided he could pawn his loot he would have enough money to start a fresh life and acquire a new identity, far from the sordid squalor of Chick Lane - and Blagg. Since he had found a 'room' to which no one had access, except via the chimneys, Jack decided to spread out a little.

Over the next few nights he acquired a small carpet and half-a-dozen cushions. These he spread over the wooden joists of his 'attic', allowing him to stretch out like a Baghdad potentate at ease in his harem. Now that he had some roof space, Jack also acquired an elaborate, gold-plated candelabrum - so large, in fact, that he had to dismantle it in order to get it up the chimney and into his Oriental 'parlour.' Lit by half-a-dozen candles, Jack could now lie back on his cushions and puff contentedly on a cigar - half of which, unknown to him, had been consumed by the celebrated writer, Horace Walpole that previous afternoon.

Thaddeus Pratt, however, was far from contented.

After the 'smoke 'im out' debacle he had taken to his bed at the top of the west wing and now lay there, hour after hour. He was used to the scrabble of rats' feet from the ceiling above and the occasional creak as the old palace shifted on its foundations, but what he could not stomach was the knowledge that somewhere deep within the building there lurked an incorrigible thief. Pratt had even obtained plans of the house showing the labyrinthine configuration of chimneys and flues. None of these tunnels were of course accessible, unless stonemasons demolished large parts of the palace - a plan clearly unacceptable if some measure of 'damage limitation' was to be properly maintained.

Pratt had, of course, also considered sending another of Blagg's brats into this Minoan maze but the idea that a *second* child might get stuck up there was too awful to consider. No, it was useless! Some other plan was needed; something that would force the boy out of the chimneys and into the palace itself where he could be apprehended more easily. These, and other worrying thoughts, occupied Pratt as he lay on his bed, staring at his ceiling.

Jack, for his part, thought only of freedom. He had now lived in the chimneys, flues and secret passages of Buckingham House for seven weeks - or so he guessed.

From where he lay each lonely day, stretched out on his back on his Turkish cushions, he could just about touch with his hand the cold slates above his head. Tantalisingly, an inch or two beyond his fingertips were the skies of London - and freedom.

Later that evening, having drunk half a bottle of His Majesty's finest port, Jack lost his footing and plunged to his knees through the floor of his secret attic.

Pratt, dreaming of sooty devils, was rudely awoken by a shower of debris from above, cascading down onto his head and shoulders. When he had recovered sufficiently to look up he saw, to his astonishment, a pair of dirty feet being rapidly withdrawn from the large hole now in his bedroom ceiling. These were replaced almost immediately by the whites of two eyes in a startled, blackened face staring back down at him.

Thaddeus Pratt, for whom the last few days had been too much for his delicate constitution, promptly fainted.

12. Rigmorden Hall, Westmorland
4th May, 1763

The river Lune rises among the remote Pennine heights of Howgill Fells in Westmorland and meanders its way through a broad, fertile valley until it reaches the sea at Lancaster. To the southeast lie Windermere and Storrs Hall, to the east the steep moorland hills of Middleton Fell and then absolutely nothing - except Yorkshire.

The journey from Storrs Hall to Kirkby Lonsdale normally took about three hours, with only one change of horses, in Kendal. For the first part of the trip Kofi had sat slumped in a corner of the carriage, lost in his own thoughts. For her part, Lady Evelyn Lowther sat staring out of the window, studiously ignoring her pet 'blackamoor'. She was glad, though, to reach the relative safety of Killington Common. The fells between here and Kirkby Lonsdale are the haunt of footpads and highwaymen. Many a Yorkshire farmer, rolling home having sold his wool in Kendal, has been waylaid, beaten and robbed. A woman of quality in a smart carriage is an obvious target - even if her coachman and groom each carried a brace of pistols.

By mid-afternoon they had left the marshy desolation of Lambrigg Fells and had begun to descend into the Lune valley. The heat had long since sucked up the mists, revealing the river below, now shimmering in the sun. Occasionally a fat trout would break the surface, then dive deep into its cool, brown depths. Smoke from a few farm cottages curled lazily into clear, blue skies.

Kofi looked up from his seat and saw his new Mistress smiling at him. She patted the seat beside her encouragingly. Somewhat shyly, Kofi got up and crossed the carriage, then sat on the cushions next to her. She took his hands gently in hers.

'Sambo, you now belong to me. Do you understand?'
'Yes, your Ladyship.'
'If you behave no harm will befall you but if you disobey me you will be whipped.'
'Yes your Ladyship.'
'Good. I'm glad we understand one another. Are you tired?'
'Yes.'
'Then you may rest you head in my lap. We shall soon be home.'

Kofi did as he was told, curled up on the seat and laid his head in Evelyn's lap. She smelled of lavender and orange blossom. He fell asleep almost immediately.

They were now fast approaching Rigmorden Hall - an imposing house in the Palladian style situated on a steep hillside overlooking the river Lune and bathed in lemon sunlight. A grounds-man at once threw open the iron gates and, with a crack of his whip, the coachman steered the brougham up a steep gravel driveway to the entrance of the house. Built by Evelyn's father, the late Sir Nicholas Lowther, this country villa had been paid for with profits from the coal industry Sir Nicholas had helped develop, building the port of Whitehaven in the process.

Almost before the carriage had stopped in front of the great house, servants ran out to receive her Ladyship, one footman lifting the still-sleeping Kofi from her lap while another helped Lady Evelyn descend. This was accompanied by the cries of half a dozen peacocks strutting about the lawns at the front of the villa. As Evelyn made her entrance up the stone steps, the footman carrying Kofi in his arms respectfully followed. Kofi was still fast asleep when another servant flung open the great wooden doors and they stepped into Rigmorden's vast, marbled hallway. Kofi was at once borne, like a sacrificial lamb, off to the housekeeper's parlour at the back of the house while Lady Evelyn retired to her bedroom to recover from the journey.

Rigmorden Hall is the product of an age in which the Italian style of Andrea Palladio still dominated architectural taste. Sir Nicholas, as a young man, had travelled to Vicenza in 1702 and had visited a number of Palladio's celebrated villas - including the Villa Malacontenta. His scholarly interest in Palladio is evidenced by his first-edition copy of Francesco Muttoni's *Architettura di Andrea Palladio Vicento* (1740) in Rigmorden's extensive library.

This youthful passion for the new, 'classical' style had, when he later married Evelyn's mother in 1728, shaped Rigmorden Hall. On her father's death in 1761, Evelyn had inherited the villa and its extensive parklands - together with a sizable fortune. Since then she had made a number of additions, particularly to the already exquisite gardens, thereby turning Rigmorden Hall into one of the most beautiful 'Palladian' villas in England. It was Evelyn Lowther's rural retreat - a place for relaxation, sport (she was a fine horsewoman and regularly rode to hounds) and private 'assignations', far from the prying eyes of her fashionable, London friends.

***

After the long journey from Storrs Hall, Evelyn is tired. Thankful to be home, she is now sitting before her dressing-room mirror.

As her chambermaid carefully removes her wig and begins to brush her mistress's hair with long, even strokes Evelyn reflects on the new addition to her household. The child is indeed very pretty. She felt a thrill of anticipation at the impact this handsome black boy, under her expert tutelage, would make at Court in London.

He would, however, require considerable training. Still, she had five weeks in which to turn this little savage into a creature that would not only enhance her own elegance and beauty but also thoroughly charm her London friends and, more importantly, her eminent cousin - King George III.

***

When Kofi finally woke up he found himself on a chair by the fire and surrounded by women, one of whom announced that she was her Ladyship's Housekeeper and, therefore, 'Sambo's' new governess.

'You be a good boy and no one will clout you. Aint that right girls?' she said, encouragingly.

The girls nodded in unison. One young girl impulsively leant forward and patted Kofi on his head but then quickly withdrew her hand and looked at her fingers, just in case they had turned black from contact with Rigmorden's new 'savage'. After his stay at Storrs Hall, Kofi was already wise to the ways of English servants and promptly gave them all a huge grin.

It seemed to work for the girls visibly relaxed, by giggling and patting Kofi on the head - as if he were a pet poodle, which, after all, was perhaps his fate although he did not know that at the time!

***

In the busy weeks that followed, Kofi was turned from black 'savage' to favoured servant.

This magical transformation began with a visit from a Kirkby Lonsdale seamstress, one Jessica Simpson. She was a withered little thing, with a pointed nose and sandy hair but she was very skilled and in no time had made a splendid suit of clothes for Kofi that gave him the appearance of a liveried flunky, gold braid and all. To top it off, she created a silk turban - from which sprouted a large, brightly colored ostrich feather. To the other servants, mostly simple country folk, this preposterous costume was something of a joke but for Kofi himself, dressed in finery that clearly marked him off from the other servants, it was simply magnificent. He was, after all, the nephew of a king so why should he not dress accordingly?

If Rigmorden's servants had any resentment towards her Ladyship's new pet then they wisely kept it to themselves - even if one of the skivvies *did* once slap Kofi for getting under her feet. Moreover, the housekeeper was a kindly soul and although quite capable of terrorizing her staff, took something of a shine to Kofi - either because she though it politically expedient or because she genuinely liked him. Whatever her motives, he received her protection - even when, shortly thereafter, he began to turn into an arrogant little prig.

***

Most of Kofi's time at Rigmorden during his first week or so was spent in the company of her Ladyship. She taught him how to open doors, scrape and bow when required, feed her titbits of food from a silver platter and generally attend to her every need.

In the morning, for example, he helped her dress. While her maids fussed about her, fastening petticoats and trying stays, Kofi fed her sweetmeats or held a mirror so that she might watch as her maids adjusted her elaborate, somewhat top-heavy wigs or fastened her rich, silk gowns. In the afternoon, she took him for walks in Rigmorden's extensive gardens, teaching him how to attend to her train or protect the hem of her cloak.

While Kofi at first regarded these duties as demeaning, he soon acquired a taste for his luxurious life at Rigmorden Hall. If, like the woman at Storrs Hall,

Evelyn Lowther was a 'witch' then she was, in Kofi's eyes, a benevolent witch. Indeed, he found his new mistress utterly beguiling. After months of cruelty and abuse from all manner of strangers, Evelyn's smiles and blandishments were as balm to his troubled soul. If her 'spells' and exotic perfumes had seduced him, then so be it. For the first time since his capture by the Dahomey, Kofi was happy - secure in the knowledge that he was now this beautiful woman's favoured servant. Armed thus with a new self-confidence and basking in Evelyn's excessive affection, all thoughts of Kumasi and his beloved mother vanished - as if by magic.

***

Whenever her Ladyship was away from Rigmorden Hall - on business perhaps in Lancaster, where her mother lived - Kofi was free to roam the estate. No one seemed to worry that he might want to escape, least of all Kofi himself. Indeed, that thought never entered his head, such was his contentment with his new post as her Ladyship's favourite' lapdog' Indeed, so secure did he now feel in her Ladyship's affections that he adopted a superior tone to the other servants, including even those who held senior posts within Evelyn's extensive establishment. Since it was clear to everyone at Rigmorden that 'Sambo' was now her Ladyship's favourite, to cross her on the subject of his insufferable arrogance was far too risky.

On those days when he was free, Kofi would throw off his silk tunic and feathered turban and escape into the fields and woods that surrounded the house. On one of these explorations he stumbled unexpectedly on Adam Badget, her Ladyship's gamekeeper - stretched out on a grassy bank by a stream and enjoying forty winks. Kofi was about to tiptoe away when, without opening his eyes or moving, the man spoke.

'What's thy *real* name, lad?'

Kofi, who had thought that the man was fast asleep, was somewhat startled by this unexpected question. However, instead of running away (which was his instinctive response) he squatted on his haunches, picked up a stone and threw it into the stream where it landed with a satisfying 'plop'.

Adam sat up on one elbow and stared at the boy.

'Well?'

It was a long time since anyone had asked Kofi his real name. Sometimes he feared he might forget it altogether, so used was he now to his English sobriquet. Latterly, all thoughts of Africa had vanished in the pleasures of his

103

new post so that Badget's question threw him somewhat. He suddenly realized, moreover, that not once in all the time that he had been at Rigmorden Hall had he thought of his mother back on the plantation in Jamaica. Was she still alive even? He therefore remained squatting on the bank, his head lowered and his eyes closed, trying to hold back tears of guilt and remorse.

'What's thy name? Thou did'na be afraid of me, my little black sparra.'
'Kofi. My real name is Kofi.'
'Well then Kofi, dost thou want to learn 'ow ta fish?'

***

If Kofi had felt guilt or remorse that afternoon, these feelings vanished with Evelyn's return. He was at once summoned to her drawing room and made to sit on a stool in front of her. From a cardboard box she took pair of Turkish slippers, which she placed on Kofi's feet. They fitted perfectly. Strutting up and down on the oriental carpet, Kofi rewarded his mistress with a smile that made Evelyn's heart flutter.

For Kofi, the acquisition of these and other 'gifts' was sufficient to banish all thoughts of Kumasi - and his mother. For her part, Evelyn was thrilled with Kofi's utterly genuine response to her gift - even if it were merely the penultimate component in a costume designed to show off her little blackamoor to best advantage. Her feelings for Kofi, initially pecuniary, were now increasingly tinged with an affection, which she herself found difficult to define.

***

At this time of the year Badget - and his lurcher, Rag - could be found most days working close to the river bank below the house. It was there that Kofi headed whenever he was free.

Although dour and somewhat reserved before strangers, Badget soon warmed to Kofi at his most uninhibited. Badget was recently married to a local girl. As there were no children as yet, Kofi probably filled a gap in his life. Whatever his motives, Adam was perhaps the only one at Rigmorden Hall who saw Kofi, not as a black 'savage' without rights or liberty, but for what he really was - a little boy occasionally having fun.

Sometimes, on particularly hot days, Kofi would strip off and swim in the river. He had swum since almost before he could walk and was able therefore to dive for coloured stones on the riverbed.

Once Badget helped him fashion a spear and Kofi, in turn, showed his new friend how to make a sling with a thin strip of leather, thereby giving the spear extra leverage. With this 'primitive' weapon Kofi promptly harpooned a young salmon. For his part, Badget taught Kofi how to tickle trout, catch young pheasants with a trail of corn soaked in gin, set badger traps and snare rabbits. He also taught him the names of the small creatures that lived on or near the riverbank - field mice, voles, marmots, millipedes and even an occasional grass snake - although Kofi's fear of snakes made him run off whenever Adam spotted one.

Thus their friendship blossomed.

***

At night Kofi slept at the foot of Evelyn Lowther's bed in a room that swirled with the heady scent of sandalwood and lavender.

No one ever thought it necessary to give Kofi a room or a bed of his own. While he had often wondered why this was the case, sleeping on silk cushions at the foot of her Ladyship's bed was clearly preferable to the hard wooden cots the other servants occupied. For that reason Kofi had never questioned this arrangement. Sometimes Evelyn even allowed him to curl up on the covers at the bottom of her bed - to keep her feet warm, or so she claimed.

Occasionally, however, he was banished to the scullery to spend an uncomfortable night on cold flagstones. This happened whenever her Ladyship had gentlemen 'guests.' They were a noisy group, mostly young blades who shared Evelyn's passion for hunting and who concluded a day's vigorous sport with food and drink at Rigmorden Hall in the company of their charming, vivacious and highly desirable hostess. Evelyn, however, was very particular with whom she slept and many a young hopeful, in his cups, staggered into the night disappointed.

Some, however, were occasionally lucky.

If Evelyn happened, on one of these riotous evenings, to actually desire one of her young companions she would dismiss the others and retire to bed with her chosen 'jockey' - having sent her maid on ahead to turn down the covers and warm the bed. On these occasions Kofi was dismissed with a summary wave of the hand - to the stone floor of the scullery.

Once, after an uncomfortable night in the scullery and consumed with a jealousy he himself barely understood, Kofi burst into Evelyn's bedroom and found her Ladyship asleep in the arms of yet another painted *beau*. The bedclothes were all over the place and the floor littered with stockings, stays and petticoats. Both Evelyn and her lover, a young man with a shock of red hair, were flat on their backs and snoring loudly. Kofi promptly turned on his heels and ran off down the corridor and out into the garden and on, up into the fells high above the house.

Some weeks earlier, unable to find Adam, Kofi had explored these hills and had stumbled upon an abandoned barn overlooking a small tarn. This desolate spot, where a modest farm had once flourished, was where he now hid. On his first visit there he was horrified to discover a dead sheep, hanging by its neck from the rafters. It had entered the two-storied barn from above and crashed through the rotten floorboards where it had hung by its neck until dead. Kofi had begged Adam to take it down and bury it. Today, though, Kofi could only think of his beautiful mistress clasped in the arms of that degenerate young man.

Kofi was fully aware of what men did to women, at night and in the secrecy of the bedchamber. In the Middle Passage he had seen women and young girls brutally abused by drunken sailors - those red-faced savages who had treated his companions with such cruelty. In Jamaica, sex was a commodity and many of the younger women in his mother's compound slept with the plantation's 'white trash', merely to obtain extra food or some minor luxury, like a comb. While Ashtari herself had disapproved of these liaisons, it was so much part of plantation life that her protests fell on deaf ears, especially amongst those women for whom casual sex bought a little comfort or provided some small luxury in a world largely deprived of either.

But Evelyn's liaisons were clearly different. She *invited* these men to her bed and appeared to enjoy their company - a fact that Kofi found disturbing. It was these, and other confusing thoughts, that swirled around in his head as he hid in the deserted barn that particular morning.

When Adam found Kofi some hours later, the boy was dragged back to Rigmorden Hall, soundly whipped for his 'impudence' and banished from her Ladyship's presence for two whole days.

***

Like most women of her class, Evelyn Lowther was not over-fastidious about her personal hygiene but she *was* inordinately proud of her long, black hair and washed it regularly. On these occasions it was Kofi's task to brush it once it had dried. He would stand behind her and caress it with long, even strokes - from the top of her head to the small of her back. From his position close behind her, Kofi could smell the sandalwood Evelyn used as a conditioner. Unseen by her

Ladyship, he would surreptitiously lean closer and closer, luxuriating in the exotic smell, redolent of an Africa he had now almost forgotten.

One morning Kofi accompanied Lady Evelyn on a shopping expedition to Kendal. As there carriage drew near to the town Kofi grew increasingly anxious. This was his first outing and the first time he would be seen in public in all his finery. They entered the town from the east, descending into the valley on the Sedbergh road, crossed the river Kent by the old stone bridge and clattered up Stramondgate. The milliner's shop was situated on the far side of the town, on a hill called Beast Banks.

On arrival, Kofi helped her Ladyship descend from her carriage then followed her into the shop where they were greeted, with much curtseying, by the milliner herself. Kofi was then introduced to the staff and managed to bow to all-and-sundry without losing his silk turban - thanks largely to the hatpin her Ladyship's housekeeper had thoughtfully provided. As Evelyn tried on numerous outlandish hats, Kofi sat quietly on a stool in one corner, trying hard not to yawn.

They eventually left the shop and began the perilous descent on foot down the narrow, cobbled lane called Collin Croft. Although accompanied by her footman (carrying several large hatboxes) it was Kofi's job to steady her Ladyship as they scrambled down the slippery steps. For his trouble he was rewarded with an affectionate squeeze of the hand. Most pedestrians they met politely stepped to one side, some bowing to her Ladyship - a well-known figure in Kendal. Others simple stared at Kofi or nudged their companions and pointed. Kofi, for his part, was too busy helping his mistress to notice their stares or hear their comments, some of which were far from complimentary.

Kofi was not the first black to be seen in Kendal. A number of other wealthy women in the county had black servants but none as young or as lavishly attired as 'Sambo.' In a society where many of the great mercantile families had connections with slavery, the presence of blacks in England itself was for some a little too close for comfort. Others (rural folk, largely) were simply superstitious, seeing such 'savages' roaming their streets as dangerous. Most ordinary people, as was the custom of the age, regarded 'niggers' as commodities - no better than goods and chattels.

Lowther Street, named after Evelyn's distinguished father, was the centre of Kendal's celebrated snuff industry. Although the shop itself was small, the storerooms and grinding-mills behind were extensive, supplying quality snuffs to all parts of the kingdom. Close by this small factory were a number of tanneries, stretching down to the river and a crucial part of Kendal's main trade - leather shoes. The stench from these tanneries, combined with the pungent scent of tobacco, was overwhelming and it was with some haste that Evelyn entered the shop.

It was the custom at this time to add flavours to the ground tobacco to give each snuff its distinctive 'taste.' Some snuff takers chose bergamot or peppermint, others violet or attar-of-roses and spearmint. Lady Lowther herself preferred 'Café Royale', an exotic blend of North American and Oriental tobaccos, specially treated and perfumed with spices, essential oils and coffee.

'This is snuff. Ground tobacco. Would you like to try some, Sambo?' asked Evelyn, proffering her silver snuffbox.
'No thank you, your Ladyship.'

Kofi, who had been staring at the jars and boxes that lined the walls of the shop, was aware that he had become the centre of attention - not only of the proprietor and those staff attending her Ladyship but of a number of men and boys who, keen to catch a glimpse of Sir James's daughter and her new 'pet', were now peering through the glass partition that separated the shop from the factory within.

'Take a pinch, Sambo. You might like it.'

Kofi slowly reached out, took a pinch of the finely ground, grey powder and gingerly raised his fingers to his nose.

'Go on, boy. It won't kill you!'

Kofi inhaled the snuff. For a moment nothing happened but then the nicotine struck the nervous tissues at the back of his nose and throat, causing a sharp yet pleasant sensation, closely followed by an enormous sneeze sufficient to dislodge his turban. The audience burst into spontaneous laughter and applause.

Kofi followed Evelyn out of the shop and into the street, with the laughter still ringing in his ears. If that humiliation was not in itself enough, he then saw above the shop a carved, wooden effigy (by way of a sign) of a grinning black boy, painted in lurid colours and crowned with an elaborate white turban exactly like his own.

***

On the journey back to Rigmorden Kofi was quiet, preferring to stare morosely out of the window rather than chat with his mistress. She, for her part, ignored him. She was used now to his moods, ascribing them to the savage disposition of an inferior race for whom manners were, undoubtedly, only skin deep.

Some radical, eighteenth-century theologians had argued that blacks were white within and that blackness was only a mask - a superficial deformity hiding an inner purity and whiteness. On the Day of Judgment, therefore, they would exchange their darkness for 'something brighter and better.' Evelyn did not share this view. Like the Comte de Buffon or Carl Linnaeus, she believed that Kofi and his race were *inherently* inferior. In their scientific classification of the Natural World, these 18th Century taxonomists correctly identified, or so Evelyn Lowther believed, 'Sambo's' essential inferiority. She never doubted, therefore, that 'mankind' was composed of several distinct species and that her little 'Sambo' - of whom, she had to confess, she was now inordinately fond - was fundamentally inferior to that superior white, European race to which she herself belonged.

One day, caught short in the great marble hall at Rigmorden, Evelyn lifted up her skirts, squatted in a corner and urinated directly onto the polished marble floor. Kofi was profoundly shocked. Such behaviour would have been unthinkable back home in his uncle's palace in Kumasi. Here, so it seemed, there were servants enough to mop up the large puddle her Ladyship had left on the floor.

On another occasion, as they sat together in her miniature pagoda at one end of the Chinese Garden, Evelyn lifted her skirts above one knee and told Kofi to retie the ribbon that fastened her stocking. The boy knelt before her on the grass and, with shaking fingers, retied the ribbon just above her bent knee. With her legs slightly apart the bare flesh of her thighs was clearly visible. Kofi, who was particularly sensitive to perfumes, secretly inhaled the sweet warmth of her lower body before returning to his seat beside her. Evelyn modestly re-covered her legs then bent and kissed her blackamoor on the cheek.

'Thank you, Sambo. That was very gallant of you!'

Kofi was left momentarily stunned by this sudden turn of events. His mistress had often been affectionate but she had never before kissed him. It was a new and, he had to admit, delicious sensation. Other kisses followed later and again Kofi's occasional resolve to remain aloof and somehow independent of the 'Witch of Rigmorden' simply vanished.

As Kofi grew ever closer to her Ladyship, so he distanced himself even further from the other servants at Rigmorden.

At first he had made friends with Molly, the little kitchen maid. Molly was only nine years old and generally regarded as simple but she was an affectionate child and was the nearest Kofi had to a playmate since his arrival in England. Sometimes she would let him play with the tiny, wooden peg-doll that she usually kept hidden in the pocket of her grubby apron. It was, in fact, her only possession. He liked Molly and she, it seemed, liked him. Together, whenever either had a little free time from their respective duties, they would play skittles in the yard at the back of the kitchen. She taught Kofi how to skip and how to make a cat's cradle and he in turn showed her how to tie intricate knots in a piece of string or carve a simple flute.

But this friendship did not last.

As Kofi succumbed more and more to Evelyn's seductive charms, so too he became increasingly arrogant. Basking in his her Ladyship's affection, he had little time for Molly. After a while even she noticed his arrogance towards her and their brief, tentative affection for each other withered and died. Kofi was not insensitive to these changes in his relationship to the other servants but after a while he stopped caring, finding sufficient solace in Evelyn's blandishments.

***

One hot, moonlit night, unable to sleep, Kofi rose from his bed of cushions and moved to the open window for a breath of fresh air. Moonlight spilled into the room, casting its cool light onto the prostrate figure of her Ladyship. In her sleep she had kicked her covers aside so that she now lay exposed. In the moonlight she looked like a beautiful corpse. Kofi stared at her for some time then tiptoed to the bed, took a corner of the top sheet and covered her up. He then returned to his bed of cushions where he lay, tossing and turning for the rest of the night in a confusion of excitement and shame.

When Kofi had first met Lady Fitzallen (the wicked 'Witch' of Storrs Hall) he had convinced himself that he had been bewitched by the potions she kept on her dressing-room table. Here at Rigmorden, however, the secrets of Evelyn's extensive collection of powders, creams and perfumes were willingly revealed to her curious 'apprentice'. Side by side, on two stools, mistress and blackamoor would sit for hours, sharing the cosmetic secrets of fashionable women of the period with a childish delight on Kofi's part that Evelyn herself found quite infectious.

One large ebony box she showed him contained the zinc paste used on formal occasions to give a woman's face the deadly white pallor considered fashionable at that time. Another box held a blue substance used to decorate her Ladyship's eyelids, giving her eyes a dark, lustrous appearance. She showed Kofi how to mix this paste from a blue powder made of finely ground, Venetian glass. Another little box contained a fine, red powder used to enhance her lips or cheeks.

Once, she covered his face in white powder.

It was, although Kofi did not realize it at the time, a symbolic act in the complex drama of subjugation in which he was now a crucial if largely ignorant participant. Not even her Ladyship, the prime mover in this process, fully understood what was happening between herself and her naïve young blackamoor. Although small for his age, Kofi was fast approaching adolescence. Could it be that Evelyn sought in his company a companionship or peculiar satisfaction otherwise lacking in the arms of her numerous lovers? Moreover, Evelyn Lowther was not the only woman in England fond of owning little black boys - as the commercial success of Storrs Hall itself proved time and time again.

That afternoon she had smacked Kofi for failing to protect the hem of her dress from a muddy patch in the topiary garden. He had sulked all afternoon, much to her annoyance. Now, as he brushed her hair before going to bed, she watched him in the mirror, his face still black as thunder. He was a very handsome child, particularly when angry - or so Evelyn mused. His eyes were large and very dark. His hair, which she had herself cut recently, was a mass of tiny curls. His lips, although thick, were perfectly shaped - even when, as now, they were fixed in a sulky, childish pout.

Kofi, absorbed in his own thoughts, brushed Evelyn's hair with long, even strokes just as she had taught him. He loved his mistress but today she had been particularly harsh, calling him a 'stupid black savage'. He was thinking about this when he glanced up and caught Evelyn staring at him in the mirror, her expression exactly mimicking his own, sullen pout.

For a second or two he stared back resolutely but then, aware of his own pomposity, grinned sheepishly.

Later that night, his humiliation forgotten, Kofi curled up in the loving arms of his mistress between sheets that smelled of sandalwood and lavender. Evelyn, for her part - trembling with inexplicable excitement - was acutely conscious that although her physical relationship with her little blackamoor was wholly innocent, she was now, by taking him into her bed, moving into dangerous territory.

13. London, England

18th May, 1763

Anyone familiar with John Rocque's fine map of London (first published in 1747 but still generally available in most good book shops), will know that London's Mayfair - once an area of fields and orchards - is filled with fashionable squares. Here Berkeley, Hanover and Grosvenor squares, each containing many imposing new houses, are reached by handsome streets, some of which are even paved. Where once, only a few years before, Earl's Court had been farmland and Chelsea a charming riverside village, Georgian London is now a great city, spreading far and wide, consuming farms and fields in its stone-clad embrace and filling its skies with the acrid, black smoke of countless, sea-coal fires.

The journey south from Rigmorden Hall to London took nearly three days and now Lady Evelyn is tired and irritable. Her two maids, also exhausted by the journey, slump in their seats opposite. Kofi, however, who has never seen a great city before, is beside himself with excitement.

It was seven o'clock by the time they left Grosvenor Square via Upper Brook Street and turned south down the broad avenue within Hyde Park. The park here is alive with elegant men and women strolling on the gravelled paths, military officers on horseback taking the early evening air or carriages trying to outdo each other in the ostentatious splendour of their equipage. Soon, however, the park will be empty of such fine folk for at night it becomes a place for pimps, prostitutes, thieves and murderers - and the occasional highwayman. Evelyn was glad to have reached Hyde Park before nightfall.

At Hyde Park Corner they entered Green Park via Constitution Hill then turned west into the upper end of St. James' Park. Buckingham House now lies directly before them, its facade a delicate rust-pink in the last rays of the setting sun. Moments later their carriage sweeps into the side entrance of the palace, whereupon liveried servants rush forward to steady the horses and help her Ladyship descend. Kofi, mindful of his training, leaps from the carriage first and offers his hand to his mistress.

'Why thank you, Sambo'.

Evelyn steps gingerly down onto the paved courtyard, relieved to have arrived safely at the private residence of her cousin, King George III of England.

'Welcome, your Ladyship' says the Head Butler, Thaddeus Pratt, bowing reverently. ' Follow me, please.'

Lady Lowther and her retinue are immediately shown to a suite of rooms in the west wing where they are to stay for the duration of their visit. Their two grooms are to live above the stables while Lady Lowther's two chambermaids, Arabella and Lisa, are given a tiny room on the floor above. Kofi has the sofa in the drawing room next to Evelyn's bedroom.

This arrangement did not suit her maids but it suited her Ladyship well enough. Kofi had no say in the matter but he reasoned, a horsehair sofa was better than an uncomfortable straw pallet in some attic.

After a restorative glass of wine and a plate of scrambled eggs, Evelyn undressed and prepared for bed. She dismissed her maids, tucked Kofi up on his sofa, kissed him gently on the cheek and retired, completely exhausted after her long journey.

Within minutes they were both fast asleep.

***

The following morning Evelyn slept late, still exhausted after the long journey south. This gave her maids time to unpack, press her clothes and generally sort themselves out.

Kofi, who now had nothing to do, used the time to explore their wing of the royal palace. He was not, however, allowed to go far for security was tight. Palace guards and footmen seemed to be everywhere, none of whom approved of a small, black child wandering the corridors of the King's residence. Indeed, Kofi's first appearance that morning caused one footman to stop in his tracks, stare in astonishment then turn on his heels and hastily run off down the corridor - much to Kofi's amusement. Perhaps the man had never seen a black child before, certainly not one in a white wig, silk tunic and sporting an elaborately embroidered waistcoat.

***

Unknown of course to either Kofi or his sleeping mistress, another child was in residence in Buckingham House. Even as Kofi warmed his hands before Evelyn's fire, Jack Fisher - the renegade climbing boy - was lurking in a dark recess adjacent to their chimney.

Prattt's dramatic encounter with his sooty adversary had taken place some three weeks previously.

It had been both sudden and alarming but Pratt had not summoned the guards on that occasion. Instead, curiosity had got the better of him. By placing a chair on the table in his room he had been able to see into Jack's secret place. Jack of course was long gone by the time Prattt's plaster-covered head appeared through the

113

hole but there were the ornate cushions and a still-smoking candelabrum - definitive proof, if any were now needed, of the boy's presence within the palace.

Although Tyburn Tree now beckoned enticingly, Pratt realised that it was one thing to know that the climbing boy was in the palace but quite another to actually catch him.

In the weeks that followed, Pratt thought long and hard as to how he might catch the diminutive sweep.

Clearly there was no point in trying to enter Jack's domain - that maze of chimneys that the boy appeared to know so well. However, the one thing the little bastard clearly needed to survive was food and water. Because of the numerous banquets, formal luncheons and private dinner-parties held each week in the palace, there was always a prodigality of food available for the taking.

This meant that it was extremely unlikely that the boy would ever lack sustenance. Unless, that is...

'Yes! That was it!'

Pratt at once summoned his staff to the kitchen and issued orders that any food that remained after the palace guests had left should be removed or thrown to the pigs. From now on, all food must be locked away and a close watch kept on pantries and store cupboards.

He would, with luck, *starve* him out!

***

With Jack's secret hideaway now exposed, he had spent the last few weeks looking for some place else to live within the palace's labyrinthine chimneys. As luck would have it, and by dint of some serious kicking, one day three weeks later, Jack inadvertently smashed his way into the largest void of all - the space beneath the palace's main roof.

This vast attic, the size of three Royal Tennis courts placed end-to-end, was normally reached by a number of trap doors but on close inspection it was clear that these had not been opened in living memory. The floors and walls of this enormous void were covered in dust and thick cobwebs. Several fanlights illuminated the area but these too had not been used for years and had rusted tight shut. They cast an opaque light across the void - like strips of delicate grey muslin suspended from floor to ceiling. The space was huge, with great big beams, grey with age, supporting a steeply pitched roof. Moreover, large parts of the floor space had been boarded over - thereby reducing the chance of Jack crashing through into someone's bedroom below.

At one end of the void was an enormous water-tank. Jack of course knew nothing of this great tank but it actually held fifty tons of water and was used to service the fountains throughout the palace's extensive gardens. It was kept topped up with water pumped directly from the river Thames - which would account for the gurgles, splashes and distant pumping noises heard from time to time. After a while Jack got used to these sounds - if only because they relieved the monotony of the normal silence within the void.

It took about six hours of tortuous climbing, pulling and shoving for Jack to gather all his worldly goods into this new home. Once he had reassembled his cushions, candlesticks and other home comforts, he sat down to plan his strategy should the guards suddenly burst in - as he was sure they would do eventually. Access to this void could only be via the trapdoors but they would need to enter all of them simultaneously to catch him. If that *did* happen, he could either retreat once more into the chimney system or smash his way through a fanlight onto the roof - he had already put aside a brick for just that purpose.

No, as long as they did not attempt a mass, co-ordinated attack, Jack was now safe - or so he thought.

***

Later that morning Evelyn took Kofi on a shopping expedition. Leaving Hyde Park, their journey took them along Pall Mall and on, by a circuitous route to 98 Fleet Street - a jeweller's shop frequented by the rich. They were met inside by a very obsequious salesman who turned out to be the proprietor, John Brasbridge. He wore an enormous, dusty grey wig and appeared to know Lady Lowther. After much bowing and scraping, he guided Evelyn to a chair and ordered an assistant to fetch her Ladyship a dish of tea.

'So this...', said the salesman, '...this is the young man, n'est pas?'

Kofi, whose attention had already wandered, received a sharp slap from her Ladyship before he realised that he was the object of the salesman's remarks.

'So, shall we try it for size, your Ladyship?'
'Very well. Sambo, face that mirror.'

Kofi, who had not the faintest idea what was going on, did as he was told and contemplated his image in the mirror.

'Do stand up straight, for goodness sake!'

Today Kofi was wearing matching jacket and breeches of embroidered green silk and a white wig that made him look like a miniature version (albeit black) of Emperor Frederick the Great. Since no one ever told him anything, Kofi was totally foxed as to why he was now part of this charade:

'Another new turban perhaps, or pearl earrings? Yes, pearl earrings would be acceptable!'

After a moment Brasbridge returned, carrying an object wrapped in pink tissue paper. He then stood immediately behind Kofi and placed round his neck an elaborately tooled, silver collar, hinged on one side and with an intricate lock on the other.

Snapping the lock shut he stepped back to admire his work. Kofi was now aware that the salesman, Lady Lowther, three assistants and the boy from the tavern with the dish of tea were crowding round his chair and staring at him in the large mirror.

'Well, Madame? What do you think? Will it suit?'
'I think it will suit very well, thank you. He will wear it now.'

Brasbridge produced a small key from his pocket and deftly applied it to the tiny lock, now positioned just below Kofi's right ear. With a little 'click' the silver collar was secured. Evelyn then took the key and dropped it into the silk purse attached by a ribbon to her wrist.

While her Ladyship wrote out a money order for her purchase, Kofi continued to stare into the mirror. While the silver collar was attractive enough, the idea that it was now a *permanent* feature was disturbing. Brief images of other collars of a very different nature worn by others back in Africa and Jamaica flashed before him. He gave the collar a tug. Although not tight, there was no mistaking the fact that it was securely fastened. Perhaps, he mused, it was only a temporary fixture and would be removed later that day.

But her Ladyship did not unlock the collar or remove it, despite Kofi's pleas. Tears and tantrums followed - for which Kofi was rewarded with a slap that sent him sprawling to the floor.

***

Kofi's relationship with her Ladyship's maids, never good at the best of times, now took a turn for the worse.

Anxious not to displease his mistress further, Kofi hid his real feelings and began to show off his collar to all-and-sundry. While the girls pretended in public to admire 'Sambo's' elaborate, hugely expensive appearance they secretly resented the lavish attention Lady Evelyn now gave this black upstart.

What soon became apparent, however, was that the new collar and Kofi's preposterous silk clothes were all part of Evelyn's preparations for the central event of her visit to Buckingham House - an audience with King George III. This formal ceremony was scheduled for 4th June, on the occasion of His Majesty's twenty-fifth birthday. 'Sambo' - in his fancy clothes, ornate silk turban and expensive silver collar - was an important ingredient in her Ladyship's plans to bedazzle her king, not only with her own elegance and beauty but with that of her darling little blackamoor.

During the next few weeks, therefore, Evelyn frequented the entrance hall to the palace - the great marbled room housing the grand staircase leading to the royal apartments. No one quite knew why she hovered in this way, not least the footmen who operated in that area, but every morning, from eleven o'clock until the palace clock struck twelve, she would be there, dressed to the nines. Kofi was also present. He was made to stand beside her, shoes polished and in his second-best silk tunic, spare turban and, of course, the silver collar prominently displayed.

Since the great hallway was decorated throughout with enormous gilt mirrors, her Ladyship spent a great deal of her time checking her appearance or, with Kofi close beside her, grouping herself and her little blackamoor in decorative poses. For those who regularly passed through this hallway, either going about their domestic duties or as Court visitors, this charade took on the appearance of a scene from a comic opera. However, despite titters and snide comments, Evelyn stuck her ground and after a week or so finally got what she had wanted all along - a meeting with the Queen.

That morning, at eleven-thirty precisely, the nineteen-year-old Queen Charlotte, accompanied by three of her German ladies-in-waiting, appeared at the top of the great staircase and began her descent. Kofi, whose attention had begun to wander after half-an-hour of waiting, at once received a sharp dig in his ribs as her Ladyship, in full sail as it were, immediately swept forward. They met halfway up the great stairs. Evelyn had the good sense to pause several steps below Charlotte, thereby displaying due deference to the young Queen. Charlotte, for her part, smiled sweetly, graciously acknowledging Lady Lowther's deep curtsey.

'And who', she added benignly, 'is this handsome young man?'
'Why, Majesty', replied Evelyn graciously, 'this is Sambo.'

At this point, with the eyes of the Queen herself upon him, Kofi had the presence of mind to bow solemnly and then provide Her Majesty with one of his special smiles. The Queen was enchanted; bent forward and gently pinched his cheek with her gloved hand.

'Why then, Sambo, how do ye do!'

With that the Queen resumed her royal descent and swept out of the great doors to her carriage in a swirl of rustling silk skirts, trailing behind her a pungent smell of perfume and an unmistakable, highly pungent whiff of body odour.

Evelyn was thrilled and once she got back to her little suite of rooms hugged Kofi until his ribs hurt. That night, still basking in her triumph, her Ladyship retired early. She had drunk rather too much wine that afternoon and it took both her maids to undress her, remove her elaborate makeup and otherwise prepare her for bed. Kofi, who usually got in the way on these occasions, was summarily banished to the drawing room where he began to play patience - a card game Arabella had taught him in a moment of uncharacteristic generosity.

***

It was well past midnight when Kofi woke up. He must have dozed off because he is still fully dressed. The casement is wide open and moonlight is spilling into the room, turning everything a deathly white. Kofi yawns, stretches and moves to the window to close the shutters but just as he is about to fasten the second one he hears a noise in the chimney behind him, closely followed by a sudden fall of soot.

Alarmed, he quickly withdraws behind the curtain and watches nervously as a bare foot appears in the chimney place, closely followed by another. Suddenly a small, black figure drops into the grate, shakes itself like a dog and steps onto the carpet. When the cloud of soot subsides, Kofi sees that the black creature is actually staring straight at him with eyes as white as ivory in a face as black as thunder.

For a moment there is absolute silence - except for the pounding of Kofi's heart - whereupon the sooty ghost speaks.

'Boo!' it says, loudly.

Seconds later it has vanished out the bedroom in a cloud of soot - or so it seemed.

Kofi's first thought is to wake her Ladyship and tell her what he has just seen but then some instinct tells him that that is *not* a good idea. She would be angry at being woken. She would, moreover, almost certainly call him a liar or tell him that he had been dreaming - and then smack him. Instead, Kofi left the safety of the curtain and moves cautiously towards the fireplace, tentatively touching the soot with his foot. The soot is real enough but what of that little, evil-looking black devil?

There were always plenty of ghosts back in Kumasi and Kofi was sure that the woods around Storrs Hall had been filled with lost souls but here, in Buckingham House? Surely not!

He decided, therefore, to tell no one. Instead, he resolved, there and then, to wait up all night. If that black devil lived up their chimney it would need to return some time and then he would catch it!

But the black devil did not return that night and when Arabella found Kofi the following morning he was fast asleep behind the curtain, inexplicably clutching a large poker in one hand.

**

Preparations for His Majesty's 'secret' Twenty-fifth Birthday Celebrations were now in full swing, although the King himself was not in residence at the palace. He had gone to Hannover on business, leaving Queen Charlotte free to make her final arrangements for the 'Great Day' - Saturday, 4th June. Carpenters and plasterers were now active in the royal gardens, building an ornate pavilion while the Master Chef and his kitchen staff planned a sumptuous feast. There would be fireworks, music and dancing and many distinguished guests at Buckingham House - including the King's cousin, Lady Evelyn Lowther and her now much-admired little blackamoor.

Evelyn's stratagem to waylay Queen Charlotte had worked splendidly for not only had she now met Her Majesty in person but the following day received an invitation from the young Queen to accompany her on a shopping expedition to Bond Street - provided, of course, that she brought the 'adorable Sambo' with her.

They set off in the Queen's carriage, accompanied by two outriders from the Royal Horse Guards. Charlotte had somehow managed to escape her dour Ladies-in-Waiting with whom, under the orders of her formidable mother-in-law, she was usually stuck. Evelyn was not quite sure how she had done this but was thrilled that, for an hour or two, she would have the undivided attention of her royal cousin's young wife. The Queen had not, however, entirely escaped Augusta's 'spies' for she was accompanied on this little expedition by the elderly Countess Effingham - a lady who suffered from bad breath, poor skin and a terminal lack of humour.

As their carriage swung into Hanover Square, Evelyn patted her skirts about her and settled back in her seat. Although Charlotte had attractive, dark hair she was hardly a beauty - short, thin and pale and with a prominent nose and large mouth. What she lacked in beauty, however, she made up for in a lively disposition and a naturalness, which Evelyn found quite enchanting.

'Stop! Stop the carriage!', cried the young Queen as they turned into Bond Street and headed north, towards Oxford Street.

'What a divine *mantua*. I must have that beautiful dress, do you not agree, Lady Lowther?'

It was common knowledge that when Charlotte Sophia Mecklenburg-Strelitz had been a mere princess she possessed only one decent dress to her name. George III was said to be mean and rumours that the Queen's hairdresser doubled as a waiter at the palace did nothing to change that impression.

'Why, I do declare, these stays are perfect with that *sacque* dress. All I need now are shoes to match. What do you recommend, my dear Evelyn? The brocaded ones or these, embroidered with silk and what I take to be metallic thread? Please advise me, my dear. You know so much more about fashion that I do?'

Evelyn knew also that Charlotte was still very naïve in matters of the heart. It was common knowledge that George's real passion had been - and probably still was - Lady Sarah Lennox. They had first met when Sarah was just seventeen and fascinating to a young man of George's inexperience. She was also something of a flirt so that the young Prince of Wales was soon besotted. Most mornings in the spring of 1761 he rode to Holland House to meet his young mistress who invariably appeared dressed in what she supposed to be 'peasant' costume. Did they still meet secretly, now that George was married? Evelyn herself was not sure. If they did, would this naïve, young Queen necessarily know? Probably not.

'Look, what a wonderful *parure*! Why, it has matching necklace and earrings of Brazilian pearls. Shall I buy it, Lady Evelyn? Shall I? Please say yes! Please say that you approve of my choice. My darling husband will surely approve, do you not think?'

Evelyn knew that George would only think what his mother told him to think or approve of that which she alone approved. Augusta, who had played little part in politics when George II had been alive, dominated her son now that he was King. Poor Charlotte! What chance did she have with such a dragon constantly lurking in the wings? At least Buckingham House provided a partial refuge for a young queen still trying to find her feet at Court.

'Sambo, I want you to carry this box for me. Careful now, it contains my new shoes for His Majesty's birthday party. Will you do that for me, my dear?'

Kofi, who had accompanied all three women into shops the length-and-breadth of Bond Street, was now tired and bored. Naturally, he accepted the small parcel from the Queen with a gracious bow and sealed the contract with one of his famous smiles but all he wanted to do now was to get back to the palace and perhaps encounter the little black ghost once more. That was all he could think about.

Their presence in Bond Street had not gone unnoticed.

While Queen Charlotte was still relatively new to Londoners, one or two recognised her and word quickly spread. Whenever the royal party crossed the street from one shop to another, men would doff their hats and women pedestrians would curtsey - all accompanied by polite applause. Kofi had himself attracted a number of such plaudits and had the sense, when accompanying Her Majesty, to turn to his Queen and applaud along with the crowd as if their applause were for her and her alone - much to Charlotte's evident delight.

When they got back to the palace they went their separate ways, the Queen having first expressed her complete satisfaction with the day's outing by kissing Evelyn on both cheeks and solemnly shaking Sambo by the hand. Kofi was of course thrilled at having met the Queen again and to have been of service to her - not least because it seemed to please his mistress.

He was rewarded later that afternoon with hugs and kisses and a little bowl of Turkish delight, which Evelyn fed him, piece by piece, with her own fingers.

***

That night, the moment her Ladyship had gone to bed, Kofi prepared himself. This time he decided to lie on the sofa but concealed beneath his blanket, with only his eyes and nose showing.

He took with him the poker - just in case.

He waited and waited but the sooty imp did not appear. Clocks in remote parts of the palace struck twelve - then one, then two but still nothing. When he eventually fell asleep he dreamt of the *Biloko* who live in hollow trees and dress only in leaves. They have no hair but sharp claws, piercing eyes and snouts with mouths that can be opened wide enough to admit a human body, dead or alive.

Some hours later Kofi was woken up by a smart tap on his shoulder - to discover the black devil sat beside him on the sofa, bold as brass, his legs crossed and noisily gnawing on a leg of chicken.

'Hullo', it said. 'My name is Jack. Wot's yours?'

Kofi was at first too startled to speak and simply stared at the creature sat beside him, conscious of its smell - a pungent mixture of soot and dried excrement.

'Cat got yer tongue?'
'No', said Kofi at last. 'They call me Sambo but my real name is Kofi.'
'How do ye do, Kofi.'

The smelly imp extended a sooty hand but Kofi, who had now stood up and moved a little way off, did not dare take it. Having finished his chicken leg, the black imp casually tossed the bone into the grate and fastidiously sucked his sooty fingers, one by one.

'Why do you live up that chimney?' asked Kofi.
'Cos I do. Now don't you say nuffink. This is our little secret, right?'

Kofi nodded, not quite sure what he was agreeing to. The black imp, shedding soot at every movement, no matter how slight, began to explore the pockets of his ragged jacket.

'You hungry?' it asked suddenly.
'Yes', said Kofi.

It was true, he was very hungry. Apart from the Turkish delight, her Ladyship had forgotten to feed him yet again.

'Let's see wot we 'av 'ere', said the imp, plunging his hand into a pocket filled with loot, including several spoons, a silver napkin ring, two knives, an assortment of gold rings - and a second rather grubby leg of chicken. The chicken, produced with the exaggerated flourish of a magician pulling a rabbit from his hat, was proffered to Kofi.

Kofi took the food and chewed on it contentedly. It may be a black ghost but at least the chicken was real enough. The imp, clearly gratified that his gift had found favour, then stood up, stuffed his loot back into his pockets, shook Kofi firmly by the hand - and disappeared up the chimney before Kofi could say a word. He was left staring open-mouthed at an empty grate, a little pile of soot on the carpet and the remains of a leg of chicken.

14. Buckingham House, London
1st June, 1763

Not long after Kofi's second secret encounter with the black imp, Lady Lowther was invited to a charity concert in aid of a new maternity hospital. The concert was to be given that afternoon by a young prodigy whose reputation had spread throughout Europe. It was his first visit to London so no one knew much about his work but all of society, not least the Queen herself, would be there. It was imperative, therefore, that Evelyn should attend.

Kofi, wearing his jewel-encrusted turban, long silk tunic and Turkish slippers, accompanied his mistress that afternoon to Ranelagh Gardens where the concert was to take place. Evelyn had pulled as many strings as she could but had failed to obtain one of the many boxes - much to her annoyance. Instead, they had to stand in the body of the hall, some distance from the concert platform. The custom here was to parade round the central column while listening to the orchestra but today it was far too crowded for even the slightest movement.

The infant prodigy is called Wolfgang Amadeus Mozart. He is accompanied by his elder sister and his father, both accomplished musicians but it is the young harpsichordist who completely astonishes his audience that afternoon.

He begins by playing pieces by Telemann, Schubert and Eckhardt, followed by a few of his own compositions - short pieces but of staggering complexity. Since London is largely unfamiliar with such 'experimental' music it is not widely appreciated. However, when he performs a *capriccio* of his own devising based on a well-known theme by Johann Christian Bach, the brilliance of his technique is clearly evident. Indeed, it brings the house down, the applause led by Bach himself. Other set pieces follow, more 'party tricks' than compositions, but each designed to demonstrate that here is a performer of brilliance. When he finished, an hour later, he left the hall to a standing ovation, the crowd parting before him like the Red Sea before Moses.

Since Kofi was close to the main exit, he was the last person to see Mozart approaching. The boy prodigy was dressed in wig, gold-braided jacket and gartered breeches and sported a miniature sword. He was, to Kofi's astonishment, a mere child and even shorter than himself. For a moment, as Mozart draws closer, their eyes met. The prodigy hesitates momentarily but then recovers, resuming his exit with a jaunty step. Kofi's eyes are as big as saucers but as Mozart sweeps out of the room the infant prodigy turns his head towards him and winks.

***

Later that night, curled up on the rug in front of their drawing-room fire, Kofi pondered his future.

He loved the adulation he and his fashionable mistress attracted. His life, particularly here in Buckingham House, was one of relative idleness and great luxury. Even her Ladyship seemed to have grown fonder of him, finding every excuse to kiss him, even in public. But would it last? Here, in London, he was an essential part of her *entourage* but would he, like the clothes he wore, soon fall out of fashion once they quit the capitol and returned to the rural obscurity of Westmorland?

Kofi was the first to recognise that he had been complicit in Lady Evelyn's plans for him. He was maturing rapidly yet part of him still resented the numerous ways in which she robbed him of his identity. Why, he scarcely recalled his own name, so used was he to being called 'Sambo'. What, moreover, would his mother think of him if she could see him - the pampered popinjay of a beautiful but unscrupulous woman? Kofi loved and admired Evelyn but even he could see that he was now something between an emotional whipping boy and a fashion accessory. He craved the cuddles and kisses Evelyn lavished upon him - even if, later, she occasionally beat him for some minor misdemeanour.

It was this curious mixture of intimacy and cruelty that confused him so and which, when he was alone, frequently occupied his thoughts.

***

Thaddeus Pratt has not been idle during these last few days. As Head Butler he is responsible for looking after the many guests staying at the palace, including Lady Lowther and her retinue. He is also responsible for the complex arrangements associated with the King's forthcoming birthday reception. He has had, therefore, very little time to concentrate on the embarrassing matter of a light-fingered sweep loose at night in the palace.

A painful reminder of this 'problem' occurred on the night of the celebrated Mozart concert.

Jack's ideas of hygiene were non-existent. Not only was he filthy but also his toilet habits beggared description. Sometimes, when on the loose in the palace, he would simply pee on the carpets - even in the staterooms. If he wanted to crap, he would do it wherever he was, there and then, and wipe his sooty bum on the nearest curtains. While he normally peed wherever he found himself within the chimneys, up there he always shat down one particularly narrow shaft in the east wing.

Besides, this particular chimney was of no other use to him because when he had explored it earlier he had found that it ended in a small iron stove that filled the hearth, thereby denying him access to the room itself.

After many weeks of crapping down this particular shaft there was a considerable pile of accumulated waste now balanced precariously on a brick ledge thirty feet below.

Agnes Millichop, dozing before the fire in her tiny room in the east wing, was unaware of the smell that lingered in the flue above. While she was always quick to upbraid her girls for their primitive notions of cleanliness, she herself stank like a glue factory. As Housekeeper she was responsible for ensuring that her chambermaids and scullery girls were well turned out yet beneath their starched aprons, caps and fresh skirts the delicate skin of these young girls was usually an unhealthy grey. Scullery maid Felicity Butcher was a case in point. Not only was she dirty all over but also her lovely brown hair was crawling with lice. Since their betters rarely washed, what possible understanding could these poor girls - most of them as ignorant as newborn calves - possibly have of personal hygiene and cleanliness?

Even so, Agnes is surprised to see an enormous pile of dried shit suddenly land in her hearth.

Her screams bring footmen and maids running to her room - closely followed by Pratt in a grubby nightshirt and clutching an enormous shillelagh. When he sees Jack's accumulated efforts sitting in Agnes' little grate his heart sinks. What if this should happen in one of the royal apartments? What if the King himself were rudely awakened one night by a dollop of sooty excrement landing on his carpet? These terrifying thoughts may partly explain why, later that night, a distraught Pratt could be found in his bedroom banging his bald head against the wall as tears of anger and frustration pour down his cadaverous, pox-marked face.

***

As for Jack, well - for the first time in many weeks of solitary confinement he has someone to talk to, even if it is only a pampered 'nigger'. To have found a boy of his own age and one willing to keep silent was a minor miracle. After weeks of loneliness, compounded by toothache in a mouth full of rotten teeth, it is wonderful to have someone with whom to share his anxieties or, better still, his adventures within the palace.

How would it end? Well, that was another matter. For the time being, however, Jack is having fun.

Later that night he found Kofi asleep on the sofa in Evelyn's sitting room. It is about two in the morning and the palace is as quiet as the grave - apart from Evelyn's sonorous snores from her bedroom next door.

'Psst!', said Jack into Kofi's ear. 'Wake up, me owd mate. Time we was out an' about.'

Kofi sits up like a startled rabbit. For a moment he is unsure whether or not he is still dreaming but the very smelly figure of Jack perched on the end of the sofa clearly suggests otherwise.

'It's only me. You 'ungry?'
'Er, yes', said Kofi, now wide-awake. 'Yes, I am.'
'Well then young 'un, follow me.'

Jack stands up and darts out of the room and down the corridor with the speed and agility of a cat. Kofi follows but in the darkness momentarily loses him. Moments later, turning a corner, he sees the sweep cheekily poking his head round a doorway and beckoning with one, sooty finger.

'In 'ere. Quick now, we aint got all night!'

Kofi follows and finds himself in a large room he has never seen before, in the middle of which is a table groaning with food, much of it untouched

'Help yerself, nigger', said the imp, cramming his face with cold meats and potato salad. Kofi, too bemused to ask any more questions, tucks into a turkey leg almost as big as his head. After a while, their hunger assuaged, Jack sits on a chair, cocks a leg on the table and stares at Kofi.

'Why you dressed like that? Are you some kind of flunky?'

Kofi is not exactly sure what a 'flunky' is but he resents the tone of the boy's voice.

'I am servant to Lady Evelyn Lowther, mistress of Rigmorden Hall'.
'Very nice too', replies Jack, somewhat sarcastically.
'And how much, I wonder...', asks Jack slowly, '...is that collar of yours worf?'

Kofi has no idea as to its actual value but he quickly gets Jack's drift. He decides to change the subject.

'Why do you live up the chimney? Can't be much room up there?'

'You'd be surprised, Kofi. Anyway, I've got no bloody choice. I got stuck up there. When the buggers tried to smoke me out I said to meself that that were no way to treat a climbin' boy so I decided to brass it out, live up them chimblies for a while and fend for meself.'

At this point Jack rises and moves closer to Kofi's chair. There is now something threatening in his voice.

'I 'ope you aint goin' to tell no one about me, Kofi? This is our little secret, right? Say nuffink to no one and I'll show you uvver secrets, right? Is that a deal?'

Kofi nods, at which point Jack abruptly leaves the room - by the chimney. By the time Kofi crouches in the hearth and peers up the black tunnel above his head, Jack has disappeared. Kofi then makes his way back down the corridor to Evelyn's drawing room. It is now three in the morning.

***

Later that morning Pratt rose from his bed, dressed, donned his dusty wig and tottered downstairs to find William Appleby.

William had been on special duty that night - hidden behind the curtains in a small room filled with a large table groaning with food. His task was to observe or even apprehend the climbing boy should he be drawn towards this gastronomic feast. It was a cunning trap laid by an increasingly desperate Pratt. Unfortunately, William had got bored and at about two in the morning had left the room and had retreated into the arms of a more than willing Phyllis in another part of the palace. Although William had had the sense to stagger back to the banqueting room before dawn and hide once more behind the curtains, he was - unfortunately - later found fast asleep by an extremely angry Pratt.

It was clear from the sooty footprints on the carpet that the sweep had taken the bait but, through William's incompetence, had escaped one again. William was summarily dismissed later that morning. Phyllis' part in this farce was also soon discovered. According to Pratt, jewellery belonging to the Queen had been found under her bed. Although the girl denied the charge, she was arrested that same day. After a less that satisfactory trial, she was imprisoned in The Bridewell where she languished for two years, during which time she died of typhoid. Prattt's part in all this was less than distinguished for it was he who had planted the jewellery in the girl's bedroom.

Meanwhile, high in his loft, Jack is as happy as a sand-boy.

For a few days he had found it difficult to obtain food, thinking perhaps that they were trying to starve him out but the discovery of the banquet had proved that this was not the case. In fact, after some weeks of loneliness, Jack is once more in his element. He has decent accommodation, an apparently uninterrupted supply of excellent food - and a new playmate. Most nights, therefore, he now meets Kofi and together they explore the palace.

Kofi even gets to sit on the His Majesty's golden throne and pee in the royal chamber pot.

In fact, Kofi is becoming more and more attracted to the reckless lifestyle of his new friend. After the tedium of society life during the day and the cloying blandishments of the ladies of the court, especially those of his mistress, his nights are now filled with adventure, excitement and danger.

***

Meanwhile, as Jack and Kofi scamper about the palace at night, plans are being made to put an end to this abuse of His Majesty's royal property. However, since no one as yet has dared to tell His Majesty, nothing is done officially. Grooms and gardeners, bottle-boys and footmen are therefore coerced into taking turns to guard strategic points throughout the palace. This rather amateurish approach - necessitated by what had become known amongst the staff as 'Prattt's Dilemma' - might explain why it fails to catch either Jack or Kofi up to their nightly pranks.

Two days later, however, just as the bells of St. Clement's struck five in the morning, Jack and Kofi come within inches of discovery.

Jack is teaching Kofi how to slide down the marble banisters of the great staircase itself - the very staircase down which Queen Charlotte had descended the day Evelyn finally met Her Majesty. The trick of course is to go down 'side-saddle' then leap off at the last moment before hitting one of the rather ugly winged messengers at the end of each marble 'banister'. With luck you can land safely on the soft carpet in the body of the hallway. It is a technique Jack had perfected after many attempts over many nights.

On this occasion, Jack's descent is fast and furious but his landing is not so good because he trips, misses the carpet altogether and, like an ungainly goose landing on ice, slides on his face across the marble floor. He ends up in a crumpled heap against the end wall. At that precise moment a small door opens on the far side of the hallway, emitting a sleepy chambermaid carrying a brass scuttle full of coal. As she crosses the hallway, yawning and clearly lost in her own thoughts, she neither sees a winded Jack prostrate on the floor nor, had she glanced upwards, the terrified figure of Kofi at the top of the grand staircase.

Frozen with fear, Kofi actually resembles one of those life-size, wooden blackamoors popular amongst women, unlike Evelyn Lowther, who cannot afford the real thing.

*****

While these futile attempts to catch Jack continue, Pratt himself is now fully occupied with final preparations for the King's birthday celebrations. In the palace gardens an ornate, semicircular pavilion has been constructed of decorated wood and plaster - designed by the architect, Robert Adams. Pathways have been paved, tables and chairs placed in the gardens and ornamental canopies rose to shield gusts from the elements. In all, everything is in readiness for the great day.

Meanwhile, in the west wing, Evelyn Lowther's last-minute preparations for the 'Great Event' are *not* going well.

For the last few days Arabella and Lisa have been hard at work, preparing their increasingly testy mistress for her presentation to His Majesty. Their little apartment and the servants' quarters above have been a hive of industry as clothes are pressed, altered, re-altered and pressed once more. By Thursday both servants are sick of the whole business and wish they were back home in Rigmorden Hall.

Kofi, who seems now to get in everyone's way simultaneously, takes the brunt of Evelyn's ragged nerves, closely followed by the bad humour of her overworked chambermaids.

His Majesty's Birthday Celebrations
4th June 1763

On the morning of the Great Day - the same day Jack and Kofi had nearly been caught sliding down the marble staircase - Evelyn is in a particularly foul mood. While the Bond Street shopping expedition with the Queen had been a triumph, other invitations have not followed quite as readily as she had hoped. Of course, Kofi has been admired wherever she has taken him but, to tell the truth, she is now a little jealous of her pretty blackamoor.

She has noticed also that he has become decidedly less attentive and is always yawning - as if her company bored him. He has also taken to retiring at the earliest opportunity rather than play cards with her or sit and chat on her bed, as they had frequently done in the past. While she is excessively fond of him and has tried, since their arrival in London, to lavish on him all her care and affection, Sambo is definitely *not* responding as warmly as he had done only a week or so before.

In short, he is *not* fulfilling the requirements of a favoured servant and might need to be reminded soon of where, exactly, his real responsibilities lie.

Meanwhile, recumbent on his cushions in his secret void, Jack has time to reflect on his recent adventures with Kofi. His close encounter in the Great Hall troubles him. No doubt the sleepy chambermaid would have constituted no threat to his person but the palace is now crawling with servants and guards, anyone of whom could have seized him had they too appeared. Moreover, he sees that his recklessness is contagious, causing Kofi to take ever-increasing risks in his company. It is a recipe that will surely end in disaster. Even Jack, whose whole life has been something of a survival course, can see that it is now only a matter of time before he and his new friend are caught.

Then what? Imprisonment? Deportation? Death? Time, perhaps, to plan an escape and quit the palace altogether. But how? Where? When?

***

By six o'clock that evening, as the hour for her presentation to the King grew closer, her Ladyship is equanimity itself.

Gone are the earlier screams and tantrums. Now, she is calm, pleasant and utterly beguiling. Arabella, who knows her mistress better than most, realises that she is about to witness her Ladyship's greatest performance. Like all accomplished 'actresses', Evelyn has prepared herself for this role with the consummate professionalism of a Sarah Siddons.

Soon the curtain will rise and she will make her entrance - to tumultuous applause. That at least is the plan.

At six-thirty precisely, Evelyn and Kofi leave their apartment and descend to the palace gardens where they see, for the first time, the elaborate 'Italian' pavilion in all its splendour. It is a beautiful summer's evening and the gardens of Buckingham House, illuminated already by countless *flambeaux*, are altogether enchanting. Hundreds of guests have gathered on the lawns and terraces and are now strolling about, enjoying the music.

Since the cream of London society is here, dressed to the nines, the ornate gardens have the appearance of a vast bouquet of flowers. It would be wrong, however, to describe all those present as self-indulgent hedonists for among the many ostentatious, fashion-conscious 'mannequins' are eminent scientists, scholars, parliamentarians, distinguished members of the church, rich merchants and even richer landowners - the veritable core of Georgian England. Yet in an age lacking those opportunities for publicity or self-promotion we take for granted, formal occasions like this are crucial indicators of one's public standing or reputation within Hanoverian society. It is therefore important to make a good impression upon those in power and upon whose patronage you are invariably dependent.

'Sambo, your turban is crooked and if I see you picking your nose once more you will be beaten within an inch of your life. Do you understand, you wicked boy?'

Sambo quickly adjusts his turban and surreptitiously wipes his snotty finger on the back of his silk breeches.

'Yes, your Ladyship. I understand'.

For her part, Lady Evelyn Lowther - looking absolutely resplendent in her fine gown and elaborate straw bonnet - now stands proudly on the upper terrace preserved for special guests, luxuriating in the admiring glances she and Kofi attract from all quarters:

'Evelyn, my dear. You are a picture, a veritable Gainsborough of elegance and beauty, I do declare!'

'Who', whispers another to their companion, 'is that gorgeous creature? The woman over there with that diminutive nigger. Is she not one of the Lowthers? Rich as Croesus, some say. Handsome filly, what? '

Meanwhile, Kofi stands beside his beautiful mistress and tries to look dignified yet appealing at the same time. When she surreptitiously takes his hand in hers he notices that she is trembling - to the extent that the feathers in her headdress quiver like the uppermost leaves of a young tree caught in a sudden breath of wind.

Kofi at once gives Evelyn's hand an affectionate squeeze, whereupon her trembling stops.

***

Meanwhile, elsewhere in the palace, Jack is fully aware that some major event is now taking place. He has seen the new pavilion several times from various windows during his regular, nocturnal wanderings during the last week or so and each time it has appeared even more elaborate.

The noise and confusion in the palace kitchens state rooms and corridors that afternoon clearly indicates an imminent event of extraordinary scale and importance.

That evening, therefore, hopeful that the palace staff would be fully occupied elsewhere, Jack emerges from his loft in search of food and perhaps some more loot to add to his collection.

***

The opening ceremony goes entirely to plan, much to the relief of Queen Charlotte who has spent weeks organising this event.

At the appointed hour, George is led up the great staircase by his wife who wears a sumptuous silk gown in white and gold. She then takes him into her darkened apartments on the first floor, whereupon the shutters of their balcony are suddenly flung open - revealing the crowded terraces, lawns and canal below. This dramatic moment is accompanied by a fanfare from the musicians of the Royal Horse Guards, followed by a spirited rendition of 'God Save the King'. George, resplendent in ermine, is so pleased that he kisses his wife in public, something rarely seen.

This produces a round of spontaneous applause from the hundreds of guests gathered in the gardens below.

Meanwhile, as the King and Queen make their way downstairs, Evelyn waits, somewhat impatiently, among the select group of guests chosen to meet His Majesty. Crowded together on the upper terrace, it is becoming increasingly difficult to retain any semblance of dignity in the scramble to obtain a good view of their Majesties, now completing their royal descent. Although surrounded by lords and ladies, bankers, merchants and slave owners, Evelyn is gratified to see that none are dressed as ornately or as elegantly as she and her little blackamoor.

Eventually His Majesty appears, walks the length of the red carpet leading to the pavilion and takes his place on a small dais in front of the crowd. Charlotte - with a smile of contentment and pride on her young features that must surely have melted the heart of her most severe critics - sits to one side of her husband, on a small yet lavishly decorated throne. Then, one-by-one, the King greets his guests, accompanied throughout by music from the orchestra. Taking its cue from the music, an elaborate fireworks display fills the sky above the pavilion with a cacophony of rockets and cascading starbursts. This too produces generous applause from the assembled guests.

Just as Evelyn's is about to step forward and greet her royal cousin something extraordinary happens.

Suddenly there is a loud noise from the far end of the garden, causing all heads to turn, including that of His Majesty. There, held by the scruff of the neck by a tall footman, a totally black child in filthy rags is screaming and shouting and swearing at the top of his voice - like an irate Billingsgate fishwife.

'Let me go, you poxy bastard. Let me go!'

So tall and strong is the footman that he is able to hold the child off the ground and at arms' length. Thus suspended, Jack - for it was indeed he - waves his arms and legs like a demented windmill and punches the air with clenched fists, generating a small, sooty cloud that partially obscures him from the astonished gathering now watching, with some fascination, this remarkable spectacle.

'Put me down, you sodding halfwit!'

Then something even more extraordinary happens.

Kofi drops Evelyn's train and runs the length of the royal carpet towards the footman holding Jack. Once there, he steps boldly up to the astonished man and kicks him as hard as he can in the groin. So unexpected is this sudden attack that the footman is unable to defend himself. He drops Jack, falls to the floor and rolls about yelling blue murder while clutching his genitals - much to the amusement of those guests nearest to him. Indeed, some have already convinced themselves that 'Sambo's' sudden attack is part of the evening's entertainment and are already applauding accordingly.

Jack, who had landed on the floor in a confused heap, is now frantically gathering up the various gold and silver trinkets that have fallen from his pockets when Kofi grabs him by the collar and drags him off towards the house. It all happens so fast that it is a moment or two before the palace guards and staff realise that the two boys are escaping. Pratt, who witnessed Kofi's attack from the back of the terrace with growing alarm, at once summons a party of palace guards and footmen and charges off towards the house in hot pursuit.

But it is too late! By the time they reach the palace kitchens the two boys have disappeared.

It was too late also for Lady Evelyn Lowther. She had watched Sambo's bold action with absolute astonishment and horror. Moreover, with her presentation to the King and Queen so eagerly anticipated and yet so rudely interrupted, she simply then fainted, ending up in a crumpled heap at the skippered feet of His Britannic Majesty and an equally astonished Queen Charlotte of Mecklenburg-Strelitz.

***

For some time now Jack has been careful, whenever he left the security of his loft, to stuff his pockets with loot - just in case! He reasoned that since they were going to hang him anyway it did not matter if they found stolen property on his person. On the other hand, it would come in very useful should he ever escape and wish to start a new life out there in the real world, far from his sooty prison. Thus it was that, amongst his collection of silver, gold and paste trinkets, Jack found a set of keys that might just save his life. With shaking hands he inserted the largest key into the iron door of the palace cellars before which he and Kofi now stand, breathless and trembling with fear and excitement.

The lock turns and the door opens. Both boys step inside. Jack quickly locks the door behind them. For a moment, at least, they are safe from Pratt and his bullyboys chasing them.

Kofi, whose abrupt actions have just saved Jack's life, is now in a state of shock. He has no idea where the courage and boldness he has displayed only minutes ago came from. All he knows is that he and Jack have escaped. None of this had been planned. Slumped on the floor beside Jack, breathless and in a state of indescribable exhilaration, Kofi now stares, wild-eyed, into the blackness of the darkened cellar.

Their escape thus far had not been without incident. They had entered the palace through the great kitchens - much to the alarm of those preparing the king's supper of one hundred dishes and an 'illuminated dessert'. No one had done anything, of course, except stare.

Leaving the kitchen and turning right along the main service-corridor they had then rounded a corner and run slap into Charity Bucket, the little pot-room skivvy. The collision sent her sprawling across the carpet, her legs in the air and her skirts flying. Charity, who had always known that the palace was haunted ever since her encounter with the sooty ghost, scrambled to her knees just in time to see two black devils disappear down the stairs at the far end of the corridor. Almost at once the pursuing footmen rounded the corner and sent the poor girl flying again. One after another, all five fell in a confused heap - with poor Charity, now wailing like a banshee, crushed beneath them.

Meanwhile, Pratt hastily dispatched footmen, chambermaids and skivvies to remote corners of the palace. Pratt himself led the largest party of footmen down the back stairs towards the cellars. It was towards these cellars that the two boys had been heading when last seen.

The actual capture of Jack, however, had been something of a lucky accident - or so it seemed.

Caught short, the burly footman had slipped into a small drawing room in the west wing and peed in the coalscuttle. At that precise moment two bare feet appeared in the chimney. These he had grabbed, pulling a very frightened Jack out onto the carpet. The boy had kicked and screamed but was soon hauled to his feet by the scruff of his neck and dragged downstairs and out into the palace gardens.

The rest is history - except that no one could explain 'Sambo's' part in all this excitement. Had the boy gone completely mad?

Plenty of people at the garden party had seen the child before, immaculately dressed and in the company of Lady Lowther. Indeed, he was something of a triumph amongst the Queen's select *entourage* for Charlotte had, by all accounts, found him absolutely enchanting. Others who had met him had found him both polite and engagingly servile.

Yet what on earth had provoked such a frenzied attack on that poor footman? Had 'Sambo' somehow reverted to his basic savage character - little more than a beast of the jungle?

As for Lady Lowther herself, she was clearly distraught and was reported to have retired to her bed.

***

Meanwhile, Jack and the 'savage' have recovered their breath and a measure of self-composure and have begun to explore the large wine cellar into which they have retreated.

This is not the first time Jack has visited this part of the palace. In fact he has been here several times before and has acquired a taste for the fine Burgundies His Majesty has thoughtfully laid down for his use. He even knows where the Wine Butler keeps flint and candle - and an illegal but convenient corkscrew. It only takes a moment or two, therefore, before the darkened rooms opened up before Kofi's astonished eyes, illuminated by the light of several candles.

These ancient cellars are enormous and consist of a number of 'rooms' down what appear to be long, brick corridor. The walls of each 'room' are lined with brick bins in which are stacked thousands of bottles of wine and spirits - the collection of King George II which his son, the present King, had inherited when his father died in 1760.

While Kofi is taking in this astonishing sight it suddenly occurs to him that they are now well and truly trapped. It is surely only a matter of time before the servants or palace guards batter down the iron door and arrest them both. What then? According to Jack, capture for him will mean being hung, drawn and quartered - a gruesome process which Jack had described to Kofi in some detail only a few days before. But what of Kofi himself? What would Evelyn say or do if he were captured? Would he be killed too? So alarmed is he by these thoughts that Kofi now sinks to the floor, buries his face in his hands and starts to cry.

When he next looks up Jack has disappeared.

Panic rises like a vulture, clutching at his throat. He is about to yell out when Jack's voice breaks the silence. In this vast echo chamber it is difficult at first to tell where it comes from but some instinct leads Kofi down the brick 'road' towards the light of a single candle now see flickering in the darkness.

'Over 'ere, young 'un. Hurry! They will be wiv us soon enough. I aint the only one with a key for this place!'

Kofi runs the length of the corridor to discover Jack struggling to lift an iron trap door set in the floor of the cellar.

'Come on, giv' us an 'and, Kofi! I can't be doing' this all on me own!'

Kofi grabs the iron ring and together they raise the trap door - to reveal a deep, black hole with a metal ladder descending into the darkness. For a moment Kofi is overwhelmed by the memory of the trapdoor on the slave ship into which he and his mother had been pushed but this quickly vanishes as the door at the far end of their corridor bursts open and footmen, armed with cudgels and candlesticks, rush into the cellars.

'There they are!' yells Pratt, peering into the darkness. 'Grab the little bastards!'

It is Jack who reacts first. Grabbing a bottle of wine from the nearest bin, he hurls it with all his might towards the rapidly approaching footmen. The bottle smashes harmlessly on the brick floor in front of them but so unexpected is Jack's action that it momentarily halts their advance. Another bottle follows and another, thrown this time by Kofi.

What happens thereafter can only be described as a vintner's worst nightmare as bottle after bottle flies through the air and smashes against the brick walls or ceiling, showering the footmen with priceless wine and shards of broken glass.

Burgundy, 1753. Crash! Chateaubriand, 1757. Crash! Chateau La Fayette, 1748. Crash!

By now Jack and Kofi, caught up in the sheer exhilaration of this bibulous carnage, are like men possessed. Whoops of glee accompany each crash as yet another wine bottle disintegrates, spraying the cowering footmen with glass and expensive red wine until they look as if they had been ripped to shreds by canon shrapnel and were drowning in a veritable sea of blood.

'Back, back you fools!' yells Pratt, more mindful of the damage being done to His Majesty's wine collection than any possible harm to his servants.

The footmen quickly withdraw into the shadows - to regroup and decide what to do next. This is just the break Jack needs. He kneels beside the trapdoor and peers down into the shaft. Far below he can hear the sound of running water. The stench suggests a sewer but since Jack has never explored this far before it is anyone's guess what lies below. Either way, it is clear to him that their only hope of escape now lies down that dark hole.

Jack boldly steps onto the first rung of the ladder and begins his descent, quickly disappearing from view.

'Quick!' says Jack in the brief silence that follows his descent. 'Down 'ere, young 'un. Follow me!'

Kofi, terrified of the darkness into which Jack has vanished, stands poised over the trap door like a frightened rabbit, frozen into stupefied immobility. It is in that position that the first footman to reach Kofi finds him. He grabs the boy by the neck, digging his bony fingers into Kofi's silk tunic. Since Jack's candle has now gone out it is pitch black. Kofi at once tries to escape, kicking out blindly in the darkness while the footman struggles to retain his grip. Others soon join him, falling over each other in the confusion.

'For Gawd's sake, young 'un, jump! Its yer only 'ope!' comes the distant voice of Jack from below. 'Jump, damn yer! Jump!'

Knowing that what he did next would surely determine his fate one way or the other, Kofi steps out blindly into the black void. For a moment he hangs there, suspended by his collar in the grip of the footman but then, raising his arms above his head - more in fear than by design - his slender body slips from the coat and he hurtles, arms and legs flailing wildly, down and down into the blackness.

15. Freedom!
5th June, 1763

When Lady Evelyn Lowther is eventually told of 'Sambo's' daring escape she is incandescent with rage.

The messenger who brings this information is her chamber-maid (the luckless Arabella) and receives a black eye from a well-aimed hairbrush for her trouble. Thereafter, Her Ladyship is inconsolable - despite the best efforts of her loyal maid. Eventually withdrawing, Arabella leaves Evelyn with her head buried in silk cushions, sobbing uncontrollably.

The intensity of these feelings surprised even Evelyn - when she recovered sufficiently to consider how she felt about the sudden, inexplicable behaviour of her blackamoor. Evelyn Lowther was not, it should be said, celebrated for her sensitivity yet 'Sambo's' betrayal, and the very public manner of his defection, had profoundly disturbed her.

Worse still, she never got to be presented to the King. Although His Majesty had subsequently written expressing his concern at her loss, adding that he was sure that the silver collar would be recovered eventually, *not* to have met him formally was extremely upsetting. Moreover, to have fainted at his feet and then to suffer the indignity of being carried from his Royal Presence by a member of the Privy Council no less was deeply humiliating. In short, after weeks of preparation, the whole thing had been a total disaster.

Meanwhile, the search continues - both in the sewer and in the palace gardens, with little success.

Although footmen had immediately descended into the sewer, the boys were long gone by the time they reached the foot of the ladder. Here the air was so foul that their candles went out. Without light, none of the footmen or palace guards could be persuaded to step further into the pitch-black sewer. Besides, no one was entirely sure where this unexpected underground tunnel led; few even knew of its existence. Where it ended exactly was something of a mystery.

Pratt himself, however, is currently more concerned about the inestimable damage done to His Majesty's wine collection than the immediate fate of the two boys. What is more, questions are now being asked as to the identity of the sweep and why His Majesty had not been informed of the thief's presence in the palace. If that were not enough, the Queen is known to be upset at the disturbance that interrupted her husband's birthday celebrations.

In short, Pratt now has a major disaster on his hands.

***

Kofi's fall into the black void had been partly broken by Jack at the foot of the ladder. For a minute or so they had lay there in a confused heap, winded by Kofi's fall but then some instinct told them to get up and move on - into the pitch black of a long, yet well constructed tunnel. It had made sense at the time to follow the direction of the stream and so, hand-in-hand, the two fugitives had set off into the darkness with the shouts of Pratt's servants reverberating down the tunnel behind them.

This tunnel was about ten feet wide, brick-lined and with a channel down the middle filled with what appeared to be raw sewage. It was black as pitch and stank horribly. They had in fact stumbled on one of London's underground 'rivers.' This one was called, ominously enough, The Tyburn. Jack had led the way, running his free hand along the slimy wall of the tunnel as a guide in the pitch-blackness. Kofi had followed, comforted by the firm grasp of his friend's bony fingers.

The stench and impenetrable darkness of this tunnel brought memories of the 'Cerberus' flooding back to Kofi. The smell was dreadful but the thought of capture, after all they had been through, was even worse. Assuming that they would be followed, they pressed on - trying to put distance between themselves and their pursuers. At least Kofi had shoes on his feet. Jack was barefoot so that he was obliged to wade through the filth without protection, the horrible green slime oozing up between his toes.

Since Jack's feet were as hard as iron, Kofi assumed that he did not mind but Jack's real fear was that he might step on a nest of rats in the dark. Jack had known rats all his life. It was part of growing up in London but he had never liked them. Numerous, close encounters with these creatures in the past, in the slums of St. Giles and elsewhere, had given him something of a phobia. Wading through a darkened sewer, probably occupied by thousands of these creatures, did little for his self-confidence.

***

Meanwhile, back in the palace, Evelyn Lowther has recovered sufficiently to summon both maids to her bedroom. She has decided, she tells them, that they are to leave London in two days time to return to the solitude and tranquillity of her country estate in Westmorland. Arabella and Lisa, relieved to be returning home, at once begin to pack. Although she said nothing further to the girls, Rigmorden would allow her to heal her wounds in peace and quiet, away from the gossip and cruel, waspish comments of London society.

Longing for her black youth and anger at his 'treachery' now struggle for supremacy in her wounded heart.

While her maids try to undress her, Evelyn fights back hot tears of anger and grief - in equal measure.

'Arabella, tell Lord Carlisle that I shall meet him at Vauxhall Gardens tomorrow night and that it is a matter of life and death. Tell him that he will be well rewarded for his trouble. Now leave me, both of you!'

Arabella and Lisa quit the room, relieved to be out of the presence of their troubled Mistress. Soon thereafter Arabella gathers her cloak about her and, summoning a sedan chair, sets off into the night to find Evelyn's former lover, Lord Frederick of Carlisle.

***

It is now about two hours since Jack and Kofi disappeared into the tunnel beneath Buckingham House. Far below St. James' Park, in the bowels of the earth, they are making slow progress. To their consternation they have reached a part where the tunnel divides into two.

Jack, who has assumed the role of leader of this exploration of London's most secret river, chooses the left branch - for no other reason than that is the side of the filthy stream on which they now find themselves. It is a fortunate choice for half-an-hour later they reach the mouth of the tunnel and are staring at the dark, swiftly moving waters of the river Thames. It is now night, and stars are visible in a cloudless London sky. They emerge cautiously from their tunnel onto the gravel beach that leads to the river.

For a moment they savour their newfound freedom but Jack, mindful that palace guards might be close, pulls Kofi back into the shadows of the stone embankment.

'Not so fast, nigger. We 'aint safe yet. Them guards will know this river and could be out there, waitin' fer us!'

Meanwhile, back at the palace footmen and under-butlers are sweeping up the shattered remains of some dozen bottles of priceless wine. Buckets and mops mingled some of the finest vintages that a war-torn Europe has ever produced. Pratt, observing the aftermath of this catastrophe, is feeling particularly morose. Like most civil servants, he is not good at dealing with catastrophes of this nature, particularly those that affect him. Leaving his men to finish their work, he withdraws to his little room beneath the slates and forlornly considers his future.

***

Evelyn, in her bedroom in the west wing, stares into her mirror and considers her future too - now that Sambo is gone. Her bedroom and the adjoining drawing room are in chaos as Lisa packs her Ladyship's extensive wardrobe and personal effects in readiness for the journey to Rigmorden.

The silver collar, although expensive, is of little consequence to one as rich as Evelyn Lowther. She had inherited from her father a considerable fortune so that such trinkets mean absolutely nothing to her. What troubles her most is that after so much kindness, after so much genuine affection lavished on her beloved Sambo, he has abandoned her - and with little evident regard for her feelings.

***

It turned out that Jack was wrong. There were no guards on the Thames embankment that night so he and Kofi were able to slip out of the shadows and disappear into the maze of muddy streets between the river and Northumberland Gardens, just east of Charring Cross.

Jack, who knew large parts of London like the back of his hand, heads now for familiar territory behind St. Martin's Church and safety - or so he hopes. Although the streets here are not busy, Kofi (in his cotton shirt, fine silk breeches and Turkish slippers, now wet and filthy) is somewhat conspicuous beside the ragged, bare-arsed sweep he is following so assiduously. Eventually they arrive at a narrow street adjacent to Moor's Yard, behind the church of St. Martins. It is now ten o'clock at night. There are no streetlights in this poor quarter - for which Jack is particularly grateful.

'We need a gaff to 'old up in, me old mate. T'aint safe out 'ere. Stick close and follow me, young 'un. I knows just the place'.

Jack leads Kofi to a ramshackle boarding house in St Giles and knocks on its door. The old woman who answers shows them to a shabby room on the first floor then pockets the gold coin Jack offers her without comment. It is far more than this rat-infested bolthole is worth but she knows, without being told, that the coin is also to pay for her silence. They lock the door behind them and crash onto the bed. They are both completely exhausted.

Jack immediately falls into a deep sleep but Kofi, troubled with feelings of guilt, tosses and turns on his side of the bed.

What will his mistress think? Will she despise him for running away? She is bound to be angry but will she hate him? Kofi, clutching at straws in his confusion and misery, convinces himself that the silver collar is of no consequence to Lady Evelyn and that all that matters now are their feelings for each other. Yes, he has betrayed her but he still loves her, still feels pride in his service to her and still believes that she will eventually understand *why* he had to escape and return to Africa - to be with his mother. Surely she can understand that?

***

Kofi woke up the following morning after a fitful, dream-filled sleep. He was alone in the room for Jack had vanished.

For a moment he was somehow relieved. To be yoked to this strange boy who stole at will and who thought nothing of filching silver and gold trinkets from even the King troubled Kofi who had never knowingly stolen anything in his life - until now, that is. The collar, that hateful silver collar, was still fastened round his neck like a hangman's noose.

For the next hour or so Kofi drifted in and out of sleep, tossing and turning on the bed. Once he dreamed that he was falling down some dark tunnel - until he landed with a sickening jolt on the deck of the slave ship that had brought him and his mother out of Africa. Later, he was lying at the foot of her Ladyship's bed, wrapped in silk sheets while a savage dog gnawed his exposed feet. When he woke up from this particular dream he found himself lying on the floor, the ragged blanket wrapped about his neck.

Jack returned three hours later carrying some bread and cheese and a bundle of clothes, which he had bought from a rag-and-bone merchant. He threw the clothes onto the floor in triumph - like a cat returning with a dead, somewhat mangled trophy for its owner.

'Right! Time you was given a new h'appearance, Sambo.'

Kofi is not interested in the clothes but snatches at the bread and cheese and stuffs the food into his mouth like one possessed.

'I'm not Sambo. My name is Kofi.' he mutters angrily, between mouthfuls.
'All right, keep yer wig on! Try these for size.'

Jack holds up a shabby woollen jacket in one hand and a pair of greasy breeches in the other.

'Best I could find'.
'I can't wear those! They are filthy.'
'You'll wear wot you is given, Sunshine. If you don't, you will be spotted in the wink of an eye. Now, get dressed.'

Kofi does as he is told. Jack, seated on the bed and chewing on a crust of bread, watches approvingly as Kofi is transformed from pampered blackamoor to impoverished street urchin. A strip of rag serves as a scarf, thereby concealing the all too conspicuous collar.

'Right, now follow me, young 'un. I am going...' (Here Jack paused dramatically for greater effect) '...for a wash!'

Kofi, startled by this unexpected announcement, followed his sooty friend downstairs and out into the cobbled yard at the back of their lodgings where there is was water-pump. A small group of women, having completed their washing, are now standing by the pump, gossiping. Several grubby, emaciated children dressed in rags are playing in the puddles while two workmen are leaning against a fence, smoking clay pipes.

Jack's recent adventure in the sewer had not only failed to remove even some of the soot that completely covered him but had made him stink even worse that usual. It was, he felt, time to remove the filth acquired during two years as a climbing boy, seven weeks in the chimneys of Buckingham House and several hours in one of London's filthiest sewers. Ignoring the stares of those gathered in the yard, he therefore boldly walks up to the pump and casts off his rags. Kofi, clutching a blanket to use as a towel, hangs back in the shadows and watches in amazement as Jack, now completely naked and with arms and legs like burnt matchsticks, squats beneath the pump.

Two small boys, themselves almost as dirty as Jack, seize the handle and begin to pump vigorously.

At first Jack puts on a brave face but then, as jets of icy water cascade about his head and shoulders, he begins to scream in earnest. Strong hands grab him and hold him under the pump while two old women, keen to join in the fun, apply their scrubbing brushes to his thin, wiry body. He tries to slither away on his hands and knees but others grab each thin ankle and drag him on his belly back across the slimy cobbles to the pump where the brushes at once resume their work.

Slowly, as the brushes do their fiendish work, a new and rather unexpected Jack emerges.

Kofi has never seen his friend other than completely black. Now, as the water does its work, Jack is turning into something very strange - a thin, etiolated figure of lurid white, rather like a scrubbed radish. When, eventually, a completely naked Jack is exposed in all his pristine glory - newborn, as it were - the women and street urchins who have helped in this transformation burst into spontaneous applause. At first Jack cowers, covering his genitals in embarrassment but then quickly warms to the situation as the crowd's raucous adulation swells. He begins strutting about in triumph, much to the lubricious amusement of his enthusiastic audience.

'Why, look at 'im!' says one of the old women. 'Aint he the fine one. Giv us a kiss, darlin'!'

As he watches Jack's shameless exhibitionism, Kofi's feelings are strangely mixed. He is pleased for his friend and for the friendly laughter and applause Jack is attracting but somehow something has changed.

His hero, he realises, is no longer black - like himself. He is now white, like all the other men, women and children in this detestable land. Kofi quickly steps forward and throws the ragged blanket round Jack's shoulders and leads him back up to their room, the applause and laughter of the crowd ringing in their ears.

Now that Jack is clean and no longer wearing his filthy rags, a further sea change occurs.

At first Kofi is slow to see it but after a while he notices that Jack is turning from anxious fugitive to a veritable 'Jack-the-Lad.' While Jack always had about him something of the cheeky, street-wise survivor, he has now become exceedingly cocky. Moreover, when Jack dried himself and began to dress, Kofi saw that the new clothes he had bought for himself were considerably smarter than the scruffy rags he had been given. Indeed, replete now in buckled shoes, linen shirt, waistcoat, short fustian jacket and smart blue breeches, Jack is actually dressed in the height of fashion - at least that was how it would appear in these impoverished parts.

'Right, young 'un', he says (admiring himself in the back of a silver spoon that had once belonged to King George III), 'I'm off out now.'

He crosses to the door with a swagger and turns to face Kofi, now sitting despondently on the edge of their bed.

'Don't let no one in, whoever they sez they are, right? I'll be back soon and tomorrow we'll 'av that collar off yer.'

With that he waltzes out of the door, shutting it behind him. As he descends the stairs he whistles a jaunty tune, his new boots clattering on the rickety, wooden steps. There is a spring in his step. After years of poverty Jack has money in his pockets and the freedom to spend it.

As Jack subsequently made his way through the filthy streets of St Giles, Kofi sat on the edge of their bed and pondered an uncertain future. When, later, he tried the door of their bedroom, he found that it was locked. Jack, either for Kofi's protection or, more likely, to secure his 'investment', had made him a prisoner on what was their first real day of freedom.

Kofi lay back down on the bed and wept.

Meanwhile, Jack is heading towards Chick Lane. He is not sure exactly why. With money in his pocket and a new identity he could have picked any inn or coffee house in the area but he chose instead the disreputable tavern frequented by his former employer - Jeremiah Blagg. The temptation to beard the old enemy on his own patch has proved irresistible and it is with beating heart that Jack now steps across the threshold of Blagg's favourite watering hole - the 'Red Lion'.

Jack, delighted to be 'home' once more, sidles up to the bar and orders a large flagon of beer.

***

Kofi is now feeling increasingly depressed.

He crosses to the window of their tiny bedroom and flings open the wooden shutters. The view from the window is even more depressing for their lodging house is situated on the banks of the Fleet Ditch - a 'river' that is little more than an open sewer. Some thirty feet below, Kofi can see - and smell - its black, sluggish waters. A dead dog - bloated and lying on its back, its legs pointing skyward - drifts slowly past even as Kofi watches.

On the opposite bank there is a row of old tenement houses, propped up by large wooden poles that criss-crossed the ditch. Without these poles the houses on either side of the ditch - including their own would - probably collapse into the filthy waters of the Fleet.

Kofi hastily closes the shutters and sits back on the bed.

***

Back at the palace, Evelyn Lowther pulled herself together, repaired the ravages of the previous night, put on a new face and a new gown and set off by sedan chair for Vauxhall Gardens in Lambeth with high hopes - and revenge - in her heart. Her companion and bodyguard for the evening is her groom, a handsome young man called Thomas Weatherspoon.

They soon reached the water's edge at Westminster Steps. Evelyn, gathering her skirts about her, settles down on her seat in the wherry that they have hired to take them across the river. It is a beautiful summer's night and as the oarsman manoeuvres the boat out into the Thames, Evelyn gazes at the stars. What, she wondered, did they portend? And where was Sambo? Was he still alive or had he drowned in that terrible sewer?

They arrived at the far bank, their boat fighting for position amongst the many others trying to tie off at the narrow landing stage. Evelyn, who wished to travel incognito, has covered her face with a black mask attached to the end of a short, ebony rod, which she now holds in one gloved hand. Since news at Court has spread like wildfire concerning Sambo's dramatic and highly controversial defection, she does not want to be recognised in public, - certainly not here in London's notorious Vauxhall Gardens.

They entered Vauxhall Gardens by passing beneath an elaborate archway covered in foliage. Here paved paths between shaped, ornamental trees run the length of the site, criss-crossing other tree-lined alleys. Near the main entrance there is a large music room, fifty supper-boxes adorned with paintings by Hogarth, a Chinese Pavilion and a circular bandstand. The park is illuminated by paper lanterns suspended from trees and *flambeaux* stuck into the grass at regular intervals. Above their heads fireworks constantly explode into a thousand fiery blossoms.

It is here, in these ornamental gardens, that the rich men and women of London regularly gather, some openly, others secretly but all masked in the Venetian style. Bawds, pimps and willing clients of both sexes mingle in the shadows or withdraw into the privacy of the curtained booths to make love or dine, waited on by discreet, eminently corruptible flunkies.

Lady Evelyn picked her way cautiously through the crowds, accompanied by the towering figure of her bodyguard.

In Vauxhall Gardens sex is everywhere. The place oozes lubricity from every corruptible pore. The narrow, secretive paths, booths and ornate gazebos scattered throughout the gardens are alive with amorous couples. Even in this part of the gardens, far from the crowded central pavilions, the orchestra's music hangs in the night air like the heavy scent of an orchid, creating a heady, intoxicating ambience.

They rounded a corner to discover Lord Carlisle and a young woman, copulating in the bushes.

'I see that you are still up to your old tricks, my Lord! Do you never tire of such debauchery?'

'Evelyn!', replied his lordship, somewhat breathlessly. 'What a pleasure it is to see you. If you are seeking my company I regret that you must wait your turn. As you can see, I am presently occupied.'

Indeed he was for his partner, bent over a table and with her pert bottom exposed to the night air, was being vigorously 'serviced' by his lordship even as he and Evelyn spoke.

'Quite. However, I need your help.'

'If it's money, my dear Evelyn, I must assure that I have none - until my famously robust father falls off his golden perch. Could it have anything to do with that little nigger who appears to have absconded with your silver collar? I'm only guessing of course but if memory serves me right, you were always terribly careless with your possessions.'

'Yes. I want them both back. You have contacts in the city. He is sure to have it removed. I doubt he has the savvy to pawn it but an object of that value cannot go unnoticed amongst your more dubious acquaintances.'

'And if I do recover both, what shall be my reward? As you know, I have always enjoyed your celebrated gifts. No doubt you will find it in yourself to satisfy me with your usual, dare I say it, professionalism?'

At this point Carlisle appears to reach a satisfactory conclusion. He withdraws and wipes his penis on his shirttails then starts to button his breeches - all this executed, without shame or embarrassment, in front of Lady Evelyn and her bodyguard.

'We shall see!' says Evelyn sweetly.

The girl, still breathing heavily, now staggers to her feet and adjusts her own clothing. She is wearing a half-mask, behind which her face is clearly flushed with her recent exertions.

'Now that your young friend appears to have recovered sufficiently to resume her place in polite society, I must leave you both. So, are we in agreement, my Lord? Can I rely on your help once more?'

'Very well. I will find Sambo and your precious collar for you but I will need money and plenty of it/ Bounty hunters are expensive - particularly here in London. Where shall I find you?'

'I leave Buckingham House tomorrow. Send word to Rigmorden. I shall contact you thereafter. Good evening, my Lord.'

With that Evelyn turned on her heels and strode off down the path, closely followed by Weatherspoon.

***

Jack did not bump into Jeremiah Blagg or any of his cronies earlier that afternoon, much to his surprise.

He took satisfaction, however, in discovering that no one recognised him in his new, lily-white appearance. None would anyway, for few at the 'Red Lion' had ever seen Blagg's lads other than a filthy black. They were, therefore, unlikely to recognise Jack now that that his face was a shiny white and he was no longer dressed in rags. Besides, most of them believed that Jack was famously dead, still stuck up German George's kitchen 'chimbley.'

But where was Jeremiah Blagg?

One theory was that he had been arrested for conspiracy to rob - something to do with one of his climbing boys falling foul of the law, or so it would seem. Nor was there any hard news of Jack's best friend, Jem.

While Jack had been somewhat circumspect in his enquiries (if only to avoid suspicion) it was clear from one or two of the 'Red Lion's more sober customers that Jem had disappeared at about the same time that Jack had vanished up the chimney at Buckingham House.

This was worrying news. Despite his age and extraordinary climbing skills, Jem was a vulnerable individual, constantly ill and with a tendency to cough up quantities of dark, sooty blood just as you were settling down to a nice plate of tripe and onions.

One rumour was that Blagg had unceremoniously thrown Jem out onto the streets the moment the callow youth's health deteriorated.

'Typical!', thought Jack bitterly. 'So much for loyalty!'

Some hours later, surrounded by a group of fellow drunks anxious to relieve Jack of his money, he ordered another round and paid for it with a large, gold coin which he slapped onto the wooden trestle that served as a tavern bar - much to the delight of the old crone serving him.

Jack's action was also observed by a dark, piratical figure with blackened teeth and a sallow complexion, lounging in the doorway.

Later, when Jack left the 'Red Lion' and staggered back to his lodgings, this man followed him - at a safe distance. With some difficulty Jack clambered up the stairs, found the right landing and unlocked the door. He fell into the room with a crash, waking Kofi.

Without a word of apology or explanation, Jack - still fully dressed - fell onto their bed and within moments was fast asleep.

***

The next morning Kofi rose and crossed to the window, leaving the sweep spread-eagled across the covers and snoring loudly. Jack had forgotten to bring Kofi any food. Not only was he hurt by Jack's thoughtlessness but he was now extremely hungry.

Something had definitely changed in their relationship - not least the sweep's familiar colour. Although their present circumstances as fugitives gave them some similarity, Jack was undeniably *white* and that, Kofi now realised, was sufficient to drive a wedge between them forever.

It was a sobering thought.

While Kofi had, through his experiences on the 'Cerberus' and on the plantation in Jamaica, come to understand how colour frequently determined the relationship of white to black, it was very disappointing now to realise, for the first time perhaps, that it could spoil a genuine friendship between one captive child and another.

Both their *souls* were white? Were they not, therefore, equal?

Even as Kofi struggled with these difficult thoughts his fate, and that of his only friend, was being shaped by others as yet unknown to him or his sleeping companion.

***

After his exertions in Vauxhall Gardens the previous night, Lord Frederick Carlisle could be found that lunch-time relaxing in a tavern off Whitcomb Street - a place frequented by as extraordinary a collection of low-life as Chick Lane itself could muster. Enthroned in a dark corner of the room, a painted doxy on one knee and a

149

pitcher of ale before him, his Lordship had fallen into whispered conversation with a dark, piratical figure with blackened teeth and a sallow complexion.

'Tell Clem to meet me at my fencing club this afternoon. Meanwhile, let it be known among the jewellers, pawnbrokers and other Jewish scum around Saffron Hill and elsewhere that I will pay handsomely for any news of Lowther's silver collar. Be discreet! Now go - I have business here.'

The man nodded and disappeared into the crowd. Carlisle took a swig of ale and turned to the young girl with the lurid white face and crimson lips perched provocatively on his knee.

'Now, my dear child, what did you say your name was?'

***

Jack rose late that morning - to find Kofi staring morosely out of the window. It was raining heavily. The streets were already thick with mud. Ragged men and women, leaning into the cold, blustery wind and rain, went about their business or loitered aimlessly in the dark courts and alleys that surrounded their lodging house. It was now their second day of freedom yet Kofi, after a restless night, was unable to share Jack's elation. The business of the locked door still troubled him. Although he had said nothing, he was resolved to watch Jack more closely.

Jack however, whose night on the town had done nothing to diminish his newly acquired *bonhomie*, leaped out of bed and dressed quickly.

'Come on, young 'un', he said cheerfully. 'Time we got rid of that bloody collar of yours, eh? Someone is bound to spot it and then we is buggered. Besides, we could badly do wiv the money. Silver, 'aint it? Must be werf a bob or two, don't yer reckon?'

Jack did not wait for an answer from Kofi but hurriedly splashed water on his face from the cracked bowl on the dresser and then grinned at Kofi, still wrapped in his grimy blanket.

Since Jack had rather taken to this washing lark, the only part of him that now remained black were his rotten teeth but in the excitement of his new-found freedom, even they had stopped hurting. His night out at the 'Red Lion' had been Jack's first, tentative step back into society - even if it was with a new identity and a degree of caution. He was, after all, a celebrated 'criminal' who had, quite literally, eaten at the King's table and partaken of His Majesty's worldly goods. It was only a matter of time - or so Jack reasoned - before word got out and he became London's 'cock of the roost' and her most celebrated criminal.

150

It never occurred to him then or subsequently that he could, at any time that previous night, have bumped into his mother - assuming, of course, that she was still alive. In fact, he had passed through many of those streets that she had frequented as a prostitute and later, as she spiralled down into alcoholism, as a beggar. She might just as well be dead - so remote was she from Jack Fisher's thoughts now that he was free of Blagg and about to start life as a 'wealthy gentleman of leisure'.

When Kofi followed Jack down the stairs, across the yard and into the street he was careful to cover his silver collar with a strip of rag. In Moors Field a valuable object like that would inevitably attract attention.

Few here would think twice about killing some black 'savage' if it meant they might profit from Kofi's death.

With his head full of such thoughts, Kofi followed Jack through lanes and alleyways ankle-deep in mud. Kofi noticed that not only were his 'new' boots too big for him but they let in water.

After half-an-hour or so Jack found the street in Saffron Hill that he had been looking for. It contained a row of narrow, medieval dwellings interspersed with small shops above which hung an assortment of painted signs - including the familiar three globes of the many pawnbrokers who inhabited this poor, predominately Jewish part of London.

'Right', said Jack, boldly leading the way into the shop. 'Say nuffing, right? He don't need to who you is or why yous got such a thing round yer neck. Git my drift, nigger?'

Ten minutes later Kofi's silver collar is removed with the use of a silversmith's tool, deftly handled by an elderly Jew whose long, oily ringlets shine eerily in the light of the single candle that illuminated his shop. Kofi noticed that the nail on one of the man's little fingers was over three inches long and curled in the shape of a corkscrew.

Although the hated silver collar was no longer round his neck, Kofi felt uneasy as they left the shop. They now had more money in their pockets than either of them had ever seen in their short lives but they were now entering dangerous territory for they were both thieves, on the run in a dangerous part of London.

It was not something Kofi cared to think about too much - not least because the colour of his skin made him so conspicuous in a world that was predominately white.

Unknown to them, their departure from the pawnbroker's shop was observed by a man with blackened teeth and a dark, sallow complexion.

***

Evelyn's journey back to Rigmorden was long and tedious and rather tense, not least because of her violent mood-swings since Sambo's departure. As their carriage left the fields and hamlets of Highgate and headed north into open countryside, Evelyn leant back in her seat, closed her eyes and thought of her little blackamoor.

Sambo's unexpected defection had touched her in ways that she had imagined impossible. That a child, a mere nigger that she owned, could treat her with such contempt and with such a total disregard for her finer feelings, proved beyond a shadow of doubt the natural treachery and capriciousness of black savages. Moreover, it patently demonstrated the inherent inability of blacks to assimilate even a semblance of culture and refinement.

Had she not lavished on the boy her knowledge and experience of the world - all that made English society the most civilised, the most refined in Europe? And how had he repaid her? Why, by abusing her generosity at every opportunity and by a public act of treachery.

Thus it was that Evelyn, torn between such anger and an excruciating sense of loss, left London that fine June morning. Would she, she wondered, ever see Sambo again? And how would she feel should they meet after all that had now taken place?

Whatever Evelyn's private thoughts, Arabella and Lisa were thoroughly glad to be going home after what had also been for them a very fraught visit. Not only had they had to cope with Evelyn's tantrums but had themselves shared with her the bitter disappointment of the aborted presentation on the occasion of His Majesty's birthday. All that sewing and ironing - and for nothing!

***

Despite the rigours of an hour or two that afternoon in the arms of an energetic, if somewhat expensive young woman, Frederick Carlisle was in prime, physical condition and parried the blade of his fencing instructor with consummate ease.

The vigorous moves and countermoves that followed were watched by a certain Clem Piggin.

It should be noted at this point that professional bounty hunters were of a peculiar breed - part thief, part mercenary, and part assassin. Indeed, Piggin had about his person enough weaponry to arm a platoon and yet his disposition was discretion itself. Dressed in a greasy coat that reached to his riding boots, he sported a cap worn at a rakish angle and of a style that revolutionaries in France were beginning to popularise. Despite these concessions to fashion, Piggin also had the ability at any time to merge into the shadows or even completely disappear. It was some time, therefore, before his Lordship, partaking of a glass of wine after his fencing lesson, even noticed the surly man lounging in the doorway.

'Piggin? Good! I have urgent work for you.'

Carlisle crossed the scrubbed, wooden floor of the gymnasium and stopped in front of the bounty hunter.

'Secure the black boy and his collar and bring them to me. There is another with him, thought to be a sweep. The King, no less, is interested in that young man and will reward us handsomely if you can deliver him, dead or alive. Quashe will show you where they are hiding but remember' - at this point Carlisle raised his foil and pressed its point close to Piggin's face, touching the man's cheek just below his right eye – 'remember, this business is between you and me. If you betray me in any way I shall remove your one good eye, n'est pas?'

The bounty hunter flinched. While Clem Piggin was one of the most feared men in London, his lordship's reputation as a duellist was also well known. Moreover, Carlisle's cruelty was legion. Once, he mutilated the face of a young groom with his sabre merely because the boy had cast lascivious eyes on one of his Lordship's girlfriends. Piggin, who had lost his left eye in a tavern brawl some years before, was not particularly keen to lose the other.

He nodded, compliantly.

'I see we understand each other. Now listen, I care absolutely nothing for the nigger but that silver collar and the sweep, well, together they could turn a pretty profit, do you follow?'

Piggin nodded then left the room - as silently as he had entered it.

***

Jack and Kofi reached the safety of their room, locked the door and spread the money out on the bed. They stared at it in silence, mesmerised at the enormity of their newfound wealth. While Jack had attempted to bargain with the Jew they had, in effect, accepted the first price offered - such was their anxiety to get rid of that incriminating collar. They were still contemplating their gold coins when a tentative knock on the door shattered their reverie. Another knock followed, somewhat louder.

'Who is it?' asked Jack.

'It's me', said the old woman who ran the lodging house. 'I've brought you some fresh water, my dear.'

'Go away. We don't want no water. Leave us alone.'

This brief exchange was followed by silence. Both boys could then hear the old woman trying to open the door with her key. This was followed immediately by renewed knocking, but louder and more insistent.

Jack gathered up the money on their bed, hastily stuffing gold coins into every available pocket. More knocks followed, this time with an insistence that clearly spelled trouble.

'It's a trap!' whispered Jack, moving towards the window. 'Time we got out. Come on, young 'un. Stir yer stumps!'

The knocking now was not that of the old woman but of someone clearly determined to batter down the door. Knowing they only had moments before the door gave way, Jack grabs Kofi by his jacket and drags him to the window. He flings open the shutters and clambers out onto the narrow sill, pulling Kofi after him. Perched now on the window ledge they both stare down into the filthy depths of the Fleet Ditch some thirty feet below. Behind them they can hear the splintering of wood as their bedroom door gives way.

'Come on!' yelled Jack above the noise. 'Follow me! It's our only 'ope!'

Jack lowers himself down the outside wall until his feet touch one of the poles that crossed the stream, like horizontal pit props. By the time Kofi reaches the nearest pole beneath their window Jack is already halfway across, moving with the speed and dexterity of a tightrope walker. Kofi, far less confident and now trembling visibly, crawls along the pole on his belly. His progress is so slow that he is only halfway across the ditch by the time Jack lands safely on the far side.

'Hurry, young 'un! Nearly there. Come on, for Gawd's sake, or we is done for!'

Eventually Kofi reaches the other side and with Jack's help scrambles over a low wall and into the backyard of a derelict house.

Suddenly a shot rings out. The ball of lead strikes the wall just above Kofi, showering his head with flakes of blackened plaster.

Clem Piggin, now clearly framed in the window behind them, raises his second pistol and calmly takes aim.

Jack, immediately realising the danger, grabs Kofi by the collar and pulls him to the ground. Keeping as low as possible, the two fugitives then scramble across the yard towards the street beyond, ironically called Blackboys Alley. Then a second shot crashes into the wall above their heads - followed by a bloodcurdling curse from Piggin. They hastily quit the yard, pass beneath an archway and find themselves in the street. Thankful for the many pedestrians, carts and horses that fill this narrow thoroughfare, they head north, quickly merging with the crowd.

For the moment they have escaped but some minutes later, pausing for breath in an alleyway off Shoe lane, the enormity of what has just taken place suddenly strikes them.

They are now desperate fugitives, pursued by a man clearly prepared to kill them for a valuable silver collar they no longer possess!

16. The Stews of London
9th June, 1763

Kofi, ignorant of the ways of Georgian society, would have been surprised at the lack of interest London had for his recent, somewhat sudden departure from Buckingham House.

Blacks, after all, frequently absconded; there was nothing new in such stories. More fool Evelyn Lowther, said her peers, for not keeping a tighter rein on her expensive pet. There was still the matter of the silver collar but for the extremely wealthy Lowthers such trinkets were surely of minor importance. No, what gripped London that week was the story of the climbing boy and his amazing escapades within the palace - under the very nose of the King himself.

Over the next few days accounts of Jack's adventures, the vast amount of treasure he had acquired and the numerous encounters the palace staff had personally experienced with the sooty black renegade, filled the newspapers and dominated conversation in coffee shops throughout London. Jack was now the talk of the town and was rapidly acquiring that status of a working-class hero. Printed pages depicting the more lurid aspects of his life of crime, culminating in his daring exploits within the palace, appeared on street corners. These pamphlets were bought, read and passed on to friends and colleagues - at least those who could read. Had Jack known of these scurrilous and largely invented accounts of his life he would have been thrilled but since he was in hiding and could not read anyway, he never knew just how famous he had become.

Even as Jack's story blossomed, writers associated with Drury Lane Theatre were hard at work devising a short, highly dramatic *divertissement* for the amusement and edification of their more discerning clientele - something about a climbing boy who 'tweaked the nose of the King of Hannover'. It would of course need the approval of the censors before it could be presented on stage but Garrick was quietly optimistic. However, not every one was happy about Jack's sudden rise to fame. Giacomo Casanova - the famed Venetian seducer, even then visiting London was alarmed to see his illustrious and highly controversial name in all the gossip columns replaced by some unknown sweep.

He left for the Veneto very soon thereafter, puce with anger.

When, King George III was eventually told all about the renegade sweep that had lived in his palace for seven weeks, he was - much to everybody's surprise - hugely amused. Nothing of real value, after all, had been stolen and even the wine, expensive as it was, did not mean that much to a man whose cellars contained over thirty thousand bottles.

No, what annoyed His Majesty was the apparent 'cover-up' that had followed the climbing boy's death' up the palace chimney in the first place.

While the King fully appreciated the embarrassment the death of a child up one of his chimneys might have caused the palace, *not* to tell him or a senior member of the Royal Household at the time was a serious mistake. Now that the 'cat was out of the bag' it required some skilful 'damage limitation' on the part of his staff to contain the wilder reports now circulating London. Thaddeus Pratt, who was questioned by the Queen Mother herself, was promptly dismissed - not for his incompetence in handling the fight in the cellar but for having covered up the sweep's assumed 'demise'. Pratt, however, immediately sold the 'real' story (with a few embellishments of his own) to the *London Tatler* magazine for a small fortune.

Jeremiah Blagg, on the other hand - once he recovered from the shock of being arrested the day after Jack escaped down the sewers - was now quite happy to bask in his errant sweep's notoriety. Although the Bow Street Magistrates were unable to prove that Blagg was behind Jack's palace 'scam', the old villain spent an uncomfortable two days behind bars - until Scab, who alone knew where the Master Sweep kept his pot of gold, bailed him out. Scab, Blagg's bandy-legged acolyte, was also under suspicion. Because of his diminutive size and athletic abilities it was generally thought that he had a sideline in house robbery, masterminded by Blagg. Again, the authorities could prove nothing, even though they searched Blagg's filthy gaff in Chick Lane.

While his neighbours in Chick Lane laughed behind his back, Blagg himself continued to dine out on stories of his brilliant young apprentice and how he, Jeremiah Blagg, had taught Jack everything he knew. This annoyed Scab since he considered himself Blagg's favourite, now that Jem had been kicked out of their house. Scab resolved, therefore, to find Jack and 'shop' him.

Thus it was that Scab, together with a few of his little cronies, began to scour Jack's known haunts in the hope of spotting the little bastard and thereby put a timely end to his current notoriety.

Jack meanwhile, ignorant of the fame accumulating about his person, was far from happy. After their close encounter with Piggin (whom Jack had long known by reputation if not in person) he and Kofi had gone to ground. They had spent the last three days under Vauxhall Bridge, on the north side of the river. This was the sordid, rat-infested abode for some of London's worse gin addicts. Here the flotsam and jetsam of London's poorest gathered at night to consume the last of their gin or sleep off a day of drunkenness. Beggars, tramps, alcoholics and even children crowded together in the darkness, wrapped in filthy blankets.

Jack had chosen this desolate spot because it would be the last place the authorities - or any bounty hunter - would think to search. These people, whoever they were, now knew that the boys had money but no one would think to look amongst the dregs of society for two relatively *rich* fugitives. That, at least, was Jack's plan.

Kofi was less sanguine about Jack's choice of hiding place.

After the luxuries to which he had become accustomed, this place was truly horrible. Besides, if the drunks around them ever discovered how much gold and silver they had stuffed in their pockets they were sure to wake up one morning with their throats cut. Worse still, the smell of gin, vomit and human excrement reminded him of the recurring nightmare that was the *barracoon* in Accra or the miserable weeks he and his mother had spent on board the slave ship that had taken them to Jamaica.

***

Lady Lowther's decision to quit London a day or so after Sambo absconded was, on reflection, a wise one. As the palace authorities, under the personal direction of Catherine Dashwood (Lady-in-Waiting to the redoubtable Augusta), probed into the affair of the palace thief, links with Sambo grew - to Evelyn's discredit. While

157

no one of course blamed *her* she was now glad to have escaped London society for the rural solitude of Rigmorden.

However, Evelyn had now withdrawn into herself, frequently plunging into one of her notorious black moods. Sometimes, in the middle of the night, she would get up and wander about the corridors of the great house - until Arabella or Lisa found her and coaxed her back to bed. Sometimes, if the weather were fine, she would take to her garden where for hours she would sit in her Chinese arbour, sighing to the wind. Once Lisa found her sat on a bench in the topiary gardens, sobbing uncontrollably. It took both of her chambermaids and her Housekeeper to persuade her back into the house where, after the application of smelling salts, she finally stopped crying. Since she resolutely refused to allow anyone to summon her doctor, her staff soon became increasingly despondent, fearing for the sanity of their distraught mistress.

***

If polite society was agog with the latest gossip concerning the now infamous sweep, London's black community took a very different view of recent events at the palace. As details of the 'Sambo affair' emerged - Buckingham House now resembling a leaky sieve - so the debate amongst Kofi's compatriots raged wherever London's blacks lived and worked.

There were at this time some fifteen thousand living in London. Some had absconded or jumped ship but most were free men or women, living quietly in London's docklands or near the city's great markets. Indeed, blacks were becoming a familiar sight in London - particularly as beggars or street entertainers. One or two were even famous, like Joseph Johnson, a beggar celebrated for his hat shaped like a fully rigged sailing ship.

The majority of London's blacks, however - once they had their freedom - stayed on in the employment of their former owners, often as cooks, grooms or even butlers. Francis Barber, servant to Dr. Samuel Johnson (the celebrated lexicographer), was among the first of London's better-known blacks to hear of 'Sambo's' escape. Since the coffee house was all the rage amongst London's professional classes, it was there that Barber learned something of the boy's origins and the young blackamoor's subsequent 'treachery'.

Barber himself regularly accompanied his master to his favourite coffee house near St. Paul's Cathedral. Here they would meet Johnson's literary friends, drink punch, smoke a pipe and at nine o'clock enjoy a plate of Welsh-rarebit, followed by apple-puffs washed down with porter. It was here too that others came to stare at Dr. Johnson, with his crumpled clothes and ill-fitting wig.

While Barber and his black friends did not actually approve of what 'Sambo' had done, they were reluctant to condemn him outright. One reason for this was that most had themselves experienced the horrors of enslavement. They knew what it was like and how great the need to escape was felt by those unfortunates still trapped in this vicious trade. While it would be many years before the formal abolition of slavery could be considered even a possibility, most blacks who knew about Kofi's escape from the Lowther household secretly applauded his courage. It is not recorded what Dr Johnson himself thought but Frank Barber quietly put it about amongst *his* friends that should 'Sambo' surface then he was to be given whatever help and protection was necessary.

For the majority of middle-class whites, 'Sambo's' defection proved beyond all shadow of doubt the inherently venal nature of blacks.

'Orang-utans do not seem at all inferior in the intellectual faculties to many of the Negro race. It is certain that both races agree perfectly well in lasciviousness of disposition.'

This was said of a child whose tribal customs and cultural artefacts predated the European Renaissance by some three thousand years.

'Their barbarity to their children debases their nature even below that of brutes. They have no moral sensations, no taste but for women, gormandising and drinking to excess.'

This was said of a child who was still only eleven years old, alone and despairing in the stews of London.

While he had of late thought little about his mother, Kofi's relationship with his family was, in normal circumstances, warm and loving. The Ashanti were celebrated throughout Africa for their highly developed clan structure and the value they placed on kinship. For the Ashanti peoples, the keystone of all social relations was the bond between mother and son.

Others, including blacks wise in the ways of their white 'masters', recognised that the biggest difficulty facing boys like 'Sambo' was that they were prized for their youth yet scorned for their manhood. 'Sambo's' future, whether he had temporarily escaped or not, was ultimately determined by the inevitable onset of adolescence. Once he outgrew his usefulness as a servile, acquiescent 'fashion accessory', deportation was inevitable.

'Sambo's' situation, therefore, was widely considered hopeless.

***

Late one night, only three days after their first, close encounter with Piggin, Kofi and Jack - their arms full of bread and cheese - were spotted disappearing down a side street near Hungerford Steps.

The man who subsequently betrayed their whereabouts was himself black. He was called Mason Quashe and was at that time groom to Lord Chesterfield whose stables were situated close by. We may never know exactly how Clem Piggin acquired this valuable information from Quashe or what money exchanged hands in the process but Piggin now knew the exact whereabouts of Jack and the boy they called 'Sambo'. It was, therefore, only a matter of time before he made his next move. This time, however, he would be better prepared. His recent failure to capture the two boys had done little to enhance his reputation as London's most successful bounty hunter.

Then there was the matter of the silver collar. While the Jew had himself informed the Bow Street authorities of its whereabouts, having first sold it on (conveniently) to another dealer almost before Jack and Kofi had left his shop, it was proving very difficult to trace it further, not least because it had now become something of a collector's item. Lady Lowther herself would have been flabbergasted to learn that 'Sambo's' silver collar was now valued at a staggering £200 - ten times more than she had paid for it only a week or so ago.

The Jew, it should be said, was *not* charged with dealing in stolen property for he was a known informant and more use to the Bow Street Magistrates *out* of prison than in. Others, it was darkly hinted, might not get off quite so lightly for while the collar may indeed have become a collector's item; it was in legal terms something of a 'hot potato.' The principal Magistrate himself was now actively involved, anxious to reassure his wealthy benefactors that their property and its recovery, if stolen, was always Bow Street's primary concern. After all, Lady Lowther was cousin to the King of England.

Since the collar was therefore proving difficult to acquire, it was up to Piggin to obtain for his client the next best thing - the sweep and his black accomplice. It was to that end that Clem Piggin, armed with that vital information from Quashe, now directed his attention.

Later that evening, Jack and Kofi prepared themselves for another uncomfortable night beneath Vauxhall Bridge. They were used now to the stench of human excrement and the sickly-sweet aroma of raw gin that pervaded the place but nothing masked the cries and screams in the night, the violent nightmares and the incoherent babble of the deranged all around them.

It had been a long time since Jack had thought of his mother but amidst the squalor of their hiding place memories of her now filled his head.

They were not happy memories.

It was she, after all, who had sold him to Blagg in the first place. It was she who had condemned him to a life in which he was forced to ascend terrifyingly chimneys and endure lacerated knees and elbows onto which Scab had rubbed brine with such ill-disguised glee. It was she who, in her desperate need for gin, had sold him into nothing less than white slavery - to be abused and exploited by Jeremiah Blagg. Now, as Jack listened to the cries of those about him, he remembered Kitty's own painful addiction; the squalor of her life as a prostitute; the ugly men she habitually embraced and the sordid rooms in which they had lived during the last few years of their life together.

He could never forgive her and yet, he now realised, he could never really forget her, much as he might try.

Suddenly, five armed men with lanterns appeared at the far end of the arched bridge and began moving towards them. At their head was the unmistakable figure of Clem Piggin, silhouetted against a distant street lamp. Kofi, at once realising the danger, leapt to his feet, dragged Jack to his feet and headed for the slimy green steps that led to the Thames embankment.

'Stop thief!' said a voice from the darkness. Others at once took up the cry until the archways beneath the bridge echoed with dozens of accusatory cries.

The two fugitives emerged from the shadow of the bridge and raced off down the embankment towards Hungerford Stairs. It was low tide and the banks of the river were pitted with holes and shallow pools of water. Every few yards they had to make their way round a small boat or barge beached on the mud at the water's edge. Behind them they could hear the shouts of Piggin and his men getting closer and closer.

Reaching Hungerford Stairs, they clambered up the greasy steps towards street level then headed north between warehouses towering above them. Jack, who knew this district well, instinctively headed for Hungerford Market.

This long, narrow market was still active although it was already quite dark. Torches fixed at intervals to the sheds and storehouses illuminated the area, casting lurid shadows across shoppers jostling for position in front of the stalls. Because of their size, Jack and Kofi could slip through these crowds easily but their pursuers found it difficult and soon began to fall behind.

With the tower of St. Martins Church now in front of them, Jack turned right and picked his way through the narrow alleyways and courts leading to Villiers Street. Thinking for a moment that they had lost Piggin and his bullyboys, Jack dived into the back entrance of the nearest house, just to get his breath back.

This was his first mistake.

Within moments they heard the sound of hob-nailed boots on stone flags getting closer and closer. Peering over a pile of rubbish they saw one of Piggin's men at the far end of their alleyway. After a moment's hesitation the man beckoned to his companions to bring more lights and, accompanied by Piggin and two others, began to move towards them, truncheons at the ready.

Jack's brief but peculiar career had hardened him to most dangers. Several times, even before his adventures in Buckingham House, he had found himself trapped in some flue or narrow, fume-filled tunnel and had survived, remaining solid when others might have panicked. Jem, who was the greatest climbing boy Jack had ever met, had taught him much - not least the need to stay absolutely calm in dangerous situations. While Jack had not always managed to follow Jem's advice, his survival within the chimneys of Buckingham House had owed much to this sound advice and may explain why Jack had eluded capture for so long.

If ever Jem's advice were needed, it was now. Jack's first instinct, therefore, was to go *up* - up to the climbing boy's familiar world of slates and tiles, rooftops and gable ends.

This was his second, fatal mistake.

The entrance into which he and Kofi stepped was the back porch of a large house, the front of which looked onto Villiers Street. This was the servant's entrance and when Jack pushed against the door it opened. They entered, closed the door behind them (forgetting to bolt it) and scrambled up three flights of stairs, encountering neither servants nor occupants on their way up. When they reached the top landing Jack flung open the shutters and clambered out onto the narrow sill. By clinging to a drainpipe and then easing himself sideways over the gable end, he soon reached a flat part of the roof.

Kofi, whose fear of heights Jack found incomprehensible, was at first reluctant to follow but the shouts of men below lent him courage. With Jack's help he too scrambled onto the roof, sixty feet above street level.

Here, on the roof of London, they were spoilt for choice for in all directions there stretched a thousand dwellings, cheek-by jowl, separated only by narrow gaps across which it would be possible to jump. With courage and some luck they could scramble across the rooftops of Villiers Street and beyond, moving from rooftop to rooftop until they found a convenient route back down to the street. That way they might just outrun Piggin's heavy, less agile thugs. For a moment or two Jack hesitated - carefully considering their options.

In the end it was Piggin himself who solved their dilemma. His face, purple with rage and exertion, suddenly emerged through an open skylight only feet from where they now crouched. The shock of this sudden entrance was sufficient to persuade Jack (panicking somewhat) to clamber up to the highest part of the roof, dragging Kofi with him. Here, together, they cowered behind a cluster of chimney pots that were belching black smoke. Several shots followed, whistling past their ears and shattering a chimney pot close to Kofi's head. Warm, sooty shards flew in all directions, causing them both to duck.

While Piggin reloaded, Jack stepped onto the rim of the steeply pitched roof and edged his way along its length until he reached the shelter of another set of tall chimneystacks at the far end.

'Kofi, quick! Follow me!'

Lacking the courage and experience to walk upright, Kofi crawled on his hands and knees towards his friend. Piggin, unable now to get a decent shot from the skylight, thrust his pistol in his belt and clambered up onto the roof and cautiously edged his way towards the first chimneystack.

In the skylight Piggin had just vacated, there now appeared the faces of his followers, fighting for a view of the proceedings and yelling encouragement to their leader. However, Piggin's slow progress along the rooftop gave Kofi the time he needed to reach the safety of the second chimneystack and crouch behind it. Below them, at the end of the roof on which they now clung, was a second, lower roof, less steeply pitched.

'This way, young 'un. Follow me!'

With the agility of a Barbary ape Jack jumped, landing lightly on the angled pitch of the smaller roof some eight feet below the chimney to which Kofi now clung. The few slates Jack dislodged by his landing slid down the roof and disappeared over the edge, followed by a loud crash as they landed in the cobbled street far below.

'Come on, Kofi', cried Jack. 'Jump! You can do it, Sunshine!'

Kofi bravely followed but his landing caused him to sprawl forward awkwardly. To his horror, he now began to slide sideways. In a desperate effort to save himself from slithering off the roof to almost certain death.

What followed was like a nightmare - in slow motion.

Jack, caught off balance by Kofi's ungainly landing, had barely recovered his equilibrium when Kofi grabbed his ankle. This sudden movement caused Jack himself to lose his grip on the chimneystack, fall onto his back and slide down the tiles, headfirst. As Kofi watched in horror, Jack clawed at the tiles, frantically trying to arrest his inexorable slide. Inches from death he suddenly stopped, his bony shoulders momentarily wedged against the gutter while his head hung in space over the edge.

'Kofi, save yourself!'

These were the last words Kofi heard. Even as he reached out a helping hand, Jack disappeared over the edge of the roof. As he fell to the street below his scream filled the night air. At that very moment Piggin reached Kofi, grabbed him by the scruff of the neck and jerked him back up the roof.

'Got yer!', yelled Piggin triumphantly.

Kofi's anguished cries, not for himself but for his lost friend, were promptly stifled by Piggin's iron grip round his throat.

17. The Journey North
12th June, 1763

SAMBO'S ESCAPE
A Theatrical Divertissement in Five Acts
As performed at Drury Lane Theatre, London on 18th July, 1763

Prologue
Just as Jack Fisher's adventures within the palace acquired, through the pamphlets and newspaper articles circulating London, a certain notoriety, so too did the subsequent adventures of 'Sambo' - despite an initial reluctance by polite society to commemorate the activities of a mere savage.

Within weeks of 'Sambo's' rooftop capture, the journey north to Preston, his dramatic escape with the help of a highwayman, Clem Piggin's violent murder and the arrest and execution of this same highwayman (one Joshua Bloom), Sambo's own adventures were represented on stage at Drury Lane Theatre - at the instigation of Mr. David Garrick.

Since no black child could be found to play the part of Sambo, Miss Sarah Talbot blacked up for the occasion. While savages are not known for their rational behaviour or mode of thought, we have - the better to improve our theatrical narrative - endowed 'Sambo' with a semblance of articulation.

Act One, Scene One

12th June, 1763. Remote country road north of Preston. The stagecoach, carrying Kofi and the bounty hunter Clem Piggin, is on the last part of its long journey north to Kendal.

Narrator

The first leg of their journey from London to Manchester - one hundred and eighty-six miles - lasted two days. After a brief stopover in Fallowfield, they continued their journey throughout the following day, finally reaching Preston by late afternoon. They are now well on their way to their next major stop - the old market town of Kendal in the county of Westmorland. From there it will be a short trip east to Kirkby Lonsdale and then on to Rigmorden Hall.

Sambo

After my close encounter with death on the rooftop in Villiers Street - a violent encounter that had killed my best friend - nothing could touch me, so wrapped up was I in my grief for Jack and despair at my own situation.

Jack's death was entirely my fault - or so I convinced myself. This, more than anything else, was what plunged me into utter despondency; that, and the cruel recognition that my short-lived freedom had been brutally curtailed by Clem Piggin and his bullyboys.

Clem Piggin

I too was despondent - but for entirely different reasons. While I was glad to have captured the little black bastard, Lowther's silver collar had vanished. No doubt it would eventually resurface somewhere in London but for the moment it, the money the boys had probably got for selling it and the sweep himself were missing.

To add to my woes, Lord Carlisle had been none too pleased with my first, entirely botched attempt to seize the thieves in their gaff. Even the second attempt had gone wrong, for by the time my men reached the street most of the crowd there had vanished, presumably taking Jack Fisher's body with them. Later that day, acting on Carlisle's instructions, I bought a ticket at 'The Bull Inn', Charring Cross for the long journey north to Rigmorden Hall, the home of Lady Evelyn Lowther.

Narrator

To save money, Piggin has elected to sit on the open seats at the back of the stagecoach. Sambo is beside him, his right arm manacled to the iron rail used to stop luggage sliding off the roof. The other passengers, snug and warm inside the carriage, are in fine fettle but Piggin, drawing his greatcoat around him, scowls into the gloom. Sambo, dressed only in rags, is thoroughly frozen - to such an extent that he can no longer feel his hands and feet.

Act One, Scene Two

Having left Preston far behind, they are now travelling on a road that winds its way across desolate moorland or plunges through steep-sided valleys, thick with trees. Darkness, like a great black cloak, has already begun to enclose the woods and hills on both sides of the track. The last, blood-red streaks of day are stretched, like claw marks, on a bruised sky.

Sambo

I had no idea what Lady Evelyn had in store for me. I knew I would be punished but that hardly troubled me. A severe whipping was nothing to the mental torment that I was suffering, knowing that my one bid for freedom had failed.

Act One, Scene Three

Two hours have passed and still the stagecoach sways and bumps along the country road, its wheels lurching from one deep furrow to the next.

Sambo

I missed Jack terribly. While I had begun to mistrust the climbing boy, even in the short time we had known each other, we *had* shared a number of exciting adventures together.

I recall with pleasure the first time we ate stolen food in the great banqueting hall in the palace and how Jack had danced a drunken jig on the polished table - before slipping and sending a large bowl of soup crashing to the floor.

I remember also how Jack had shown me how to slide down the palace's marble banisters and how to swing from the chandelier by first standing on a sideboard then leaping boldly into mid-air, thereby causing the chandelier's tear-shaped pendants to shimmer wondrously in the moonlight!

The sun has now set and the June moon - a great orange orb - is rising sedately over the rim of the sky.

Act Two, Scene One

The carriage itself is full of noisy, animated conversation. Laughter spills into the night - like bright sparks from a blacksmith's anvil.

Narrator

There are three men immediately below where Sambo sits - and a young woman. The men are rich, well dressed and clearly besotted with the pretty, dark-haired girl sitting opposite them. Like a young actress making her stage debut, she is all blushes, giggles, and fluttering eyelashes - a stage princess afloat upon a sea of voluminous, crimson taffeta.

Of course, their interest has nothing at all to do with the low-cut bodice she wears, revealing firm breasts of a peachy complexion.

First Gallant
Why, madam, I wager you have turned many a pretty fellow's head with those wonderful brown eyes of yours, what?

Girl
Why sir... [Demurely] ...I truly have the eyes if you have the stomach!

Sambo
Lost in my own thoughts, I had neither the interest nor the understanding to follow this conversation yet the young woman's voice, clear and spirited on the night air, reminded me of my mother's laughter.

Mysteriously prompted by this unknown girl's silver voice, my mother's smile glides towards me through my tears and across the vast distances that separated us both.

Act Two, Scene Two
The stagecoach is now approaching a shallow stream that crosses their path. The coachman, Ned Twist, steadies his team.

Ned
Steady, lads! Steady Robin, steady our Bess. There's Claw Hill yonder. T'aint no time to shed shoe or break thy fetlocks!

Thin wisps of mist hang in the numerous nooks and crannies of this gloomy hollow, like ghosts that have lost their way. As the wheels of the stagecoach clatter across the stream, the mist turns and spins like so many tiny whirlpools.

Ned
Now then, Dicken! Let's see that blunderbuss of your'n primed and pointed! This t'aint no place to be caught nappin'!

Narrator
The man to whom these cautionary words are spoken is a thin, shifty-looking fellow perched next to the coachman and clutching a very large blunderbuss. Dicken Spicey is the guard.

Dicken

I got this job because it was assumed that I was a good shot, being a professional poacher. However, the only man I ever killed was my neighbour whom I mistook one moonlit night for a rabbit. It is my task to protect the lives and property of the four rich passengers in the carriage below. As for the two on top, especially that little black devil - they can go to hell for all I care!

Dicken proudly wipes the stock of his battered blunderbuss on one greasy sleeve of his bloodstained, moleskin jacket.

Dicken

Tis ready and primed, Ned!

Dicken boldly raises his ancient weapon and takes aim at an imaginary rook perched in the trees above them.

Ned

Aye, and don't be afeared to use it!

Bang! says Dicken to himself - and an imaginary rook explodes, showering the coach with twigs and feathers, sticky with blood.

Ned slaps the reins on the backs of his four brave horses and boldly steers them towards the steep hill that now lies before them.

Narrator

This sudden surge of speed caused Dicken to fall back in his seat and grab wildly at the rail - to stop himself toppling sideways into the ditch. He now hangs on to the blunderbuss with his free hand, much to the consternation of his companion who quite expects it to go off at any minute and blow his hat, closely followed by his head, to Kingdom Come.

Clem Piggin, who had been dozing, wakes up with a start and reaches instinctively for his pistols. Thus armed, he stares about him in the darkness with such a fearsome look on his pock-marked face that shivers of fear run up and down Sambo's spine.

Act Two, Scene Three

The stagecoach has now reached the foot of the hill and has begun its tortuous ascent.

Narrator

Claw Hill is steep and treacherous, bordered with dark trees whose branches reach down with black, bony fingers. Despite the coachman's liberal use of his whip, the four horses make slow progress.

Inside the carriage the passengers fall silent and cling to straps - or each other. Great attention is given by all three young blades to the immediate comfort and safety of the girl, to the extent that two of them insist on squeezing into her seat, on either side - like a pair of amorous bookends.

Act Three, Scene One

The moon has now lost its orange tinge and has become a pale globe, balanced precariously on the dark rim of the horizon. The road here is steep, narrow and overhung with trees through which shafts of moonlight shine, turning the coach and its powerful horses a deathly white.

Suddenly, a figure on horseback appears before them, silhouetted dramatically against the moon. It is a highwayman! With one gloved hand he holds the reins and with the other waves an enormous pistol.

Narrator

It is a very theatrical entrance and one which would not be out of place in a play by John Gay, celebrated author of *The Beggar's Opera*. Having raised the curtain, as it were, of our expectations, the highwayman's great black horse rears dramatically on its hind legs and lets forth a loud whinny that echoes down the track towards them.

Highwayman

Stand and deliver! Or I'll blow yer bleedin' brains out!

Narrator

Reactions on board the stagecoach to the dramatic nature of this new and startling development are mixed. The coachman himself swears loudly and pulls hard on the reins while Jack, his knees already trembling, looks about desperately for some means of escape.

Piggin

Behind them, partially hidden by the luggage, I silently cocked my two trusty pistols.

Sambo

Not knowing much about highwaymen, other than what Jack once told me, I cowered in my seat, ready toe any eventuality.

Narrator

Inside the carriage itself there is confusion and panic as each of the gallants struggle frantically to conceal watches, gold coins and other movables down the back of their seats or under cushions. The girl, clearly anxious to help, stuffs whatever is offered down the front of her ample cleavage.

The stagecoach has now stopped; close enough for all those on board to get a good look at their assailant.

The mounted highwayman - as one would expect of a member of that infamous profession - wears a long, black cloak; a tri-cornered hat with a plume of black, ostrich feathers and thigh-length boots. Beneath his jacket can be glimpsed a fine, silk waistcoat over a cambric shirt - and a large dagger.

His face is completely obscured by a white mask - in the Venetian style. It leaves only his eyes visible.

Narrator
Having taken in his general appearance, attention is then drawn, inevitably, to two pistols now pointed menacingly at them. One is levelled at the flushed face of Ned Twist and the other at a spot equidistant between Dicken Spicey's beady eyes.

Act Three, Scene Two
Dicken stares back down the muzzle of the highwayman's pistol - like a startled ferret.

Highwayman
No monkey business, Ned - or you'll be the first to get it!

Narrator
Ned glowers back at the man but bites his lip and says nothing.

Highwayman
And don't even think of firing that blunderbuss, Dicken Spicey. This ball of lead has your name on it! I carved it meself.
Dicken
[*His face suddenly drained of all colour*].
How do you know my name?

Narrator
Dicken is now shaking violently - so much so that there is a distinct danger that his ancient blunderbuss will go off of its own accord and kill everybody in sight, including himself.
Highwayman
Never you mind, Dicken. Put up that bloody gun - h'afore I peppers yer with mine!

Narrator

The guard hastily lowers his blunderbuss and lays it across his trembling knees. Two trickles of urine begin to fill his boots.

Ned

How did you know we was acomin' this way? Tell me that, you blackguard!

Highwayman

Now then, Ned. There h'aint no call for hinsolence! Besides, a driver of your hexperience should know that we gentlemen of the road knows heveryfing. Now, stop bletherin' while I hintroduce meself to your passengers!

Narrator

Ned falls silent, painfully aware of the pistol still levelled at his large, red nose. The four horses, grateful for this un-scheduled halt, pick and paw at the muddy grass by the roadside.

Act Three, Scene Four
Sambo

From my vantage point high on the roof of the stagecoach I watched with great interest as the masked man ordered the other passengers out of the carriage and onto the road. At first the three gallants protested noisily but a sudden, sideways movement and a clatter of hooves from the large, black mare startled them and they quickly stepped down into the mud.

Narrator

The young woman, whose hooded cloak conveniently fails to conceal a face of quite exquisite beauty, is the last to leave. She coyly lifts her skirts and steps down, revealing an elegant ankle covered in pale, cream silk. Her descent is executed with the grace and charm of a professional courtesan which, had they but known it, is what she really is - especially between weekday theatrical matinees and after most evening performances.

The men, with a great show of reluctance, empty their pockets and place their few remaining coins, watches and rings into the leather pouch that the highwayman now extends towards them.

With delicate fingers the girl drops her own bulging purse into the pouch, punctuating her action with a neat curtsy. Her smile - practised to perfection before her mirror - has frequently graced the stages of The Grand Theatre in Lancaster and other local fleapits. It is no less effective here.

Highwayman

Madam! [*Courtly flourish*], your generosity hoverwhelms me!

Act Four, Scene One
Narrator

Suddenly Piggin draws his pistols and aims them at the highwayman, momentarily distracted by the pretty girl.

Sambo

I abruptly spring to my feet and lunge at the Piggin's extended arm. Both guns explode with a deafening crash, causing a splintered branch to fall about our ears. Another shot immediately rings out and Piggin, clutching his shattered face, falls backwards off the coach and down onto the road - dead as a door nail.

I then scream with horror for my hands and face are splattered with Piggin's blood and brains.

Narrator

Then a third shot rings out, this time from Spicey. The blunderbuss, unequal to the task of dispatching the highwayman, partially explodes in Jack's face before sending a few pellets whistling past the highwayman's ears and causing his horse to rear violently.

Jack, his face now as black as soot, is still staring in astonishment at the splintered weapon in his hands when the highwayman, coolly taking aim across his horse's neck, fires his second pistol.

Highwayman

The ball of lead - with Jack's name on it - passes through the side of Ned's portly neck, severing an artery in an explosion of blood and tissue and then on into the guard's right temple, killing them both instantaneously.

Act Four, Scene Two

Narrator

By now the male passengers have fled into the bushes, leaving the girl alone at the roadside. For her part, she screams hysterically and waves her arms about - like a deranged windmill.

Gun smoke, trapped in the lamps' pale beams, swirls briefly in the trees before disappearing. The coach itself shakes and rattles as the horses, alarmed by the sudden noises, pull and buck within their traces. The smell of gunpowder hangs pungent on the cold, night air.

Highwayman

I drew my musket from my saddle holster and edged my horse closer to the small, black child cowering fearfully on the carriage roof. The boy tugs desperately at the rail to which his right arm is manacled. I raise my musket and take aim.

Narrator

For a moment their eyes met but then Sambo closes his own and calmly waits for death. He can smell it, for its acrid scent swirls about them both - manacled blackamoor and violent robber alike.

The shot rings out - blasting part of the carriage roof to smithereens. The rusty iron rail, to which Sambo is attached, disintegrates in a shower of metal splinters. Sambo is free!

Act Four, Scene Three

Narrator

Rising in his stirrups, the highwayman leans forward and seizes the startled boy by his lapels, lifting him bodily up into the air. For a moment Sambo hangs there but then the man lowers him onto the mare's neck. With one leg on either side, the boy promptly slides down the animal's sleek, black mane and lands in the saddle - but facing the wrong way.

At once the horse rears, swerves to one side and gallops off into the woods like a beast possessed.

Narrator

For a mile or so it crashes on through the undergrowth, briers and branches tearing at its chest and flanks. Soon the stagecoach and the three dead men are far behind, lost in a tangle of shadowy trees.

Sambo

It was some moments before I fully realised what had happened. The violent movement of the mare, charging deeper and deeper into the forest, caused me to clasp the highwayman about the waist and hang on for dear life. With my nose thus pressed into the man's chest, I could taste the gunpowder that still clung to his clothes.

Suddenly I remembered Piggin's face abruptly disintegrating into a broth of blood, splintered bone and brains. My head began to swirl and darkness descended upon me like a swarm of locusts - until there was nothing but black, impenetrable silence.

Act Five, Scene One

Somewhere deep in the forest. A large oak tree occupies stage centre, its green canopy towering above. The scene is lit by a single storm lantern hanging from a branch of the great oak.

Narrator

When Sambo comes too he is seated on a pile of leaves, propped up against the trunk of an enormous tree. A storm lantern, suspended from a branch, swings gently in the breeze above his head, creating a small pool of moving light. Before him stands the highwayman. He is looking down at him intently.

Sambo

Behind him and tethered to a tree, I could see the highwayman's mare. Steam rose from her back and her flanks were scratched and bleeding. The man moved closer, until he towered above me. I cowered back against the tree and felt the bark press sharply into my shoulder blades. I tried to pray but the familiar spirits of my childhood had disappeared, vanquished by darker, more powerful forces. I lay there, staring helplessly at my captor. The highwayman then leant forward until he was quite close and removed his mask to reveal - the face of a black man!

There is now a broad grin on the highwayman's thick lips and his eyes and teeth shine a lurid white in the light of the lamp.

Then, to Sambo's further astonishment, he opens his mouth and removes a large pebble, which he holds for a moment between two fingers before dropping it onto the ground. When he next speaks his voice is quite unlike the voice Sambo remembered from the hold-up.

Highwayman

Hello Sambo! Is you scared or is you not?

Narrator

Kofi keels over sideways, yielding once more to the darkness of a thousand locusts.

Act Five, Scene Two

The blue of the sky is intense, like pain. Two great vultures circle high above, sensing death. Sambo rises slowly from the ground, suspended between heaven and earth. He has often dreamt of flying but never like this. There is a sharp pain under his arms and a constriction about his chest that makes his lungs ache.

Narrator

When he opens his eyes the vultures have vanished and there, above him, kneels the black highwayman on a crude platform constructed in the upper branches of the great tree. The man is pulling on a rope.

Sambo

For a moment I could not understand what was happening but then I realised that I was tied to this rope and being hauled up into the tree. Although a loop of the coarse hemp encircled my chest, I reached automatically for the rope above my head and clung to it frantically with both hands. I tried to scream but when I opened my mouth nothing emerged. For a moment, therefore, I hung in absolute silence, conscious only of the pounding of my heart and the yawning space below, above which my feet dangled and danced - like a man on a gibbet.

Far below him, at the foot of the great tree, stands the girl from the stagecoach, holding the other end of the rope and steadying Sambo's ascent.

Nan

Hello Sambo. Never thought you'd see me again, did you?

Narrator

Sambo stares down in astonishment at this unexpected vision in crimson taffeta, lit by the light of the storm lantern. It is the pretty girl from the stagecoach - the highwayman's accomplice.

.

Highwayman

Well, don't just hang there. Start climbing, boy. We ain't got all night, 'av we Nan?

Sambo looks back up at the man on the platform above and is about to speak when the highwayman reaches down and grabs him by the lapels and hauls him onto the platform. Sambo now lies on the wooden planks, crumpled and bent like a discarded doll. The highwayman unfastens the rope and throws it over the side of the platform.

Narrator

As the highwayman sinks back on his haunches and rests, the girl shins up the rope with the agility of an acrobat - bringing the lantern with her. On reaching the top she promptly falls into the outstretched arms of her lover. When Sambo next looks they are rolling about on the floor of the platform, giggling and kissing.

At first the black highwayman showers the girl with kisses but soon he begins to tickle her and her screams of laughter redouble.

Nan

Each time Joshua plunged his arms into my voluminous gown or encircled my waist, his hands as quickly re-emerged, grasping some valuable object - like a gentleman's watch or purse full of gold coins. I responded by laughing even louder and kicking my heels high in the air to expose my shapely legs in a froth of white petticoats stained with mud.

Eventually their laughter subsides and the two robbers lie exhausted on the floor of the platform, surrounded by their booty. Silence.

Sambo

Why did you not kill me?

The highwayman, having momentarily forgotten Sambo, sits up on one elbow and stares at the boy.

Highwayman

Because you is black, like me. And because...well, you saved my life. That bounty hunter of yours would have killed me if you had not moved so quickly. Besides, niggers is family and we must all stick together.

Sambo

I'm not your family. My name is Kofi and my uncle is King Kwasi Obodum. I am an Ashanti prince. My mother is a pricess.

Nan

No you 'aint, Sunshine. [*sitting upright and re-arranging her skirts*]. You are called Sambo and you ran away - with a silver collar worth a fortune. That poxy villain, wot Joshua shot, told me so last night in the Crown Inn at Preston. You, my boy, is a wanted willain of the first order!

Highwayman

Leave 'im alone, Nan. Even if we 'aint kith-n-kin, we've got to stick together. 'Aint that true, Kofi?

Narrator

Sambo wriggles from beneath the man's embrace and crawls to the far side of the platform. He crouches in the leafy shadows cast by the lantern and stares back at his two captors.

Highwayman

Very well. I can see you is still scared. Here....

He rummages in the pockets of his voluminous cloak and magically produces a crust of bread and a large pickled onion.

Highwayman

Eat this. I bet you 'aint eaten for a month of Sundays!

Narrator

Sambo scuttles forward and grabs the food and stuffs it into his mouth. It is true! He has not eaten since the change of horses in Preston and even then Piggin only gave him a few stale biscuits.

As he eats, Joshua and the girl gather up their booty from the floor of the tree house and place it in a saddlebag that hangs from a convenient branch. Although small, the tree house gives ample coverage and is invisible from the ground. It is clearly designed as a temporary hideaway.

With the horse well hidden in the thick bushes below, no one would ever find them up here - in this great oak tree deep in the forest.

Sambo

For a moment or two I cherished the notion of living up this tree but the fresh memory of Piggin's shattered face and the guards' feet twitching convulsively as they lay on the ground in a pool of blood made me quickly reject this idea.

Narrator

Suddenly the girl stands up, bends down and kisses the black highwayman full on the mouth. Then, with the agility of a performing monkey, she slips over the edge of the platform and shins down the rope.

Nan

I'll meet you at Gisburn. On Friday. Goodbye, beloved Joshua. Goodbye Sambo.

Narrator

She lands lightly on the ground and looks back up towards the highwayman, who is now leaning over the parapet and peering down into the darkness below.

Nan

Take care, darling. They are sure to double the guards - after what you done this evening!

With a brief wave to her lover she runs off and is quickly consumed by the dark shadows of the forest.

Act Five, Scene Three

Narrator

That night Sambo sleeps at Joshua's feet, partly covered by the hem of the highwayman's great cloak.

The moon rises higher still and casts its deathly light onto the upper branches of their tree.

The two fugitives lie stretched out on the hard, wooden planks, their bodies mottled with leafy shadows. In this dappled moonlight their flesh shows the leprous marks of death.

Sambo

When eventually I dozed off, my sleep was full of violent dreams. Blood dripped from the dark branches above me, falling upon my upturned face. Sometimes, Dicken Spicey's blackened face peered out of the shadows, his look of astonishment, even in death, still frozen upon his visage. His final scream, as he fell slowly backwards from his seat on the stagecoach, hung in the air above my head like the scream of a screech owl hovering above its prey.

Act Five, Scene Four

The following morning. It is already light when Sambo awakes. A slight breeze stirs the uppermost leaves, causing them to quiver and shake nervously. It is now Thursday, 16th June 1763.

Narrator

Kofi sits up and looks at Joshua, still sleeping and wrapped in his rumpled cloak like an Egyptian pharaoh.

Sambo

If these people are professional robbers, I reasoned, then perhaps they can help me. Joshua had, after all, killed the bounty hunter - with my help. Now that I am free and out of Clem Piggin's clutches, Joshua and his doxy could help me get back to Sunderland Point...and Africa.

Narrator

This startling idea, rapidly growing like a giant tapeworm, expands in Sambo's imagination. Unable to contain it any longer he grabs Joshua by both shoulders and shakes him violently.

Sambo

Wake up! Wake up, mister! Wake up!

Joshua awakes with a start, stares about him wildly. He quickly draws both pistols, cocking them simultaneously.

Highwayman

What is it boy? What have you heard? Are we discovered?

The highwayman scrambles to his feet and rushes to the edge of the platform, peering down into the forest clearing.

Sambo

No, there is no one. It's just that you must help me. Will you? Will you help me find my mother? My family? Will you? Will you, Joshua?

Narrator

Joshua stares down at the small boy crouching at his feet and clutching the hem of his cloak like a Bedlam beggar. The child's face is wet with tears and there is a wild look in his eyes.

Highwayman

Of course I will help you, boy. We'll leave today. But where is your mother? Where can we find her?

Sambo

Why, Jamaica, of course. Where else would she be?

Epilogue

Narrator

This short, dramatic *divertissement* ran for three nights only at Drury Lane Theatre and attracted mixed reviews, certain critics regarding the narrative as ridiculous and far-fetched.

Some members of the audience were even prompted to question the veracity of that which they saw enacted on the stage but the events herein described were later corroborated by Bloom's whore Nan, who herself gave King's evidence at Bloom's subsequent trial. Besides, in these enlightened times and in a nation that prides itself on the freedom of its press and the intellectual rigour of its dramatic representations, who could doubt the truthfulness of this epic tale of heroism, youthful courage and violent murder?

Thereafter, as is often the case with such melodramatic re-enactments, Reality slid inexorably into Myth and Truth soon disappeared, forever, into historical oblivion.

If Time were a shattered mirror, each shard a fragment of the Truth, then it now behoves our Author, in the few chapters that remain of this historical narrative, to gather these splintered fragments together and to provide, for your edification, a *true* account of the final adventures of Kofi and the Climbing Boy.

18. Lancaster to Sunderland Point

16[h] June, 1763

News that 'Sambo' had been captured reached her Ladyship in Westmorland two days after Piggin had reported to Lord Carlisle. The London-Kendal mail coach had carried a letter from his Lordship, informing Evelyn in some detail of the first abortive attempt. Since both he and the climbing boy were now hot news, any information relating to their supposed whereabouts in London and Sambo's subsequent capture, was quickly disseminated. News always travels fast, especially if it is bad.

Evelyn was not pleased to learn that her silver collar had vanished and that, surprisingly, no money - or so Piggin claimed - had been found on the boy. The climbing boy's miraculous survival, having fallen some sixty feet from the roof of the house in Villiers Street, was vaguely interesting but since the child had now vanished, spirited away by a crowd of apparent supporters, it was of little relevance. How a number of these same onlookers had managed to break his fall and therefore save his life was itself remarkable but Evelyn Lowther was not remotely interested in such trivia.

What interested her was how she would feel when re-united with her beloved blackamoor. The journey from London would take Piggin about three days so she could expect them both at Rigmorden Hall by Thursday at the latest. That was tomorrow. Tomorrow she would have her darling Sambo back in her arms once more.

These intense feelings - so unexpected, so inexplicable in a woman twenty-four years older than her young blackamoor - were difficult to comprehend or contain. These were emotions that she had long considered dead or inappropriate in an independent woman of her superior class and position. Feelings, moreover, which she had never found in the embraces of her numerous lovers. These were emotions that troubled and disturbed her and yet they were feelings that now filled her with an indescribable pleasure and excitement.

Evelyn placed her silk shawl around her shoulders and stepped into her garden to still her beating heart.

The sun had now vanished behind the hills but across the river, far beyond the house, the last rays struck the tops of the moors above the hamlet of Barbon. The intense yellow of scattered patches of late broom was clearly visible, even in those areas already in shadow. The river itself, meandering through lush meadows of wild flowers in the valley immediately below the great house, shone briefly before vanishing in the evening gloom.

Evelyn had no desire to marry and have children; the very idea was abhorrent to her. Although she had been courted many times and had found some comfort and pleasure in the arms of her lovers, she had always stopped short of any real commitment - such as marriage. Besides, she was far too selfish to accommodate in her heart that warmth and generosity of spirit children expect of their parents. Her mother, whom she resembled in many ways, was a profoundly selfish woman and riddled with financial insecurities, despite her late husband's enormous wealth.

Like her mother, Evelyn was incapable of any natural expression of love or regard that was not wholly motivated by a wish to dominate. However, her feelings for Kofi were a curious blend of desire and an impetuous need to mother him, as if he were indeed her child. It was, she now realised, this dangerous combination that she found so disturbing and yet so exciting.

Evelyn shuddered, turned and quickly walked back towards her house and the security of her drawing room.

***

It was early evening by the time Kofi and the black highwayman reached Lancaster. The castle glowered down at the two weary travellers as they skirted the edge of the town and headed towards the river Lune and the bridge that would lead them to Sunderland Point. Kofi, wrapped in the folds of Joshua's cloak and seated in front of him on the great black mare, was hidden - except for his feet, which hung down the mare's flanks and bounced against her with each step.

Joshua had thought it best to avoid the town itself. News of the murder of the coachman, guard and bounty hunter on the 'North Star' had quickly spread throughout Lancashire. Soon there would be reward notices pinned to the doors of inns or pasted on walls in towns and villages throughout the county. There was already talk of soldiers scouring the area. Moreover, the search had spread to include the girl who was now generally believed to have been the highwayman's accomplice. If caught, both would surely hang. While no one as yet could connect Joshua Bloom with the masked highwayman, it would not take an Isaac Newton to put two and two together if a missing blackamoor were seen with a big, black 'nigger' on horseback.

The River Lune shone fitfully in the sun's last rays and the shapes of tall ships moored close to the Customs House on St. George's Quay made an impressive sight, their black hulks silhouetted against water tinged with gold. Kofi had never been to Lancaster before but he sensed that each hour, each new mile of their journey, brought them closer to Sunderland Point - that desolate spit of land sticking into the sea where he had first stepped ashore three months ago.

From Sunderland Point he could begin his great trek home.

Joshua paused for a moment on the old stone bridge and gazed at the ships moored along the southern bank.

'Kofi, are you sure you don't want to find a ship? There aint nothin' at Sunderland Point. 'Famine Point', they call it round here! Why, if you was to seek passage on one of them ships down there, who knows, someone there might take pity on yer!'

Joshua's wise words fell on deaf ears. Kofi *had* get to Sunderland Point. That was where he would find his way back to Kumasi.

It was painfully clear to Joshua that there was no chance whatsoever that a black slave, implicated now in a triple murder and on the run, could ever find sanctuary, let alone get back to Africa. He knew instinctively that Kofi's situation was desperate so he buttoned his lip and let the boy chatter on about Kumasi, his tribal village and all his relatives who would be waiting for his triumphant return – or so the poor child imagined.

***

They left the bridge and turned south, following the river on their left as it meandered past the town and on, towards the Irish Sea. On the far bank, beneath the shadow of Lancaster Castle and the Church of St. Mary's, the dockside area was busy, even at this late hour. A wooden crane swung crates aboard a frigate while labourers manhandled bales of cotton or tobacco from a sleek schooner. On either side of the newly built Customs House were tall, brick warehouses - stuffed with the booty of a rapacious and expanding colonial nation.

Kofi turned his face away from the sight of the ships and focused, resolutely, on the great trek that now lay before him.

Soon the road left the northern bank of the river and veered off into a flat expanse of marshland. The flickering lights of Lancaster were soon lost, obscured by tall reeds that rustled in the evening breeze. Stunted trees, windblown and twisted by the prevailing winds, lined the track. The sluggish streams that criss-crossed these boggy wastes were thick with brine. Meadows, clogged with rank weeds, were like muddy sponges - soft and pliant under foot. Kofi sniffed the evening air. He could smell the sea.

Back in London, news of the capture of 'Sambo' and the climbing boy's dramatic escape spread like wildfire.

Jack's escape had indeed been miraculous. For an agonising few seconds he had hung there on that rooftop by his fingertips, convinced that he would soon be dead. He had heard Kofi's desperate cries and Piggin's obscenities but nothing then could save him. He remembered, vividly, the moment when his fingers finally gave up and he plummeted down into the street, some sixty feet below.

But the fall did not kill him!

Instead, eager arms and hands reached upwards, cushioning his fall and protecting him from the harsh reality of the cobbles. He was then born aloft, suspended high above the heads of the crowd and carried down the street like some sporting hero. They had saved him only because they saw him as their hero.

'Had not this climbing boy, against all odds, bearded the King himself in his own palace? Had not this humble sweep defied the authorities and cocked a veritable snook at the aristocracy - and survived?'

The crowd took their hero to the nearest tavern and placed the startled boy on a table in the middle of the room. Tankards were filled and toasts offered, accompanied by thunderous cheers.

These celebrations were rudely interrupted by the sudden appearance of Piggin's bullyboys.

When the boisterous crowd realised what was happening a fight immediately broke out. Within moments the inn was a shambles as fists flew, flagons were smashed overheads, tankards sailed across the room in great arcs, spilling their contents, and chairs and tables upturned. In the confusion, Jack was able to drop to the floor and crawl on his hands and knees towards the door and out into the yard at the back of the pub. He then jumped over the rickety fence and was off down the lane before anyone noticed that the hero of the day had ignominiously scarpered!

***

It was dark by the time Kofi and the black highwayman reached Overton - the hamlet closest to the estuary that separates Sunderland Point from the marshes of Colloway and Middleton.

They passed the village in silence – there was no one about, thankfully - and then found the narrow path leading to Sunderland Point itself.

To Kofi's bitter disappointment, the tide was in.

Only a few months before, under the watchful eye of Grundy, he had travelled in a cart along this track. Now it was covered in deep, tidal water. Here and there a few elongated strips of mud covered with bright green grass stood proud above the swirling water but otherwise it was impassable. The wooden posts marking the track were barely visible. The few remaining lights from the fishing village on Sunderland Point were like distant stars in a watery galaxy. Even as Kofi and Joshua watched, these lights went out one by one as the fishermen and their wives of 'Famine Point' took to their beds.

Joshua realised at once that there was no way Kofi could reach Sunderland Point that night. He would have to wait until the tide turned and the deep water covering the track had subsided.

It was, however, time to say goodbye.

He lowered Kofi to the ground and watched him walk to the water's edge. The boy gazed out across the tidal water, lost in his own thoughts. High above their heads a flock of geese, their wings moving slowly and in unison, headed south in silence. A pale, sickly moon hung in the sky.

'Time I was ago'in, Kofi.'
'I know', said Kofi, his back to the highwayman.

Kofi continued to look at the water, now flecked with moonlight. There were tears in his eyes. Joshua dismounted and moved closer to the boy. The mare bent her head and began to lick the salt that had formed a thin, yellow crust at the edge of the road.

'Are you sure you don't want to stay?' asked the highwayman. 'You knows you is always welcome to ride with old Joshua.'

The silence between them was now palpable, like the pressure Kofi had first felt in his ears when diving deep into the cool depths of the great lake at Kumasi.

'There's plenty more booty where that last lot come from. What do you say, boy? Would you not rather stay?'

Kofi's heart was torn between regard for his new friend and the compulsion that now drew him to Sunderland Point and the start of his great trek. Suddenly, in his mind's eye, the lake at Kumasi vanished and was replaced by Clem Piggin's face - a mass of blood and shattered bone. With that sudden memory Kofi's doubts evaporated. Besides, there was about the person of Joshua Bloom the unmistakable stench of death. Joshua was a man condemned. Doomed! His fate was sealed. Kofi knew this – even if Joshua himself was ignorant of the destiny the Gods had chosen for him, dangerously adrift in a sea of violence.

Kofi stepped towards the highwayman, looming above him, and solemnly shook him by the hand.

'Thank you, Joshua. My uncle, Asatehene Kwasi Obodum, honours you for your kindness to his nephew. We will both remember you in our prayers.'

Kofi then turned and walked back to the water's edge and peered fixedly into the darkness. Joshua, taken aback by such formality, turned on his heels and strode back to his horse in silence and climbed into the saddle. He was angry and hurt by the boy's proud, insensitive manner. He jerked at the reins, causing the mare to wheel in a tight circle, ready to gallop off up the lane. As he turned he saw that Kofi was now facing him. For a moment they stood there, in silence, staring at each other. Then Kofi raised one, thin arm and waved. Joshua saw at once that he was no longer a proud king's nephew but a sad and lonely little boy.

'Good luck, Kofi!' said Joshua, his voice trembling. 'May your gods protect you on your great trek!'

***

After his miraculous escape (his second!) Jack had gone to ground in a filthy court off Cockspur Street. Here, crouching behind a pile of builder's rubble, he grabbed a moment or two to catch his breath and decide what to do.

It was clear that he had lost Piggin's men in the confusion in the tavern but what of Kofi? Obviously Piggin had captured him but where was he now? What would happen to the poor nigger now that the valuable silver collar was gone? Although he had lost a few of his gold coins, silver trinkets and other royal portables in the fall from the rooftop in Villiers Street, Jack still had plenty of money about his person to survive. But where? Where could he hide, now that they knew what he looked like? If Piggin did not get him and club him to death then the Bow Street constables surely would. If he should survive their beating, then what? Tyburn's triple tree?

It would be absurd - even in a work of fiction such as this - to believe that there existed, roaming the back-streets of London in 1763, a gang of bandy-legged midgets intent on mischief. But that is precisely what Jack now saw coming towards him. He was even more astonished to see at their head the diminutive figure of Blagg's young acolyte, Scab.

'Well', said Jack, emerging from behind his pile of rubble, 'fancy seeing you here! And who are these little vermin? Not friends of yours, surely? You never had no friends, Scab - unless it was that old bastard Jeremiah Blagg. How is he, Scab? Still employing bandy-legged retards like you?'

The little band now stopped and formed themselves into a tight group behind their leader who was holding a thick stick almost as big as himself.

'Your days is up, Jack Fisher. No more gadding about, robbin' 'is Majesty blind and bringing the 'onourable name of sweeping into disrepute.'

'Bollocks!', interrupted Jack. 'You is just after me money. Well, you aint gettin' it, so shove off!'

With that Jack picked up a half brick from the pile of rubbish beside him and hurled it at Scab. Much to his surprise, it struck him full in the face and with such force that Scab was lifted momentarily off the ground before crashing to the floor. Jack waited for Scab to get up but there was no movement. Indeed, Scab remained where he had fallen - flat on his back. Almost as surprising was the speed with which Scab's little band of followers promptly turned on their heels and scuttled off, callously abandoning their leader now lying in a lurid pool of blood.

'Well, that was easy!', thought Jack as he casually walked over to the prostrate figure and prodded Scab with the toe of his boot. The boy was still alive for he let out a groan but showed no sign of getting up, whereupon Jack gave him a resounding kick in the ribs.

'That's for the time you first brined me and this...' - kicking him in the groin - 'is just for luck!'

****

Jack's natural instinct for survival had begun in the womb and had continued throughout those desperate years with his drunken mother when starvation or even death loomed. Nothing had changed since then except that now he had money and a measure of freedom - even if his life was still under threat from both Piggin and the Magistrate's constables. That instinct had kept him alive in those tortuous chimneys and would save him now. Or so he thought.

Two hours later, therefore, Jack bought a ticket for the next coach north - and the desolate wastes of Sunderland Point.

How, you might ask, could Jack possibly know that Kofi had escaped Piggin's clutches and was planning with Joshua's help to travel to Sunderland Point? How could Jack be sure that Kofi was not already back under the control of his owner, the redoubtable Evelyn Lowther? How, above all, did Jack know for sure that Kofi was not still in London, banged up perhaps in Newgate Prison and waiting deportation? Well, the truth is that Jack had absolutely no idea whatsoever on any of these highly speculative issues. All he knew now was that he had to get out of London and somehow rescue his friend in the process.

Irrational? Yes. Foolhardy? Certainly. But of all the people in England that day only Jack Fisher knew where Kofi would probably head for, given half a chance - Sunderland Point and then Kumasi (wherever that was!). God knows, Kofi had talked enough about 'his great trek back to his tribal lands.'

The least Jack could do was get there just as soon as he could and find his friend. That much he surely owed Kofi.

**

That night Kofi crouched by the waters' edge at Sunderland Point until the tide finally turned and the sea subsided, leaving a thin deposit of mud across the track.

Thoughts of Evelyn and those moments of intimacy that had marked their relationship had filled Kofi's troubled mind all night as he crouched in the darkness. While he had never knowingly encouraged Evelyn's affection, he had basked in it in ways that he now realised were indulgent and probably inappropriate. Although he was still only a child, alone and far from home, he had found in Evelyn's love a comfort and a pleasure that was both troubling and, on reflection, exquisite. Whatever Evelyn's real intentions, their relationship had been, for him at least, a defining moment in his young life.

He wrapped his ragged coat around his thin shoulders and set off towards Sunderland Point - and home!

**

Jack's journey north - begun only a few hours after Piggin and Kofi had first boarded the 'North Star' - was as long and tedious as it had been for the ill-fated bounty hunter. Unlike the parsimonious Piggin, Jack could afford to sit inside the carriage and was thus able to sleep for a good part of the journey. He was also able to enjoy, for the first time, true anonymity since absolutely no one on board realised that he was the infamous climbing boy who, for nearly seven weeks, had run amuck in Buckingham House.

This realisation was viewed with mixed feelings for Jack had thoroughly enjoyed his brief moment of fame back in the pub, even if it had ended abruptly. The journey north also gave him time to reflect on why, of all people, he should want to 'rescue' some worthless nigger. It was not as if they were close - like he had been to Jem back at Blagg's gaff. Indeed, should he not even now be looking for *him* rather than Kofi? Jem, at least, was 'family' and his recent dismissal from Blagg's establishment was cause for concern, even among Blagg's little fraternity of sweeps.

There were no easy answers to any of these questions. After a while Jack, not used to such introspection, stopped thinking and fell asleep

***

It was not quite dawn when Kofi ventured along the narrow track towards Sunderland Point, his boots squelching through liquid mud. In some parts the road dipped and he had to wade knee-deep through swirling water to reach the other side. As dawn broke, the thin streaks of light at his back grew longer and the night wind dropped to a fresh breeze, stirring pools of water left by the retreating tide. After a cold, sleepless night Kofi's arms and legs were stiff but his growing excitement warmed his heart.

Sensing somehow that the sea - and freedom - lay at the end of this muddy path, Kofi began to run. A startled cow looked up as Kofi ran past and followed his exit with her mournful gaze. By the time he reached the path's end his arms and shoulders were wet with dew but before him there now stretched a vast, stony beach and beyond that a grey, inhospitable sea - and Kumasi!

`***

It is now late morning of the 17th of June and Jack's coach has reached Conder Green, a tiny hamlet between Preston and Lancaster. Jack steps down, thanks its driver and watches as it trundles off up the lane.

The last part of Jack's journey, from Preston to Conder Green, had taken nearly two hours. Jack had spent an hour or so the previous night in Preston. Here he had discovered the town buzzing with talk of the recent murder of three men on the 'North Star'. Someone had shown him the notice promising a handsome reward for the capture of the highwayman concerned.

There, clear as day, was Clem Piggin's name and although Kofi was not mentioned, Jack knew instinctively that somehow he had escaped!

Since Kofi had spent that same night in Joshua's tree house, Jack - although he could not know it at the time - was only an hour or so behind. He knew also that he was now close to Sunderland Point, assuming of course that he could get a ferryman to take him across the Lune estuary. That, according to his driver whom he had asked for directions, would be the quickest route.

Jack left the road and followed a stream, reaching the estuary some twenty minutes later. The tide had turned and the river's muddy banks were now exposed and glistening in the early morning light. The ferryman - an old man with a mean, sallow face - argued long and hard over his price. Jack knew that he was being robbed but in the end handed him the two coins the ferryman demanded. The man took the coins, bit them one by one then grinned - revealing a mouth full of rotten teeth.

Jack clambers aboard and the narrow, black boat drifts into mid-steam - where a combination of river water and ebbing tide suddenly seizes it by the throat. Like a scrap of wood or a leaf in a gutter swollen with rain, it is immediately swept, with ever-increasing speed, towards the sea. Jack has never been in a boat before and clings nervously to its sides with both hands. The ferryman, who seems to enjoy the boy's discomfort, laughs and shakes his head in disbelief at Jack's evident terror.

They soon reach the great bend in the river below Overton and Jack can now see the cluster of black cottages on Sunderland Point. Far out to sea a schooner in full sail suddenly appears from the mist - like a ghost ship completely ensnared in gossamer.

Perhaps Kofi will not be there? Perhaps, after all, he has found his ship and is already on his way to Africa? These are thoughts that had troubled Jack on his long journey north and now that he is so close, trouble him even more.

The great ship - its sails a lurid white against dark, rain-threatening clouds - suddenly vanishes, as quickly as it had first appeared.

***

Meanwhile, Kofi is wandering dejectedly along the beach towards the tip of Sunderland Point. Here the fields of scrubby grass end abruptly in a steep, exposed bank of reddish soil - like bleeding gums. The beach consists of rounded stones, worn smooth by the sea. Wood, shrivelled hemp and gobs of tar litter its surface. Kofi steps carefully across the bleached skeleton of a cormorant, splayed out obscenely on the ground. Feathers still adhered to its anatomised carcass although its eyes have long since disappeared.

Far out at sea, gulls swoop and dive against a dull, grey sky. Apart from their distant screams, Sunderland Point is strangely quiet.

Kofi scrambles up the bank and squats beneath a hawthorn bush that is gnarled, knotted and bent double with age. He is cold. He rubs his hands together and hugs himself to try and get some warmth back into his body. He narrows his eyes and stares out to sea - longing for a sign!

***

Jack's boat has now crossed the estuary and is within sight of the fishing village at Sunderland Point. For some reason - probably laziness - the ferryman is unable to stop at the stone jetty by the village so Jack has to scramble onto the beach then pick his way towards dry land by moving from one grassy clump to the next, stepping gingerly between pools of slimy green water and patches of sulphurous mud.

His landing is watched by a group of fishermen preparing their boats but Jack decides to avoid them and instead strikes out, instinctively, for the southern beach.

***

Kofi, still crouching beneath his tree, stares seaward - to where sky and sea merge in a confusion of countless shades of grey and white. His eyes are sore for he has been staring now for at least three hours. His prayers have produced nothing. No sign has given him the comfort he needs and hope itself, like the tide in front of him, is ebbing fast.

He remembers how once, praying for rain at his grandfather's side, he had seen a snake suddenly split in two, each separate creature wriggling off across the sand then disappearing into the bush. The old man had clapped his hands, thrown back his head and laughed for joy. That night rain had fallen, its heavy drops dancing an intricate pattern on each withered leaf.

Kofi closes his eyes. Suddenly there is a distant sound, no more than a pulse perhaps but something strange and remote.

At first Kofi confuses this sensation with the beat of his own heart but then, as if by magic, it becomes a rhythm stirring long lost memories. The sound of many drums dance and skip, like spangled light on water. Then, with the rush of a gathering storm, the sound gains momentum, moving closer and closer until it crashes about Kofi's ears in a triumphant, exhilarating explosion of primordial thunder.

190

He opens his eyes.

The sun, a great golden globe, at once sends daggers of light hurtling towards him, shattering - like splintered glass - into a thousand colours.

When next he looks the grey sea has parted - revealing a broad avenue of shimmering sand, undulating in the heat. Tall, black shapes twist and turn, like elongated ghosts dancing freely. Their bodies grow thick, and then mysteriously thin like pearl divers moving through water but always, as they change shape, dancing to the drums' insistent rhythm.

Then figures step boldly from the sun's golden orb and, in stark silhouette, move in stately procession towards Kofi. The dancers, now clearly visible, crowd behind them - cheering and shouting. Kofi can see that these black men wear ceremonial skins of leopard or lion. Bracelets of silver and gold adorn their arms and round their necks hang beads and ornaments of great craftsmanship and beauty. Their bodies and faces are painted with brightly coloured clays. Each warrior carries his shield and spear, waving the spear ecstatically above his head in time to the beat of countless drums.

The procession, moving closer and closer, is now fully visible and there, in their midst, is the Ashanti king - Kofi's uncle - resplendent in a great cloak of burnished gold.

Kofi at once leaps to his feet and runs as fast as he can towards the noisy, exultant crowd. The sound of the drums and the cries of welcome from the assembled tribe ring in his ears. His head spins as he runs towards them, faster and faster.

Suddenly, a figure steps forward, hesitates but then, with outstretched arms, runs to meet him.

Kofi, his heart fit to burst, gives a great cry of recognition. He runs on and on until he falls, at long last, into the warm and loving embrace of Ashtari, his mother.

EPILOGUE
Sunderland Point, Lancashire
17th June, 1773 - ten years later

Jack Fisher was a successful young man of twenty-two when next he came to Sunderland Point.

The money left in his pockets after his long journey north ten years before had enabled him to start a new life in Kendal - as apprentice to a snuff manufacturer.

There, at the sign of the Blackamoor in Lowther Street, Jack had prospered and at the precocious age of eighteen had become a junior partner in the firm, earning the respect and affection of his patron, a kindly old man who had taken pity on the distraught, twelve-year-old he had found on his doorstep.

Now - in June, 1773 - Jack has come back to Sunderland Point. With money of his own in his pocket he is now ready to pay his last respects to a lost friend.

***

Much had happened since that fateful day in June 1763 when Jack first came to Sunderland Point, hoping to save Kofi.

Joshua, who had played a dramatic part in rescuing Kofi from the clutches of Clem Piggin, terrorised the highways near Preston for two more years before Nan (Joshua's lover and partner-in-crime) betrayed him one drunken night. They subsequently hung Joshua not far from where he had murdered Piggin and the coachmen.

Nan was never charged with complicity to murder, not least because she gave King's evidence at her lover's trial. Thereafter, she fled the area and shacked up with a young butcher called Pilmot. Soon afterwards, under an assumed name, she married a rich, young fellow from Ribchester. She produced five handsome children before dying of gonorrhoea in October, 1770.

But what of Nathaniel Grundy, agent to Sir Charles Fitzallen and manager of his master's plantation in Jamaica?

Well, Grundy was, much to his surprise, sacked the day after he delivered Sarah Fitzallen's sealed letter to her brother back in Jamaica. It was said Grundy died of a broken heart a few months later but most people in Falmouth put it down to the three pints of the Jamaican rum he drank one night, merely for a bet.

And what of Sir Charles Fitzallen himself, Master of Hyde House and owner of some three hundred slaves?

Well, I'm sorry to say he continued to terrorise his blacks, becoming immensely rich in the process. In 1768 he left Jamaica and returned to England, buying a large house and estates in Derbyshire. He soon became a wealthy gentleman farmer, comfortably married to the local squire's daughter and generally regarded throughout the county as a man of exceptional probity. Such are the vagaries of history.

As for Kofi's mother, she was first cruelly abused then abandoned by Sir Charles and sent to a brothel in Kingston, Jamaica where she languished for a few months before dying, mysteriously one night. It was widely believed that she had taken poison.

But what of Jeremiah Blagg and his little family of climbing boys? What became of them in this salutary tale of abuse and exploitation?

Sad to say, Blagg also prospered. Although Jack's apparent death up the chimney at Buckingham House had been somewhat inconvenient at the time, a trip the following day to the Foundling Hospital in Chiswick quickly supplied a replacement and before you could say 'Jack Robinson' another young, undernourished child was shoved up a still-warm chimney.

Jem, Jack's best friend, died of cancer of the scrotum. His demise, which was long and painful, took place some months after Jack had eluded Clem Piggin's men in Villiers Street. Jem died alone, in an abandoned outhouse near Puddle Dock. Blagg, anticipating the worse, had thrown him out of their home in Chick Lane only a few weeks after Jack had disappeared.

Scab, whose deft hand with a cloth had soon introduced the new climbing boy to the restorative powers of brine, was kicked in the face by Blagg's donkey two years later and nearly died of a brain haemorrhage. When, some months later, he had recovered he resumed his place at Blagg's side and together they embarked on a new, spectacularly successful career as burglars - Scab using his climbing skills and agility to break into some of the most important houses in London.

Blagg's donkey herself lasted another year or so before expiring. Indeed, Blagg himself was lucky not to drown at that time for it was when crossing a rickety bridge over the Fleet Ditch that the poor beast had collapsed, neatly tossing her cruel master into the river.

And what of his Lordship? What became of that syphilitic degenerate, Lord Frederick of Carlisle?

Well, he eventually recovered Evelyn Lowther's silver collar from a pawnbroker in Golden Square, Soho. However, he got no thanks for his pains for when he tried to deliver it in person to Evelyn at Rigmorden Hall she refused to see him and sent him packing, back to London. He therefore kept the silver collar and abandoned all hopes of obtaining his 'reward' - finding consolation in another aristocratic wench he seduced two nights later in Vauxhall Gardens. After several more years of debauchery, Carlisle married the singularly unattractive daughter of someone called Lord Vaughan. Some weeks later Carlisle entered politics, eventually becoming the highly respectable member for Leeds.

But what, finally, of Evelyn Lowther?

News that Kofi was still alive but had been abducted by some highwayman near Preston had filled her with a mixture of elation and despair. Search parties were immediately despatched to the area and rewards for 'Sambo's' safe recovery published in every tavern and market place throughout the region.

As anxious days of waiting for news of her Sambo turned to months, Lady Evelyn, in the seclusion of Rigmorden Hall, withdrew into herself.

For her loyal staff these were difficult times. No longer was she the handsome, vivacious creature that everyone in society knew and admired. Where once she had worn fashionable clothes and outrageous wigs, she now took to wandering the darkened corridors in nothing but a shift. Her long black hair, once her pride and joy and which Kofi had often brushed with such loving care, was now a tangled mess. Her beautiful face, usually vivid with the makeup of a woman of fashion, was now pale and wan. Her eyes, once her most striking feature, became tearful and lacklustre.

Although occasionally tempted to purchase another black child from Sarah Fitzallen at Storrs Hall she never did, preferring to cherish instead fond memories of her precious, sorely missed 'Sambo.'

Which brings us to Jack himself.

Settled now in the sleepy market town of Kendal and far from London and its horrors, Jack has tried these last ten years to forget Piggin and Blagg and the others and expunge from his memory his terrifying experiences as a renegade climbing boy.

It has not been easy. Dreams have a habit of catching you unawares and plunging you back into some horror from your distant past, some painful memory of unrequited love or betrayal.

Moreover, since Evelyn Lowther continues to purchase snuff from the factory in Lowther Street, where Jack now works, their paths cross frequently.

At first Jack found this difficult, knowing what he did of her Ladyship's affection for her 'Sambo' but later she became just another distinguished customer. Evelyn of course knows nothing of Jack or of his association with her 'Sambo'. Now calling himself John Alexander, Jack carefully guards his new identity, not least because of his notorious past but also because he wishes to cherish and protect his feelings for Kofi.

Jack Fisher has come, albeit belatedly, to appreciate his friend more and more as he reflects on his adventures in Buckingham House and their escape together through the slums of London. He now regards that friendship - even if flawed - as a defining moment in his life.

One day though, when dark chimneys and choking soot no longer fill his nightmares, Jack's adventures in Buckingham House might perhaps make a story to enthral a child of his own but until that time he prefers to remain silent, telling no one of his secret past - least of all Lady Evelyn Lowther.

* * * *

Ten years ago, to the day, Jack had arrived at Sunderland Point in a desperate attempt to rescue his friend but the moment he saw the small, black figure crouched beneath a twisted tree at the water's edge he knew that he was too late.

Kofi was dead - even though his eyes continued to stare out to sea.

A local farmer, taking pity on both boys, had helped bury Kofi in un-consecrated ground close by where he had been found. Now, ten years on, that same farmer helps Jack erect a modest headstone over Kofi's unofficial grave. It is all that Jack can afford but at least it now marks the place where his friend still lies, unknown and unloved.

Having said his last, sad farewell Jack returned to Kendal. He never came back to Sunderland Point.

He was not the only one to visit Kofi's grave that year. Had he returned a few weeks later he might have seen Evelyn Lowther herself staring out to sea - a solitary figure against a dull, grey sky. No one knows how she discovered that this was her little blackamoor's last resting place but each year thereafter she placed on his humble grave a small bouquet of flowers picked from her gardens at Rigmorden Hall.

Today, nearly two-hundred-and-fifty years after his death, that same flagstone still marks Kofi's grave.

Sometimes kind visitors, moved by little more than the inscription itself, place a few wild flowers on this modest gravestone - even though they know nothing of the real black child whose sad life and untimely death it commemorates.

The End

Printed in Great Britain
by Amazon